The Painted Lady Inn Mysteries

Book One
Murder Mansion

By

M. K. Scott

Chapter One

A YOUNG OFFICER tied yellow crime scene tape to the rusty metal railing leading up to the porch. Donna's eyes narrowed as she considered the leaning rickety handrail. Definitely would have to go. Not only an eyesore, but also a legal liability if someone should stumble, grab the railing, which could snap off and send the would-be customer hurtling to the hard cement. Not good. *Mental note to self*: Remove the liability suit waiting to happen. Whenever a banister wasn't present, she made an effort to be more careful. With any luck, others would do so too.

A few of her new neighbors stood bundled up in coats with their pajama legs and slippers peeking out the bottom. The weather was nippier than usual for Legacy, especially since the small city straddled the border between North and South Carolina.

The other residents probably hid behind lace curtains watching the scene unfold, unwilling to chance the brisk winter morning air or the possibility of looking rude. Politeness served as a prerequisite in the restored Victorian neighborhood often masking people's true intentions. It was the reason she had jumped on the foreclosed home. It would be the perfect place for her dream bed and breakfast.

The front door swung open, drawing attention. A medic backed out of her front door, guiding a gurney. The second medic handled the back end. The series of steps leading away from the door made it difficult for the leading medic, a slender male. A couple of times, he lost his grip, bouncing the front end of the gurney down a few steps while the muscular woman on the back end chastised him.

"Come on, Barney. Grab the bar and lift. Give the man some dignity."

The residents bold enough to venture out in the morning chill leaned toward one another and whispered. She wouldn't be surprised if someone commented about the neighborhood going south. *Not good.* Time to establish her reputation and The Painted Lady Inn's, before they both ended up with unsavory ones. *Suck it up, Donna.* Go do what you need to do. Damage control.

Her lips lifted in a parody of a smile as she crunched across the frosted lawn. An elderly woman glanced up at her husband and took a step back. Seriously, did she look that bad? Okay, no makeup and her father's old pea coat paired with a ball cap worked for her initial purpose of cataloging repairs, but was hardly appropriate for making a good first impression. Even still, the woman's reaction didn't make sense.

"Hello. I bet you're wondering what's going on." She held out her hand to the man since the woman's pinched mouth and panicked eyes didn't encourage neighborliness.

He hesitated for a brief second before taking her hand and giving a brief, firm shake. "Stan Whitaker. Yes, I did wonder what was happening. The sirens interrupted our breakfast."

Ah yes, a complaint. Somehow, she had ruined their breakfast. Finding a dead man in her newly purchased home put her off her cereal too, especially considering there wasn't one there yesterday when she did the walk through with the real estate agent. "Um, sorry about that. I came over early to start on the renovations."

The man's bushy eyebrows lifted with the word *renovation.* Yeah, she knew the type. They didn't think a woman could do anything besides cook and clean. *Forever single,* she had termed herself after being left at the altar at twenty-two. Telling people that she wasn't getting married after her fiancé found someone he liked better was one of the hardest moments in her life. However, it gave her the opportunity to do many things most would consider man's work, including renovating a neglected Victorian. Ignoring his attitude, she plowed on. "I wanted to get a rough feel for what I need to do first."

She nodded her head while considering ripping out walls as opposed to holding up paint chips and looking for mouse droppings. Her brother, Daniel, a construction supervisor, agreed to give his professional opinion and should be arriving any time now.

A car door slammed. "Hey, Donna!" Her sibling's voice cut across the chaos ensuing on her front lawn.

Her hand went up to acknowledge the greeting. She wished Daniel didn't have to yell everything, probably the natural result of working with power tools. "My brother," she explained, noticing the frightened woman had no trouble peering around her for a look at her brother. Donna rolled her eyes. *Geez, seriously.* The octogenarian was checking out her brother in front of her husband. The animated look on the woman's face demonstrated her brother's attractiveness. "I'm Donna, if you couldn't tell."

She forced out a little chuckle as if commenting on her brother calling her by name was humorous. It wasn't. Knowing any chance at meaningful conversation disappeared with Daniel's appearance, she spoke faster. Not only did the universe bless him with the wicked good looks of a fallen angel with blond hair and dark thick eyelashes all women envied, but also he had charisma. Women, men, children, even dogs loved him. As a sibling, it would be normal for her to hate him, but his constant concern for his older, single sister cancelled out the uncharitable emotion. Well, at least most of the time.

Her new neighbor stepped forward with an avid expression, earning a dark look from her husband. Ignoring the interplay, Donna spoke Yankee fast. "Anyhow, in the upstairs room, the attic really, thinking about making that into a parlor, great view, found the dead man."

A backward glance revealed her brother about two feet away and a man in a sports coat clutching a cell phone to his ear, strolling behind him. *Great.* Who could that be? Don't let it be the local news.

"How do you know he was dead?" The woman managed to tear her eyes away from Daniel's wide shoulders long enough to ask the question.

She inhaled deeply. *These people don't know me. Be patient. I need their goodwill.* "I'm a nurse. Have been for the last twenty-seven years."

The husband and wife looked at each other and smiled. The man met her eyes first. "A nurse would be handy as a neighbor. My Hilda has spells."

Oh great, another couple who expected free medical services, a common reaction when she announced her profession. At least it wasn't as bad as the men who announced they'd like to play doctor. That nonsense ended about the time she turned forty.

"Glad to help," she offered, not really meaning it, knowing she'd be saddled with a hypochondriac all hours of the day and night. *Give a little to get what you want* were her father's famous words about getting along with others, but it always seemed like she gave a great deal and got very little in return.

The scent of tobacco rode the air, causing her to pivot, searching the crowd for the offender. The man behind Daniel let out a puff of smoke as he returned her glance. At least he wasn't polluting her inn with his vile smoke. Since her window of opportunity would slam shut in about thirty seconds, she blurted, "I was wondering if you knew the man. Why he might be in my house?"

They shook their heads in unison, although the man replied, "Absentee owner. I heard he resided in another state. No one ever came around the last couple of years except for the real estate agent and the lawn service."

Lawn service. A possible lead, but there was little to do in the dead of winter. "Hey," Daniel called out, turning all attention on him as he usually did. Well, at least she'd had seven years of having her parents' sole attention before her baby brother showed up.

"Oh," she added, rushing her description. "Good-looking man with brown hair, expensive haircut. Preppy clothes, oxford shirt, khakis and windbreaker. Probably in his late thirties."

Odd that's all he had on in the dead of winter. Plenty of people drove from a heated garage to their destination with almost no braving of the elements.

Hilda looked away from Daniel briefly, her mouth partly open, ready to answer, when Stan did it for her. "Nope. Don't know anyone like that."

Daniel nodded to the couple giving them an easy smile that had them beaming back like recently picked sweepstakes winners. Presenting his hand, he shook both of theirs. Hilda had no trouble shaking his hand. Donna stepped back, realizing her time was done, but she needed her brother, who engaged in chatter about the weather.

Mr. Smoky eased up next to her. "I heard what you said about the dead man."

Her eyes cut to the man beside her. His skin, upon closer examination, appeared weathered and wrinkled, not at all the appearance of a reporter. Too old, too rough, not one of the pretty boys who ended up in front of the camera. His tweed coat sported wide lapels, indicating the man was no slave to fashion, or he was cheap, or possibly both.

Surreal. Everything had shifted at some point in time to left of normal. It could have happened while she slept. The man puffed away on his cigarette, getting the last drag before he dropped it and ground it underneath his loafer. Good thing they were standing in the neighbor's yard and not hers.

She tried for the world-weary voice of a sexy 1940s silver screen siren. "Yeah, what about it?" The scratchy tone of her coffee-less voice grated. Somewhere, between finding a deceased trespasser and calling the police, she'd put down her hazelnut coffee.

Her eyes remained on Daniel as he effortlessly charmed the older couple. Why couldn't she do that? It would be a useful skill for running a bed and breakfast, but her practical nature saw small talk as a waste. She had considered making her brother a partner, but his wife Maria quickly put the kibosh on that plan.

The man spoke, reminding him of her presence by her side. "You have a good eye. You remembered a great deal while only seeing the man briefly before you called the police."

Yeah. True, she tended to remember things. Was he complimenting her or accusing her? "When a dead stranger shows up in a newly purchased house, it makes a big impression."

"Understandable," the man agreed, patting down his jacket. Finding a box-like bulge, he pulled out his cigarettes. "Do you mind?"

"Yes."

Her quick answer stopped him in the middle of shaking out a new smoke. He pushed it back in with his index finger, replaced the pack and shrugged his shoulders. "Need to quit. Nasty habit."

Her top teeth rested on her bottom lip, keeping her from agreeing as much as she wanted to. She didn't know who the man was. It would be rude behavior anyhow. As an innkeeper, she'd have to learn to hold her tongue. Critical B and B owners probably earned very few return customers.

"Name's Mark Taber, detective."

"I'm Donna—" She never got to finish her introduction before the man finished it for her.

"Tollhouse, the owner, I know."

Her top teeth clamped down on her lip again. While she could use some lessons on the art of small talk and social etiquette, Detective Taber could benefit from an extensive four-year course. At one time, she played with the idea of naming the inn *The Tollhouse Inn*. Daniel discouraged her by pointing out most people didn't associate the words *Tollhouse* and cookies together. Besides, customers might believe there was a hidden charge if the word *toll* appeared in the name.

The detective reached back into his jacket, despite the significant look she gave him. His fingers withdrew a long narrow tablet instead of the dreaded smokes.

"Ms. Tollhouse, can you run me through your day?"

Naturally, he assumed she was single. Was it the man's coat she wore or the ball cap? Did he think she was playing for the other team? Then it hit her. *Oh yeah, Ms.* The outdated term identified women whose marital status was uncertain or those who bristled when asked. Hard to say which one applied to her.

She cleared her throat. "I left my coffee in the house. Could I go get it?" If she was going to recite her morning of feeding her dog, grabbing the paint chips and her short wait at Great Awakenings coffee shop, then she needed something to soothe her throat.

"No."

No, really? It was her coffee. She was the one who had overpaid for the meager paper cup of the sweetened brew she used to jumpstart her day. "Why?"

He furrowed his forehead, allowing his eyebrows to meet. Sure, he measured a few inches taller than she did, but definitely not a giant. If he thought to intimidate her, the man needed some work. She had the dubious privilege of working with numerous doctors who considered themselves gods, not to mention dozens of truly arrogant patients. Eyebrows in need of grooming did not do it.

"It's a crime scene." He said the words slowly, enunciating them as if she were either deaf or stupid.

Donna's nose crinkled in response to his condescending tone. "I know that. I called 911 when I found the dead trespasser." Someone might have considered her tone abrupt also. Her brother glanced at her, turning away from his enraptured audience and mouthed the words *watch it.*

"Trespasser?" The detective pushed his jacket aside and placed his hand on his hip, exposing his holstered weapon.

Was the move supposed to scare her? To prove he was a big bad cop who carried a gun? Somehow that made him better, smarter than her. Not happening. "That's what you call somebody who is on your property without permission. The fact he's dead just makes it more mysterious."

"Dead. Yeah, he's dead all right. Murdered."

Hilda gasped and grabbed her husband's arm at the detective's overloud words. The tiny woman directed a baleful glance Donna's way, acting like she had something to do with the dead man. Home values in the neighborhood immediately plummeted with Taber's pronouncement. Everyone looked at her, including her brother.

"Hey, I didn't know he was murdered." She held up her hands waist high, but dropped them when she realized it looked too much like she was surrendering. "I checked his pulse and called the police. There wasn't any blood that I could see."

"That's because…" The detective halted his words, noticing everyone's intent stares. "Never mind. Forget about it."

Taber stopped talking, aware he'd given out too many clues. Plenty of serious crime drama watching had her adding them up and unraveling mysteries was the one thing she could do better than her brother. For one, the murderer would know how he or she had killed the man.

Donna mentally retraced her steps through the house. She had opened the back door, plugged in the small radio she'd brought and tuned it to a top forty countdown. Not a recent one, but a prere-corded rerun of a previous countdown. The local oldies station played it every Sunday, one of the highlights of her weekend.

A small handheld recorder kept track of her comments as she moved through the house. Much more efficient than pen and paper. People tended to forget things when writing. Her coffee was in the other hand, the fragrant steam beckoning her, when she heard a sound.

At the time, the possibility of mice had her regretting she hadn't borrowed Daniel's cat, Miss Faversham, although the overweight, spoiled cat would be more likely to hide behind her when confront-ed with a rodent. She'd crept up the stairs, certain she would see the mother of all rats waiting for her at the top. No rodent was going to take up residence in her house. However, coffee and recorder didn't provide any suitable instrument to ward off a vicious rodent. At least she had on her pink steel-toed work boots. If she'd needed to, she could kick the dirty creature out the door, but she hoped it wouldn't come to that.

A creak of the wooden floor had the hairs on her neck standing, but as an inn owner, she'd have to be bold. Couldn't have vermin on the premises. An open door greeted her as she reached the landing. She *always* closed every door, an OCD quirk. Her brother often teased her by leaving doors standing wide open to see if she'd shut them. She *always* did. For a second, she suspected her brother had sweet-talked the real estate agent into going into the house and leaving a bunch of doors ajar, but that possibility disappeared when she entered the room. The body stretched out on the floor stopped her inner diatribe against the agent and her brother. Possibly a homeless squatter sleeping off a drunk? Plenty of vacant houses served as impromptu shelter of the opportunist. Another reason the bank had allowed such a low closing bid, that and she was the only person to bid on it.

Most people had looked at the peeling paint and leaning porch and envisioned dollars flying out the windows and up the crumbling chimneys. For one brief moment, her no-nonsense attitude fell away and she saw the realization of a dream. The building restored to its former grandeur with polished wood floors accented with floral oriental rugs. A tasteful mix of modern and antique furniture would create a welcoming atmosphere that would convey both luxury and coziness. Adorned in a fancy apron befitting a television cook, she'd serve a delicious gourmet breakfast to appreciative customers. She'd been perfecting her recipes for years. Usually the lucky recipients were herself and her co-workers, as she occasionally took muffins and pastries to work. Most assumed she picked them up on her way to work, even though she placed them on a crystal platter in the middle of the lounge table.

The man stretched out on her topmost floor stood between her and her vision. Panic overwhelmed her hard-earned calm perfected during a two-year stint in the emergency room that most beginning nurses endured before working their way up to the more coveted floors. Her current job, on the post-op floor, she'd eyed years ago thinking it would be a plum assignment until she acquired it. Whatever could go wrong after surgery from infections to cardiac arrest often did. Her phone sat useless in her purse two floors away. Unfortunately, she'd dealt with her share of dead bodies and recognized the signs mentally screaming, *No! Not here, not now.*

She'd inhaled deeply; realizing death was never part of anyone's plan. Maybe he was just sleeping. *Yes, that must be it.* The hand of fate that had grabbed hold of her secret fantasy of opening a bed and breakfast let up a bit. Sleeping vagrant, while not good, was something she could handle. She hadn't earned the unflattering nickname of Sergeant Abrupt for her gentle and soft manner. She'd placed her coffee and recorder on the wide windowsill.

The toe of her pink boot nudged him, not hard, just a gentle push, enough to get most people's attention, but not his. Her position allowed her to examine his clothes. Expensive name brands and a Rolex watch caught her eye. A number of the doctors sported similar watches. She had heard a co-worker mention that Rolexes could cost as much as a car or even a modest house down payment. Weird that such a man would stumble into her place for a nap. *Drunk. Great.* Still had to get him out. Kneeling, she'd shaken his shoulder, rolling his head side to side, but received no response.

Her index and middle fingers automatically measured his pulse while she looked at her watch. No pulse. Training had kicked in as she rolled him to his back and checked his airway. *Clear.* Her hands pushed down on his chest in a familiar CPR rhythm. She cursed her inability to call for help. Why had she decided to go into the house before Daniel arrived?

The pale white face and slack jaw told her what she already knew. The man was dead. She'd galloped down the stairs, taking three or four at a time, slipping once or twice. A grab for the banister had saved her from tumbling all the way down. She'd called 911 and her usual calmness she prided herself on had vanished.

"Dead man. Stranger. My house. Come quick." The operator made her repeat the address twice. The police came and ushered her out to the sidewalk while her purse, phone and keys had remained inside.

The moment she touched his wrist forced its way back into her mind. Even though she turned on the electricity for the home inspector, she hadn't cranked up the furnace. It wouldn't make sense trying to keep the uninhabited place warm. His skin wasn't cold to the touch, meaning he hadn't been dead long. Would they lift any fingerprints besides hers from the body?

The red and white ambulance moved away slowly. No reason to hurry since the man had expired almost two hours before, according to the medical examiner. The detective's voice broke into her mental review.

"I can see the wheels turning in your head. Care to share?"

"Glad to. Could we sit somewhere?" Far from glad, but lawyering up would make her appear guilty. Besides, innocent people didn't need lawyers, did they?

Chapter Two

THE DETECTIVE PLACED a hand on her elbow and guided her to a non-descript sedan. The male hand on her arm was about as close to a date as she'd had in the last three years. Odd thought to have when a murdered man had just been removed from her future inn.

He opened the passenger door, releasing the odor of stale smoke. Donna balked at the scent. It would be like sitting in an ashtray. Why did she want to sit again? Oh, yeah, the realization that the murderer may have still been in the house when she entered. Her top teeth clamped on her bottom lip as she slid into the seat. Taber moved to close the door, but she put out a flat palm to stop the swing. "I'd like it open."

The eyebrows moved again, questioning her actions, but he left the door open as he moved to the driver's side. Daniel followed them and stood about six feet from the car. Close enough to keep her in view, but not close enough to attract the detective's ire.

Taber slammed his door, evidently having no issue with the cigarette stench. He was probably immune to it after smoking for years.

"Sorry for the smoke smell. Don't usually have people in my car."

"I understand." She mumbled the words as her bottom shifted on the textured upholstery, uncomfortable with her reason for sitting in a police car. Make that a detective's car.

"You thought of something, back there on the grass. I saw it on your face." The detective's words sounded so normal, a simple comment her brother might have made.

"I did. Yep, I've been told I'd never make a good poker player or criminal." She added the last part for good measure, just in case, even though his actions didn't resemble any police dramas she'd watched. No roughing her up or getting her to drink huge amount of liquids and then denying her the right to the restroom.

The scent of coffee penetrated the smoke scent as Taber opened up a thermos and poured the fragrant liquid into the plastic lid. He held it out to her.

His thermos, his cup, which his lips touched, maybe recently. No telling how much bacteria danced on the rim of the cup. Still, it was coffee. Her right hand wrapped around the warm cup, bringing it up to her lips for a large gulp. Black, not unexpected, but strangely sweet. The detective went heavy on the sugar.

"Ahh." The deep, appreciative sigh acknowledged that java was her drug of choice. She even forgave him his nasty habit of smoking, probably brought on by seeing the worst of human nature. She took another appreciative sip before handing it back to Taber, who drank after her, not even bothering to wipe the rim of the cup. Her earlier charitable thought died a quick death at the man's stupidity. She could have a communicable disease. Her inner tirade came to an abrupt halt when she realized she had done the very same thing. Still, that was different; stress from finding a murdered guy caused her to shortly abandon her hygienic principles.

She watched the detective with half-hooded eyes as he finished the cup with two gulps, wondering if that was the last of the coffee. As if hearing her thoughts, he tilted the thermos, allowing the brown liquid to splash into the cup, tantalizing her. Instead of offering it, he held it close to his torso.

"Tell me what you're thinking first. Then coffee."

Oh my goodness, he was as devious as the television actors were. She swallowed hard. Her intentions were to tell him anyhow, but she didn't like being manipulated. A slight sniff clearly announced how she felt about his actions. "I told you I took his pulse. The man was cool, not cold. I've taken pulses on colder, living people. He also had on a Rolex."

"Good information. Excellent observation on the watch." He moved the cup away from his chest, but kept his fingers on it as her fingers touched the plastic exterior. "There's more."

His grip held firm on the cup. Her fingers crowded his, trying to find purchase. Her eyes met his over the steaming brew. "Coffee first." Her words were low and delivered in an ominous tone that usually had student nurses scrambling.

Taber laughed and loosened his fingers. "Okay. Remind me to never get between you and your caffeine. I may have encountered someone worse than me. No wonder you were so anxious to get your abandoned coffee from inside."

Donna gulped the brew, half ignoring his comments. Sure, she liked coffee, who didn't? The coffee flowed down her throat and into her body, thawing out portions that had frozen at the sight of the dead man. She'd have to talk eventually and if any danger existed with a murderer lurking nearby, the detective would simply eliminate it and put things back to the way they used to be.

Her lips tilted up in an appreciative smile as she handed the empty cup back.

He peered inside the cup, looking for leftover coffee and then he whistled. "Definitely a coffee hound. You wanted to tell me what?"

The prompt, she recognized it. "I didn't know the man was murdered. Didn't know he was dead until I took his pulse."

She stopped, wondering how to frame her words. Taber motioned with his hand for her to continue. "At first, I thought it was a rat, a large one. I could hear the floorboards squeak the way they do when something or someone steps on them. Since I was cataloguing what I needed to do to the house, I was talking as I went up the stairs. Whoever was there could have just completed the murder and left minutes before the police arrived."

Taber's hazel eyes flicked over her shoulders to the house. He grabbed his cell phone and hit a number. "Taber here, home owner has reason to believe perp was in home when she arrived. Check back entrance for footprints."

He listened to whoever was at the other end. He grunted his agreement a few times, but then added, "No, no I don't think so. Not the hysterical type at all. I believe her."

It didn't take a stretch of the imagination for her to realize she was the topic of conversation. He believed her. He didn't think she was a hysterical female. Of course, she wasn't. Her appreciation for the man grew. It took some doctors months to get to that point. Others never did. Pompous fools. Her eyes moved over him as he spoke. He had a grizzled, weathered look. His thick hair, liberally laced with silver, had appeal but her eyes drifted to the overflowing ashtray. Smoking cancelled it all out.

Flopping back into her seat, she tabled her observation. Too much was happening for her to develop an inappropriate attraction to a man who offered her coffee. He could be married. No wedding ring on his left hand, but the lack of ring didn't necessarily equal no commitment. In the end, there could be nothing between them, anyway. Romance had given her the boot long ago. Certain women ended up in happily-ever-after tales with the mandatory one child of each gender, complete with a minivan and the annual pilgrimage to Disney World. Her lips twisted to one side as she considered the path she hadn't traveled. Not her rodeo and much too late to get a ticket.

While they sat there, more neighbors had emerged from their houses. What she assumed was decorum turned out to be a reluctance for frostbite since they took the time to dress for the weather. A handsome male couple, dressed in coordinating sweats, casually sauntered by, pretending to walk their pet, a standard size poodle. The dog pulled constantly on the leash, showing its impatience at the leisurely pace.

Two children spilled out of a nearby house, clutching baseball mitts with their father following behind them attired in a sweatshirt, ball cap, plaid pajama pants and slippers. He took his position facing her inn while tossing the ball. His children missed catching the easy lobs that arced high in the air waiting for the child to center underneath it. The car clock registered 8:15. Yeah, most men would be outside on a frosty Sunday morning to play catch with the kids. Her snort emphasized her disbelief. The returned ball bounced off the man's mitt, hitting him in the face. Looked like no one in the family was athletically inclined, making her wonder why they bought the mitts in the first place.

Taber pocketed his cell phone, glanced out the window, before pointing to Daniel. Is he your husband or boyfriend?"

A tired laugh escaped her lips. It wasn't the first time someone had made the same assumption. It confirmed her belief that they looked nothing alike. People never assumed they were siblings. He'd be the prince in a fairy tale while she'd be the sister of an ogre since she topped five nine easily. "No, that's my brother. I asked him to meet me here."

"Oh, I guess that explains why he looks so worried."

Worried? Daniel? The way he rocked side to side, varying his weight on each foot, did suggest anxiety, unlike his usual all-is-right-with-the-world mien. Of course, all wasn't right with the world, at least not hers.

"Yeah, I was wondering how soon we could get this tied up. Daniel and I were going to go over the house and…" The detective's long whistle interrupted her question.

"You are one cool cucumber. You're going back into the house after finding a dead man?"

Was this a trick question? She sucked her lips in, wondering if there was a correct answer. "Yes, today is my day off and I need to decide what needs to be done to order materials."

He shook his head slowly side to side in disbelief. "Donna," he said, then stopped and arched his eyebrows. "May I call you that?"

It seemed like a moot point since he already had. "Yes." Her glance swept downward to her fingers woven together. Their tight hold confirmed her mental state.

"Most women would be in hysterics by now."

A possible lecture on the fragility of the fair sex took form as the dashboard clock ticked off the seconds. It wouldn't be her first, but she could skip this one. "Please, this isn't the 1960s. Women aren't delicate creatures. Many are doing the same jobs as men. I imagine you even have female co-workers."

The detective stopped whatever he was going to say. He retrieved the coffee cup and screwed the lid back on the thermos while muttering in a sotto tone. "None as tough as you."

Not sure if the words were supposed to be a compliment, she chose to take them that way. Her shoulders went back as she pasted her *I Will Not Be Moved* expression on her face. Her babe days were over, although she wasn't overly certain she'd ever had any. Any phrase that pointed out her strength, intelligence, calmness in the face of adversity and even rightness, she'd take.

"Can I get back in? Half my morning is already gone. I have things to do."

The detective's lips twisted to one side as his brow bunched then smoothed, as thoughts chased across his face. To think he called her transparent, when his emotions broadcasted as clear as a flashing beacon. "Ah." He opened his mouth wide, holding the one word as if warming up for a choral performance.

The urge to tell him to get on with it was overwhelming. She barely managed to keep it behind her teeth. Her lack of theatrics could somehow incriminate her. *Nah,* it didn't make sense since she'd never met the man stretched out in the *bird aerie*, the name she'd given that room. Each room had a name. Of course, now it might be renamed *murder site* or *dead man hideaway*. The possibility of her rooms needing renaming caused her to shake her head violently in denial.

"Hey, you don't even know what I was going to say. No reason for you to be shaking your head at me," Taber complained, pulling out his pack of smokes. Noticing Donna's attention, his long fingers carefully turned the box over, but returned it to his pocket.

The uniformed police officers gathered outside her house. Another cop walked toward the huddled group with a long flat box with the familiar colors of a popular donut shop. Seriously, donuts? Could they be any more stereotypical? Worse, if they brought breakfast, then they weren't leaving soon. The town's finest resembled a blue blot on her frosted lawn, a cancerous tumor signaling the demise of her modest dream.

"It's not what you were going to say. It's all this." She flung her arm out the door, indicating the whole assembly of people, including her nosy neighbors. "How can I ever expect to open a bed and breakfast with all this notoriety attached to it?"

"Is that all?" His bent index finger rubbed the line at the bridge of his nose.

The incredulousness in his voice indicated his ignorance of B and B ambiance. People wanted comfort, indulgence, something different from their normal routine. No one ever mentioned going to a murder scene. Donna's nose wrinkled as she scented something repugnant beside the stale smoke. Oh yeah, there were people who flocked to murder scenes, but they were not the types to pay $160 a night for a room in a restored Victorian.

"Yes, it is. Considering my entire premise of opening a B and B involved paying customers. It's not enough that people drive by it slowly to gawk."

His closed eyes made her doubt he'd even heard her. His eyelids shot up as he pinned her with a direct gaze and held out his index finger while folding the other three down. "It may not be as bad as you think. My sister is into these legends and ghost stories and travels the country to stay in some iffy places just because she heard some contrived story. You could make up some story about a ghost inhabiting your house. It's bound to draw folks. Tack on a disclaimer that the story may not be true; it's just what you heard."

The idea had merit, although she couldn't say she'd ever wanted to stay anywhere haunted. "Did your sister ever see a ghost?

"No, much to her disappointment. She tried to convince me that strange things happened on her last trip. Things moved around. The items were not in the place she put them, but my sister has a lifelong habit of losing stuff. Not exactly convincing evidence."

"No reason to call out the ghost hunters then." She readily agreed, discounting the allure of having her own ghost. "Besides, people like romantic ghosts. Maybe a jilted lover who waited on her beloved to return or threw herself off the widow walk when he didn't."

"Yeah, that sounds real pleasant, better than some unknown rich dude killed in an abandoned house." His crow's feet showed in the early morning light as he grinned at her. Macabre humor, but probably par for the course in his line of work.

"Yes, it does. Most of the ghost stories are probably not true. People can accept a melancholy spirit, but don't want a spectral mass murderer hovering over them as they sleep." The ghost angle lost more and more appeal the more she examined it. Not the type of tidbit you'd type up in a brochure, along with clawfoot tubs and period-accurate furnishings.

"You got me there. How long before you expect to open the inn?" His thumb and index finger casually stroked his chin as if realizing his failure to shave this morning. It was hard to say if his stubble itched or if he tried to hide the beginning of a beard.

"Good question. The original home inspector told me there were some roofing issues and dry rot. New windows and a heating system would be necessary. The interior needs paint, wallpapering and refinishing the wood floors. Exterior needs a new porch, paint and a re-bricked chimney. I spent my small inheritance buying the place. That's why I asked my brother to look it over."

She removed her hat without thinking about it and shot both hands through her chin-length blond bob. "I was planning on six to eight months. Anything I'm doing will be done in the evenings and on my days off. It might take more time."

"That long, huh? No problems then." He shrugged his shoulders, his left hand rested on the car door handle.

It looked like the man would bail on her without answering when she could go in the house. "Wait. Why does the time matter?"

His fingers stilled on the handle. "Things happen every day. New scandals, murders, this will be old within a month. No one will remember, except your neighbors, who'll be more concerned about property value. Keep the place up and they'll forget also."

"Hmft." It sounded so easy when he said it. Spruce up the front yard with azalea bushes and tubs of colorful blooms and her neighbors would forgive her for anything as long as resale prices stayed high. "You're right. So when do I get back in the house?"

He expelled a long sigh. "You're a regular terrier once you get your teeth into something. It's not going to be today."

Not today? Her mouth fell open with his declaration. That would set the timetable back. A wasted day. Still, the image of the stranger stretched across the floorboards in need of varnishing would not leave her mind soon. "Okay." She managed a breathy reply, stunned by the sudden barrier between her and her dream. Not forever, she mentally reminded herself, just a detour. That's all.

"You look like someone killed your best friend." His brows lowered as his eyes rolled up. "Forget I said that. I meant someone stole your favorite toy."

Donna managed a slight smile for him. Sticking her foot in her mouth was something she did at least monthly. Usually, it was due to her intolerance of tiptoeing around a person's ego. No time for playing nice when you were dealing with human lives. A fellow nurse described her abrupt manner as masculine. She recognized the insult, but decided to accept it as praise since it implied she never apologized for speaking the truth.

"I know what you meant."

He rolled up on his left hip to pluck his wallet from his back pocket. The stress lines across the worn leather suggested the wallet might be as old as its owner. Taber dug out a dog-eared business card.

"It's a little worse for wear. I've being meaning to get new ones, but these will do until I run out."

She reached for the card, but Taber pulled it slightly out of reach. "I want to put my cell number on it. It only has my desk number and I'm seldom at my desk." He rested the card against the dusty dashboard before grabbing a pen to write.

"Feel free to call me tomorrow to see when you can return to work on your B and B. I'll need the keys, of course." He pocketed the pen and held out the card to her.

Needed her keys. She didn't like the sound of that. Everyone and his brother would be tromping through her house, not that she had anything to steal. "My keys are still inside with my purse, recorder and coffee."

"The recorder," he said the words more to himself than to her. "That could be helpful. Maybe some of those sounds might be on it."

Who knows what was on the recorder? All her rambling comments with a side commentary on how she hated rodents. It wasn't exactly something she wanted to share, but in the end, she probably didn't have a choice. If it helped find a killer, that's all that mattered. "Yeah. Okay." She agreed with a slight sigh that somehow didn't convey her frustration over a dream circling the drain before being sucked down.

A flash blinded her momentarily. Her vision cleared enough for her to view a camera-wielding teenager with some card clipped to his puffy vest. An officer scurried up to him, but not before, he aimed the camera at her inn for a shot. The open car door allowed her to hear the exchange.

The uniformed officer pointed away from the scene as he spoke. "Sir, you need to leave. This is a police matter."

"I know that." He snarled, not even trying to soften his disdain, echoing the same arrogance some new doctors displayed, proving that the attitude must be inherent as opposed to developed. The kid with the camera had it in spades. "That's why I'm here." His thumb motioned back to the white card on his vest. "I'm press. Here to cover the story."

Seriously? The kid who should be worried about arrest for trespassing on her property? Instead, he had the stupidity to argue with a police officer. She leaned forward, narrowing her eyes, trying to focus on the miniscule writing on the white card. *Blurry.* Still, it might be nothing more than something he copied and pasted from an Internet search.

The officer managed to stay calm while insisting the teen leave. Instead, the boy crossed his arms while angling his head back toward the car. "Is that old woman the murderer?"

Old woman! She had just turned fifty. Most of her fellow nurses insisted she looked great for her age. A few credited the absence of a husband and kids for this. Unwilling to confess to her nightly ritual of facial-tightening exercises that she usually agreed with their initial conclusion. Her lips firmed as she regarded her nemesis. Obviously, the officer didn't know how to deal with his ilk.

She scooted across the seat, ignored Taber's inquiry about where she was going and stood. For a second, she stared at the offensive creature, locking onto him as if she were a heat-seeking missile. In some ways, she was. Her muscles tensed for action as she marched toward the two males engaged in a battle of wills.

"You there!" Her index finger stabbed in the direction of Clueless and Offensive. "You are on my property. Get off." Her menacing tone often sent lab technicians scurrying for cover. The officer straightened a little, recognizing the ring of authority.

The boy-child sent her a dubious glance and then shrugged his shoulders. "Haven't you heard of freedom of the press, lady?"

Was he really going to play that card? Murdered man in her house, neighbors gossiping on the lawn, barred from the house she'd just purchased with every penny of her inheritance and now this. Anger raced through her body with liberal amounts of endorphins in the mix. A right hook would bloody the curled lip, but all the police milling about would get her jailed for assault. They might actually consider her unstable enough to be a suspect.

"Yeah, I've also heard of little boys who print off fake press passes doing two to five years in prison for fraud." She gave him a long, considering look from the top of his stylish haircut to the bottom of his expensive athletic shoes. "Lots of guys would appreciate some sweet, young thing like you to brighten up their dull days. I imagine they'd be standing in line."

Donna watched as his eyes enlarged and wondered how much she'd have to elaborate before she rattled him. His one hand felt for his vest pocket, pulling out a phone.

"Got a call I have to take." His long legs carried him across the street and into a nearby Victorian. The Federal Salt Box brick style home that squatted next to it stood out like a bleeding wound among the more elaborate Victorian mansions. No problem remembering that home or its occupants.

"Two to five years for fraud?"

The question rattled her and she turned to find Taber standing with the officer, hands in pants pockets. He gave her a knowing smile. The officer nodded and pivoted, showing former military experience in the one simple move. Either that or he was a member of a marching band.

"Okay. I made it up figuring from his 'I'm King of the World' attitude that intelligence wasn't his strong point."

"Hmmm." His murmur served as an answer. "I could do with a real bulldog like you on my team. I bet I'd get a lot more answers from dodgy witnesses."

Bulldog now, was that any better than old woman? The men who inhabited her piece of the world today were full of compliments. Normally, the bulldog statement would please her. Donna wanted people to view her as determined, confident, competent and unwilling to take attitude off anyone, sounding somewhat like a bulldog.

"Plain as day the kid was lying. I'm not sure why the officer didn't call him on it." Her grumbling covered the goulash of emotions crowding into her body. Did every emotion she owned decide to make its presence known in the space of a few hours? "All air and attitude. I know the type."

"Haynes, the officer, has to be very careful, especially in this neighborhood. Every other home is owned by a lawyer and the rest are owned by people who know lawyers and aren't afraid to use them. The woman three houses down from you called the police because she could hear the neighbor boy bouncing a basketball in his backyard court. Even sued because of it."

A chill passed over her body that had nothing to do with the frosty temps. The auction ad never mentioned anything about litigious neighbors, only that the zoning would accommodate a bed and breakfast. What if that wasn't even true?

"Did she win?" She forced the words out, afraid of the answer.

"Of course not, the judge threw it out as a waste of time. Frivolous lawsuit. However, it hasn't stopped the woman from calling the police on her neighbors or filing lawsuits. She has time and money to do both." The detective grinned, most likely finding the whole topic amusing somehow.

"What type of lawsuits?" Better to know and be prepared.

"All stupid stuff. Parking mainly. She's always out front measuring if her neighbors' cars or guest cars park too close to her area. Even had one towed away."

Visions of her guests parking in the wrong place and having their expensive vehicles manhandled while they searched for the inn terrified her. Originally, she thought a large sign would mess with the ambience of the neighborhood. Neon suddenly had merit. "Isn't that illegal?"

"Yes, it's a public street and there's no signage designating towing as a possibility. In the end, she not only had to pay the tow driver, but the legal fees of the case against her. No parking complaints have resulted lately. She did recently accuse one of her neighbor's male dogs of getting into her yard and becoming friendly with her prized spaniel."

He moved his eyebrows up and down in a comical fashion, making her laugh and she forgot about her initial fears for a second.

If the man wasn't a smoker and didn't consider her a bulldog, he might have potential. Unfortunately, he was both and served only as a reminder of the dead stranger murdered in her topmost parlor.

Chapter Three

DONNA STOOD BESIDE the detective's car staring at the personnel milling around The Painted Lady Inn. Initially, she thought the name provocative since it could have several meanings. The exterior would sport varying hues of lavender, pink and blue similar to the homes she saw when she visited Savannah.

An errant cold breeze tugged at the ends of her hair, blowing a lock across her face. The dropping temperature and gathering clouds heralded a weather change. *Perfect*, exactly what she needed to make her day complete. The way her luck was running, it would be a blizzard. Curious neighbors drifted back indoors due to a combination of falling temperature and no immediate scenes of blood and mayhem. Only a few gawkers remained. The non-athletic ball-throwing father herded his progeny into the house. Pajama pants worked for a casual look-see but didn't make the long haul. An overly made-up blonde attired in a tight sweater, jeans and stiletto heel boots kept Daniel from making his way to Donna's side.

Her brother didn't seem to be trying too hard to get away. His natural charm insisted he speak to everyone who talked to him, which made it difficult to go anywhere with him. The majority of the people eager to exchange a word were women. His wife, when she accompanied her husband, could stop female traffic with a single icy look. Maria's initial meeting happened because of an inane question she'd posed. Not surprising, she questioned other women's motives when they did the same. It was tough to keep the women away when her brother seldom wore his wedding band due to his job in construction. More than a few men lost a finger and even their life when a ring caught while using power tools. Maria accepted his explanation but didn't like it. Donna suspected the truth had more to do with he liked attention, always had.

Taber promised to retrieve her purse and coffee. So far, nothing indicated a search. A couple of police officers jogged from the impromptu gab session huddled on her front lawn and headed for cruisers. The whine of the siren indicated the possibility of a crime somewhere else. Yep, the party was over. A lone person attired in a parka with a trailing crocheted black muffler shuffled along the sidewalk with the help of a cane. Someone could possibly be out for an early morning walk. People did that even when a murder didn't happen in the immediate vicinity. Whoever it was dressed more appropriately than the woman talking to Daniel. She kept dancing on one foot and then the other until her brother predictably offered his jacket. A sigh escaped her lips as she shook her head. Yeah, her brother meant well, but sometimes he just didn't get it.

Like a good sister and even better sister-in-law, she'd have to intervene before the woman invited him in for coffee and a pastry on the side.

"Looks like Delilah has located another good-looking sap."

Her indignation over an insulting summation of her brother's behavior, even though she'd mentally already done the same, heated her blood. She threw the newcomer a dismissive glance. The man marched right up to her, without bothering to pretend he wasn't on an information-gathering mission. She had to admire such forthright behavior.

"That's my brother you're talking about." Her declaration didn't have the desired effect on the man. No excuses, apologies, or general bluster. Instead, it had no effect. He kept talking.

"Best save him now before she pulls him into the house and throws him out a few days later, just a shell of a man after she's done with him." His rusty laugh sounded more like a cough than amusement. Only his twinkling eyes announced he found some humor in his statement.

His words created an image of a pale Daniel with sunken eyes and beard stubble staggering out of one of the surrounding houses. His shirt would be misbuttoned and untucked. An angry Maria would be at the end of the walk casting daggers with her eyes not at Daniel, or the floozy that lured him into her home, but at Donna. As the oldest, the responsible one, her parents informed her early on that it was her job to look out for her younger brother.

"No worries, he's married." She hoped her words would reassure her as much as the man.

His eyebrows lifted high, disappearing behind a thick wedge of white hair peeking out beneath the rim of his fur-lined parka hood. "She's lured more than one married man inside her house. I'm not even sure she's above using a stun gun to immobilize them when her surface attractions don't do the trick."

Would the man ever shut his yap? His constant commentary annoyed her, especially when she wondered if there might be a grain of truth in any of it. The idea of her brother wandering wasn't one she wanted to examine. It took forever for him to marry after having a buffet of potential mates thrust upon him. Her mother gave up on Donna early, but with Daniel, she had hopes for grandchildren.

She just wanted the man to leave her alone, but then an idea occurred. The man knew the neighborhood and its occupants and had time to spy on them. If he could detail the goings-on, he might be able to give her some history of the house and even better, the dead man.

She thrust out her right hand in the man's direction. "Donna Tollhouse, your new neighbor." He took her hand in his glove-clad one and gave it a surprisingly firm shake.

"Herman Fremont. I see you overcame your desire to throw me off your property. Was it my sparkling repartee that did it?" His eyes danced above his drooping mustache.

"Ah, thought it would be good to get to know my neighbors."

His snort and crossed arms demonstrated his disbelief. "Okay, Donna. You strike me as a woman of sense and determination, which should make you stick out like a sore thumb in this neighborhood. Nothing but frivolous females more concerned about looking good than contributing anything while on the right side of the ground. Oh and there is one bitter, old biddy who'll sue the pants off anyone who crosses her."

"So I heard." She recognized Taber's voice as he talked to the few remaining officers standing nearby. He'd be here any minute, ending her conversation with Herman and any chance of getting needed information. "I'd like to know more about the neighborhood and its history."

"Uh-huh." He cut her a sly glance before continuing, gesturing to his head. "You saw all the snow on the roof and decided this old geezer probably knows a thing or two."

Donna stretched her lips into what she hoped was a smile. Normally, she didn't do it all that much. The fact that it felt strange and awkward meant it resembled the desired expression. "Oh no, I noticed you were a keen student of human behavior."

"Knock off that fake smile. Looks more like you're constipated and trying to pretend you aren't." He thumbed in the direction behind him. "Live over that way." A perfect location if he had any need to spy on her house.

Her smile faded. Did he think she acted as if she found him attractive? No, never. She just wanted to stroll through his collective memories.

"Better. I like an honest female. None of this fluttering eyelashes or phony expressions. What is it you want to know?" He shoved his gloved hands into his pockets, shuffled his feet and hunched his shoulders.

Taber would arrive in seconds. So much, she wanted to ask, but one question would have to do. "Do you know who owned the house?"

His eyes rolled upward as he worked his jaw from side to side, popping it once. "Hard to say, lots of people owned it, passed through hands several times. A few folks were attracted to the legend. A couple, like you, had hopes of making it into a B and B."

How did he know what her plans were? She'd told the real estate agent who initially walked her through, who must have mentioned it to someone else. The gossip train must make a regular stop at Herman Fremont's place. *Legend, interesting.*

"What legend?" Her imagination raced ahead, creating romantic triangles, suicides and consequential hauntings and even disappearing residents. Such things could either hurt or help her business. It'd be best she knew the story, too.

"Temp sure is dropping." Herman used his gloved hands to slap at his arms.

She'd doubted the man would stay considering how cold he was. "I want to hear it!" The words came out more like a demand than a polite request. Still, Herman didn't act offended.

"It's more of an urban legend, a rumor that stuck around a long time, from the end of the nineteenth century. Construction had started on your house. A sea captain commissioned the house for his beloved wife. He wanted to broadcast his financial success in the form of an elaborate home. People at that time didn't live in McMansions they couldn't afford but managed to finance. Nope, they paid cash for homes, primarily to build one. Loans existed but weren't popular. Peculiar belief that you shouldn't live in a house you couldn't afford."

Donna nodded her head while she fisted her hands inside her jacket pockets. What she really wanted to do was shake Herman and yell *Get on with it!* A brief history of the home loan wasn't necessary.

"The young wife of the original owner had a brother, James Bancroft, a dashing fellow who always had plenty of money, looks and charm. The prevailing gossip was he was a scam artist. Squired all those loaded old broads around and their diamonds vanished. None of them would point a finger at him although most people thought he helped himself as payment for his services." Herman stopped, punctuating the story with a wink.

"I got it." She volunteered that she understood the brother doubled as a gigolo to prevent Herman from explaining what services the man offered. *Ick.*

"At the time, a major crime occurred in Charlotte." Herman stopped his story as Taber approached the two of them.

The detective held out the coffee cup to Donna. "It's probably cold now. You could nuke it when you get home."

Herman looked at the detective, then back at her, then around her, pointing. "Look, there he goes!"

The three of them watched Daniel follow the blonde with more wiggle in her walk than gelatin poured into a pair of pantyhose.

"No!" The word exploded out of her mouth as she darted across the lawn. Her hand landed on Daniel's arm before he reached the porch stairs. "Stop! I need you."

The frustrated blond-haired woman put both hands on her hips and glared at both of them. Oh, the annoyed stare. *Really, she thought that would work on her. Think again, sister.* She stepped in front of her brother, cutting off his view of the siren, channeling her disdain into a freezing look directed toward the female. "My brother needs his jacket back, too. I imagine a turn in the washer will eliminate the stink of cheap perfume."

"Donna!" Her brother's use of her name reminded her once again she'd stepped over the line of polite behavior. The door of the house slammed as the angry woman's response.

Here she thought she could run a B and B. After staying at one in The Netherlands, the idea of becoming a host to various travelers captured her. Their talkative host appeared to enjoy his role. As a nurse, the people she met were heavily medicated, resentful at being in the hospital, or dying. The prospect of meeting a happier portion of society appealed as well as being her own boss, cooking for an appreciative audience and a change of scenery.

"Daniel," she snapped back. "What were you doing marching into Delilah's house?"

He blinked a couple of times. "Delilah, who's Delilah?" He angled his head in the direction of the house the blonde had slipped into. The front door opened suddenly and Daniel's jacket flew out. "You must mean Deidre. She had a creaky door she wanted me to look at once I explained I'm in construction."

Her brother must have missed her eye roll as she reached for his jacket. "Daniel, I love you, but how many houses have you entered to fix lonely women's leaky faucets, stuck windows and cabinet doors that resulted in something extra."

Daniel took the offered jacket and shrugged it back on. His habitual *aw-shucks* grin appeared, melting some of her ire. "I'll admit I've had a few run-ins with lonely women. A few might even rate up there as succubus status, but I'm married now."

"Exactly." She held her hands in front of her, making a clapping motion. *He got it. Finally.* "That's why you don't check out the various household problems."

"All right. You don't have to go all big sister on me. I understand, but what if she really did have a squeaky door?" He shook his head as if she were somehow the person at fault.

Everyone in their family readily accepted that Daniel received the looks and charm. That must have been all he got because his intelligence was MIA sometimes, or he was thinking with a different head. "If the door bothered her that much, there are plenty of people she could have called to fix it. She could have used a YouTube video for instructions. She could have gone to the hardware store and asked for help. All perfectly acceptable ways of dealing with it. So much better than allowing a total stranger into her home."

Her brother looked chastened, which didn't make her feel any better, but somehow her point may have sunk in. All the same, why not hammer it home. "Maria wouldn't like you going into a strange woman's home."

A huge laugh exploded not from her brother, but Taber, who looked silly carrying her oversized handbag. "You'd be lucky not to be bunking on the couch for the foreseeable future," the detective told him.

Daniel acknowledged the detective with a nod. "You're right."

Really. He basically repeated what she said, although he used different words and suddenly it's right coming from a man's mouth. Maybe he needed someone different to point him in the right direction. Her brother did have a tendency to tune her out after years of helpful directives. She should know better than to offer advice since unsolicited help was not always welcome. It was a habit. One she'd honed over the years.

The two men conversed as if they were old friends. Donna's lips twisted as she considered what they had to discuss. Murder. Mayhem. Women. All of her neighbors had disappeared, including the informative Herman.

Donna inquired, "Where's the old man? He was in the middle of a story."

Taber stopped guffawing long enough to answer. "He went home complaining about it being cold."

The wind chose that moment to expel an icy gust, rattling the few leaves stubbornly clinging to their branches, despite being dead. Leaves staying on a tree signaled the tree was dead, rather like a ghost, sticking around and being unaware it was a ghost. Maybe the two weren't the same. Her botany information might not be totally on the level either. The tidbit came from a man she went out with once on a coffee date. The tree bit had served as the highlight of their conversation. She shook her head, realizing her thoughts had followed a mental rabbit.

Great. Now she'd never know about the legend. *Wait.* She knew his name. Shouldn't be that hard to look up his address. At his age, he wouldn't be the type to have an unlisted phone number. The street name she knew. All she had to do is bake some of her trademark macadamia and chocolate chip cookies and show up with a plateful. The idea had merit. Her lips went up, imagining the elderly man confiding all the needed facts to catch the killer. Of course, she'd be the real hero and would merit a small blurb in the paper mentioning her inn.

"Why are you smiling?" Her brother's question alerted her that both men's attention had switched to her.

Smiling, really? She must have done it right that time.

Taber stared at her, his hand resting on her purse strap draped over his shoulder. No reason for levity, especially in a murder investigation. It gave her the appearance of being some insensitive, macabre figure. "Ah yes, well honestly, it's you holding my purse. You look so..." Before she could finish, he pulled the bag off his shoulder, holding it away from him as if he'd discovered an open vial of smallpox inside.

"Don't drop it." She darted toward her purse, snatching it by the shoulder strap. "That wasn't a cheap bag, even on clearance." Hands wrapped firmly around the strap, she hoisted it to her shoulder. "I was only joking."

The detective nodded and then winked. Was that a wink? Difficult to tell with those bushy eyebrows. Could be the morning sun was too much or something flew into his eye. Didn't mean a thing. "Am I good to go?"

"Sure. I have your number and you've got mine. Give me a call." He lifted his eyebrows a tiny bit before adding, "If you think of anything else."

"Will do." She nodded before stepping close enough to her brother to elbow him. "Let's go, Dano. We can reconvene at The Good Egg while I explain your incredible effect on women, again."

Her brother wrapped an affectionate arm around her shoulder. "I remember the lecture. Women expect ordinary guys to be friendly, polite and helpful. They expect handsome men to be arrogant jerks. When a woman encounters a handsome, charming man, like myself, they go a little bit crazy."

"Ah, spoken like a condescending jackass. There's hope for you yet. It would help if you managed to insert the word *wife* in every other sentence. My beautiful *wife* enjoys the sound of a squeaky door. My resourceful *wife* can fix a leaky faucet. I can't wait to get home to my beautiful *wife* because every moment spent away from her is agony."

Daniel chuckled slightly as she knew he would. He tightened his grip and then relaxed his hold. "You're right. I've been single so long I haven't got the marriage behavior down yet."

"Hmm, I noticed, as has Maria, I'm sure." His truck sat close to her small car on the crowded street. Parking would be the first issue for her. A discreet parking lot in the back would be a necessity. What was she saying? "Oh, just assume every woman is hitting on you because 99 percent of the time they are."

"Will do. Do you believe every guy is hitting on you?" He made a wry face at her.

Her brother thought he had made a funny. "Good one. Of course, not. I'm not you. Rumbling over the hill into fifty-one, no man looks twice at me unless he has a heart attack."

Nope, men didn't go for tall, intelligent women who spoke their minds, especially if they had some mileage on the odometer. They preferred the petite fluffy females who flattered their fragile egos. It certainly explained why her covert attempts at online dating never resulted in anything, something never mentioned to anyone in the family. They already feared she'd die alone and be eaten by her non-existent cats.

"Donna, I know I'm the little brother and you think I'm clueless. Sometimes, you're the clueless one."

A snort and a vigorous shake removed his arm. "Are you out of your mind?"

He laughed, "Maybe to disagree with you might be classified as insanity. I'm a man and you aren't. I noticed plenty of men over the years giving you the once-over. The only problem was you never stared back."

The thought made her bark with laughter. Her laugh resembled a seal's somewhat instead of the usual *haha* most people had. Her amusement always sounded like *har, har, har*, rough and discordant to the ears. It made her self-conscious and unable to laugh at most things she even found funny. It also firmed up her reputation as a serious, no-nonsense nurse.

"Yeah, right. What is this; throw your sister a bone? I know who and what I am. Name me one man who showed significant interest in me." Her brother's hesitation made her suspicious. "No making up people either."

"Donnie," he said, the use of her childhood name surprised her, "for a smart woman, you miss a lot. As for knowing yourself, you're overlooking a great deal. As for men, that detective who just left had more than a professional interest in you."

Taber? No way. She squashed the idea before it could take form. Daniel couldn't stop himself from being nice. It was who he was. A parade of women from Girl Scouts to grandmothers congregated around the rare creature, a pleasant man with a devastating smile. Maria, since marrying Daniel, often referred to him as too nice and cautioned him against letting people take advantage of him. The same advice Donna used to give her brother before she realized he enjoyed playing the hero.

Chapter Four

A POLICE CRUISER made a leisurely turn at the corner before she opened her car door. No rush, no urgent matter to attend to, it was just time to move on. Apparently, the entire force wasn't needed for the issue of an unknown dead man. A quarter of a mile later, the sight of a smiling, oversized egg perched on the edge of the restaurant roof announced her destination. As a kid, she used to confuse The Good Egg with Humpty Dumpty.

Daniel stood by the entrance, holding the front door open for two blue-haired ladies. One even patted his cheek. Donna chuckled at the action, knowing it would annoy her brother. She turned off the ignition, cutting the singer off in the middle of a word. Weird, she didn't even remember turning the radio on. Her chaotic thoughts, including a mysterious murdered man and the possibility Taber found her attractive, made enough mental noise to drown out anything else.

"C'mon, slowpoke." Her brother gestured in her direction. "I'm not going to hold this door open forever."

Actually he probably would, but the diners inside wouldn't appreciate the inflow of frosty air. Donna jogged to where her brother stood, but pointed the key fob back in the direction of her car. The horn beeped indicating the doors had locked. Good. She didn't need any more surprises today.

They grabbed a table in the back, leaving an empty table between them and the next diners, where parents battled with three young-sters under four. Their primary goal consisted of keeping the children seated as opposed to being under the table. No worries about the parents eavesdropping. They would be lucky to eat.

A bored college-age female brought them water and laminated menus. She muttered something about a breakfast special before pivoting away. Donna didn't quite catch the special, but she did notice Daniel's perplexed expression. Oh yeah, a female he didn't impress. That happened now and then. The menu hid her amuse-ment. Could be her handsome brother had reached a cut-off age where he no longer appealed to the younger set.

"Lesbian." Her low-voiced comment reached her brother as she had intended. He nodded once, concurring.

"Yeah, that's what I thought, too." Daniel worked his chin to one side, then to the other side.

Faded color photographs of huge breakfasts complete with hash browns and pancakes absorbed her attention. Usually, she told them to hold the pancakes, not feeling the need for such a substantial meal, but the unexpected murder had a way of working up an appetite. Probably would go with the pancakes then. Sure, she was feeding her anxiety, but it was hers. Made sense that she'd feed it.

Her brother grumbled about something. "Un-huh," Donna acknowledged, without listening.

"Yeah, you see it too. I wonder what the numbers are." Daniel squirmed in his chair, craning his neck to view all the diner's occupants. "What do you think the statistics are?"

"What statistics?" She didn't have a clue what Daniel was yam-mering about. "Dead men in vacant houses?"

He held out his flat palm next to his face shielding his words from the nearby lively children. "Lesbians."

Her eyebrows lifted as she realized she'd lost the conversational thread somewhere. "Daniel, I don't think there are any more or any fewer than previously. People are just more open." What did this have to do with anything? If she were a cartoon character, a lightbulb would have materialized over her head and flickered to life. Her casual comment meant to save his ego started it all.

Her brother would be forty-three in two months, not old, especially for someone who just turned fifty. His job and a gym membership kept him in shape. As a natural blond, the gray wouldn't show as much. As for his skin, a little weathered, probably from not using sunscreen as much as he should have. Still, he carried it well and it gave him rugged appeal. He had a good five to seven years before most women would see him as too old to be interesting. Would it devastate him when his good looks no longer merited superior service or enhanced opinions? Would the halo effect, where people assumed attractive people were smarter, kinder, just better than average people, dim as her brother aged? She remembered reading about it. At the time, she wondered if ugly people were perceived as meaner, more stupid and vicious. Didn't seem fair considering neither group could determine their parentage.

"What?" Daniel swept a hand over his face. "Is there something stuck to my face? Toothpaste, a bit of shaving cream?"

Shaving cream? The man actually shaved before he came. No wonder he was late. "No, I was just thinking how lucky Maria was." Good thing she wasn't Catholic. That whopper of a lie would be a confessable sin.

A huge smile stretched his lips and reached his eyes. Her off-handed comment made him happy. Maybe she should lie more often. This might be the secret to getting along with people. Besides, it wasn't a real lie. The server came back while Daniel was still beaming, but she kept scowling down at her pad. "Whadya have?"

Another flunkie from charm school. *At least I'm not the only one.* Her brother gave his order while inserting an inquiry about the server's well-being. She ignored it. Daniel's smile slipped a little. The server turned to her.

"I want the lumberjack breakfast, eggs over easy, sausage, wheat toast, grits and pancakes. Bring hot sauce and a coffee pot, while you're at it."

The server scribbled down the order and turned without a comment. Daniel watched her go with a perplexed expression. "She must not be feeling good, or she's still asleep."

Was he still stuck on why he didn't get his usual response? *Seriously.* "Dead man in my upstairs room, remember?"

He shook his head vigorously, trying to rid himself of his funk. "Of course, I remember. It was impossible to overlook the police cars and the medics wheeling out a body bag."

"Wish you would have got there earlier."

"Me, too." He covered her hand with his warm one. "It must have been hard for you seeing the body."

She kept her hand under his, which reminded her of their connection. Often as the older child, she thought of her brother as a guest, an interloper, not part of who she was. Her role was to look out for him, not terrorize him. She managed a few practical jokes, but that was the extent of it, especially when all he did in return was idolize her. Geesh, no wonder people liked him.

"The body wasn't the problem. I see dead bodies all the time." The mother wrestling her toddler gave her a startled look that had her amending her statement. "I mean, occasionally people don't survive the surgery. A few stroke out in recovery." She was sure that didn't sound like a stellar endorsement for the hospital.

Chair legs screeching and childish laughter heralded the departure of the nearby family. One child escaped his parents and ran around their table screaming in the process. The curly-headed boy smiled as he lapped their table. Cute, probably another Daniel, who'd discovered the power of good bone structure and great hair.

The mother, with one child planted on her hip, managed to snag the speedy youngster about the same time Donna replied. "It's not the dead body that's the issue. It's the location of it."

A small gasp drew their attention to the mother who held the toddler against her body with wide eyes as if she and her brother would turn into brain-hungry zombies. Daniel, always faster on people skills, remarked, "She's a mystery writer."

"Oh." The woman's arm, banding her son against her lower body, relaxed as the hunted look left her eyes, replaced by interest. "What have you written? Maybe I've read something of yours. I'm a big mystery fan."

Yeah brother, what have I written? Daniel recovered well, never letting his distress show even after caught in an out-and-out lie. "Oh, nothing's published yet. Still, I'm sure an agent will pick up her latest book."

"Oh." The minor excitement at meeting an author fizzled out of the young mother as quickly as air escaped an untied balloon. Her husband called, giving her the excuse to leave without any more conversation.

Donna watched the little family leave and head for a minivan. She'd be willing to bet it had a stick family on the back window complete with a dog or cat. "Couldn't you have made me a successful author?"

The server returned with two thick white stoneware cups and an insulated coffee carafe. She placed them on the table without pouring as she headed off toward an arm-waving patron.

Daniel angled his head in the direction of the server. "I love it when a waitress fusses over me."

"Yeah, you probably do, but I'm more concerned about the dead man in my inn." It was hard to solve issues if you couldn't stay on topic. She picked up the coffee pot and filled both cups. Sweetener packets had been laid on the table, but no cream. A saucer of creamer pods sat on the table the family had abandoned. Using a bent index finger, she pointed without speaking. Daniel retrieved them, proving their connection.

Daniel stirred the cream into his coffee. "Did you get a good look at the man?"

"I did." The man's pale face transposed over her brother's, making her shudder. "He was face down, which made me think he might be sleeping off a drunk. When I couldn't shake him awake, I ended up rolling him over. Even attempted CPR. Yeah, I got a good look at him." The stranger's face faded, leaving behind her brother's contemplative one as he sipped coffee.

"Was it anyone you recognized?"

He sounded like the police. "Of course, it wasn't anyone I knew. I could have ID'ed the man if I knew him. No one I knew. Just as well, too. If I had known him, then I'd have a possible motive."

Her brother glanced over her shoulder, causing her to turn as the server arrived with their breakfast. Daniel's plate landed with a clatter. Luckily, the eggs had congealed enough not to slide off the plate. Her plate received equally rough treatment along with the added benefit of a glare for each additional side dish. Bowl of grits, *stare*, pancakes, *even more put out* and the bottle of hot sauce, which came with an *I hope you choke on it* look.

No stranger to snarky attitudes, Donna smiled sweetly. "It all looks so good. Thank you so much for your excellent service. It was a delight being served by you."

The waitress slowly backed away, picked up her round tray and headed for the kitchen. She threw a backward glance as she went.

"Donna, that was mean. You messed with her head."

"Yep," She stared at her hash browns, then the table. "No ketch-up."

Daniel reached over to the other table and retrieved a bottle. "Doubt that the server will come back now. She'll probably have someone else bring us our bills."

"I wasn't scary." She chewed on the mouthful of sausage, savoring the spicy pork patty since she had lost the conversational thread once she started eating. Fixing, eating and even analyzing food numbered among her favorite activities. Lucky for her a fast metabolism and being on her feet all day counteracted her hearty appetite. Although lately, she'd noticed a tightness in her uniforms that hadn't existed previously.

"Un-huh." Her brother took a bite of his eggs before continuing. "Even though you were smiling, you had that *don't mess with me* look in your eyes. The one that lets people know you'll rip their arms off if they cross you."

She gave the ketchup bottle a vigorous shake without any result. "I think you got me a dud bottle." The continual shaking didn't help.

"Use your knife." Her brother waved his knife. Did he think she couldn't figure out what a knife was?

Her hand grasped the knife similar to a chimpanzee in some nature video about apes using tools. The knife served as tool, but not in the usual fashion. After several scrapes against the glass, ketchup trickled out in red splotches. The bottle exhaled, spitting out a bit with each breath. She looked at the red dots coating her potatoes when a realization occurred with such explosive clarity that it resulted in her volume increasing. "No blood."

A couple of patrons turned their heads and Daniel kicked her under the table. "Lower your voice."

A spark of anger flared. She had a strong desire to tell Daniel what he could do with his foot and advice. She tamped it down once she realized a diner was not the place to shout her murder observations. In a sotto voice, she leaned across the table. "There was no blood. Nothing to indicate homicide, but they still put it down as a homicide. The body was still warm when I touched it."

The fork dropped from her brother's hand. "I lost my appetite."

She hadn't. Picking up the syrup dispenser the server actually brought, she doused her hotcakes. Something was missing. Apparently, the medics had come in and noticed it was a murder immediately. That could just be the blood leaving his skin. "*Poisoning.*"

Their server, who was almost to their table, stopped and headed back to the kitchen. Daniel picked up the coffee pot and swished it, demonstrating its almost empty state. "I think you scared the server away again. I could do with more coffee."

"Me too." She took the coffee pot from her brother and held it in the air as she counted under her breath. An older server showed up with a fresh pot when she'd hit thirty-one, placed it on the table and scurried away.

"Nifty trick. Got service without saying a word." He reached for the new pot, refreshed his cup, then hers.

The stench of burnt toast drifted on the air, causing her to flip over her toast. Nope, not burned. Someone else was the unlucky one for a change. Just as well, she didn't feel like dealing with Miss Sullen right now. Her mother probably owned the place and rousted the teen out of bed when short a server.

"It's attitude. People give you what you expect to get. You are the absolute king of this method." Did he even realize he got different treatment or did he just assume everyone was treated the same?

"Okay. I agree." He waved his bare fork for emphasis. "I usually get good service, but not today. Can you explain that?"

"Nothing is a hundred percent. Trust me. I didn't expect a dead man in my house, but I got one anyhow. Not sure how long that will keep us out of the house or even if I'm a suspect." Her fork cut into fluffy pancakes as her brother choked on coffee when she mentioned being a suspect. She knew he would. *Predictable.*

"You. A suspect!"

"Technically, yes." The mix of buckwheat and maple syrup satisfied her need for comfort food. She chewed slowly and swallowed before answering. Her mother may have despaired of teaching her social skills, but table manners she got. It didn't stop her from talking about medical procedures while dining, but she kept her mouth shut while chewing, which was more than some people.

"Anyone who is at a crime scene must be investigated. I don't think Taber believes I'm a killer. I called, volunteered too much information, even let him take my handheld recorder. Then there's the fact I didn't know the man, tried to save him with CPR. It doesn't sound very killer like."

"Hmm." Her brother nodded as he chewed, demonstrating similar good manners. Most people didn't mind his construction talk while chowing down either. "You could be an incredibly smart criminal if doing all those things would divert someone. Still." His eyes narrowed as he paused. "I think you're right about Taber not taking you seriously as a suspect, but not for the listed reasons."

"Okay. Why?" *This should be interesting.* She moved the empty pancake plate to the center of the table while eyeing the grits and eggs. Neither one tasted that good while cold.

"Taber's a seasoned veteran cop. Couldn't get where he is without experience. He has an instinct about when someone is telling the truth. He also knows when someone is holding something back. He felt that with you."

"All good. It makes sense." She had a similar instinct in knowing when people were lying to her, especially when she confronted the spouse of a patient who denied sleeping beside her husband and the impression of her body remained on the sheets. Despite it being against hospital policy, she didn't make a big deal out of it. The sense of the familiar calmed the patient. Occasionally, she felt a twinge, especially with an older couple when one of them confessed they'd never spent a night apart since they were married.

"Thank goodness, you didn't bring up any of that nonsense about Taber wanting me."

"He does." Daniel shoveled in a mouthful of hash browns as his eyes twinkled at her.

She shook her head, unwilling to entertain the topic. "It couldn't be poisoning. I thought it was at first, but there was no vomit near the body."

"Donna." Daniel's forehead furrowed with his complaint. "Usually I can take your medical small talk, but I am eating here."

"Me too. I'm trying to figure this out. The sooner the killer is caught, the sooner the suspicious shadow hanging over my inn disappears." At least that was how she hoped it would work. There'd still be people in the neighborhood willing to rehash it, but they weren't her future customers.

The ping from the fork hitting the platter drew her attention. Her brother regarded her with a resigned expression and folded arms. "Go ahead. Tell me why it couldn't be poisoning. I'm done eating anyhow."

"I bent over him to administer CPR. As you may know, it's CPR only as opposed to mouth to mouth when you're unaware of what caused the person to be unconscious."

"No, I wasn't aware." He circled his hand for her to continue.

"As I leaned over him, there was no smell of poison." Her brother's eyebrows shot up. She continued before he could ask. "Arsenic smells rather like garlic. Cyanide has the aroma of bitter almonds. Diethyl glycol smells like maple syrup. Even though it's in everything from cough syrup to toothpaste, enough of it can kill you."

"He didn't smell like any of these?"

"No." Her eyes rolled upward as she gathered her impressions from the unknown stranger. No splotching on the face or sallowness that would be indicative of various poisons. "At first, I thought he was some homeless guy sleeping off a drunk, but then I noticed the quality of his clothes, the expensive haircut, the Rolex. When I rolled him over, I caught the scent of a high-end cologne, a complex one with notes of musk and citrus in it. At the time, I thought he was the type I wanted to visit my inn, preferably while not inebriated. I didn't know he was dead then. When I put my head near his face to see if he was breathing, he smelt fresh like mouthwash or toothpaste, not like alcohol at all. Instead of being a drunk, he was more like a man on his way to a secret tryst. Hadn't thought about it before, but what if he were there to meet someone, a romantic rendezvous?"

Her brother's lips turned down, but his gaze went past her shoulder as he spoke. "If it were romantic, then it ended badly. Makes you wonder why the secret meeting place? Better yet, how did he get in?"

How did he get in? With everything going on, she hadn't even considered this. When she opened the locked back door this morning, nothing seemed amiss. He could have come through the side or front door. Before she could relate this information, a red-faced, middle-aged woman appeared at their table. The hairnet along with the oversized apron indicated she might be the cook, or owner, or possibly both. The woman pursed her lips, fisted her hands on her hips, before giving them each a baleful glare.

"I don't appreciate all this talk about poisoning and dead bodies in my restaurant."

Donna rather admired the show of indignation. Couldn't have done better herself. Her brother smiled up at the woman, expecting the woman to soften toward him. She didn't. He hurried to explain, "We weren't talking about you personally poisoning people."

The woman's lips grew into an even tighter line that Donna would have sworn five seconds ago wasn't possible. Waving a chipped-nail index finger in Daniel's face, she announced with venom dripping from her words, "I know your type, pretty boy. Think a smile and a wink will get you out of trouble. Not here."

The woman's face reddened as she held a rigid arm in the direction of the door rather like the angel with the flaming sword barring the entrance to Eden. Yep, not hard to read that message.

Donna unhooked her purse from the back of the chair and favored the grits with a longing look before she stood. Normally, she'd put up a fuss, but too much had happened already. Daniel got up slower, probably not sure what had happened. Definitely his first ejection from anywhere, especially by a woman, not that Donna was an expert on getting the bum's rush, but she had more of a tendency to rile people up. Her brother tossed a twenty on the table, which is more than she would have done since they hadn't finished their meal.

They both walked out without comment under the silent scrutiny of the handful of diners who remained. No doubt, they'd burst into conversation as soon as the door shut. Outside in the frigid air, she winked at her brother. "First time I've ever been tossed out. I think I like it."

"I don't." His grumpy tone and woebegone expression made her laugh.

"C'mon, Dano, get in my car and we can finish our conversation, which was so rudely interrupted." Instead of answering, he went to the passenger door and waited for the unlock click before trying the door.

Once in the car, she debated turning on the engine but decided only to fire it up when it became too cold. "I guess what I want to know is how they knew it was murder. I saw no visible signs of poison. Most of the time they have to do a toxicology report to find that out anyhow."

"Do you think they may have said that to cover all the bases before they determine the cause of death?"

Weird. "It wouldn't make sense. Normally it would be the opposite. Not sure who the person was, but obviously he had money. Possibly someone important. Would the police call it murder if he weren't wealthy? Homeless people tended to die from natural causes and misadventure."

Daniel's phone chirped. He palmed it and read the text before replying. Donna knew who it was without asking. Sunday morning was probably the only day off he had to spend with his wife and she was hogging it all.

"That was Maria."

Pretend surprise. Her hand landed on her chest as she made an O with her mouth. "Really?"

"No wonder you never got the lead in any of the school plays. You're a lousy actor. She wants to know when I'll be home."

Reasonable question. "Nothing more you can do here. Maybe you can make it home in time for a second breakfast."

"Hilarious. I'm not a hobbit."

His hand was on the door handle as a familiar sedan pulled into the empty space between her car and Daniel's truck. Taber unfolded himself from his car and, seeing the occupants of the car, threw a wry smile, then walked over to the driver's side.

Donna motored the window down. "Hello. Imagine seeing you here. How can I help you?"

"A call came in from the owner of the diner." He angled his head back in the direction of the building where the apron-wrapped woman stood, legs apart, arms akimbo, itching for a fight. "Suspicious characters in the parking lot. Same two she'd thrown out for making remarks about killing people, poison and frightening her customers. She was afraid they might be concocting some type of revenge, even robbery. Typically a squad car would handle it, but I was in the area and thought the description fit you."

Description, huh? Had the bitter server described her as a tall woman with a commanding presence? A handsome woman on the upside of fifty? "What did she say?"

"Pink work boots and an attitude." His demeanor remained serious while the corner of his eyes crinkled a tiny bit.

Damn. She'd hoped for something a little more elaborate or even flattering. "I can see how you thought it might be me."

He nodded. "The yakking about a possible murder was a tip-off too. Do the two of you even know what discreet means?"

Daniel looked down at his hands, acting properly chastised. Donna wasn't having any of it. Wasn't everything happening to her?

Wasn't she getting the sharp end of the stick? No one had it worse, well, except for the victim. "We weren't talking all that loud. I know one diner had a recent hernia operation. Another one is checking her husband's texts to see if he's cheating on her. The family next to us had no control over their children and the husband was no real help, either. The only difference between them and us was our conversation was more interesting. Besides Daniel told her I was a mystery writer."

"Oh, what an inventive excuse." He exaggerated his eye roll. "That one has never been done before. How many police dramas do the two of you watch?"

Daniel looked up, recognizing an opening. "I need to go home. My wife needs me." He held up his blinking cell phone as evidence.

Taber nodded, which was all Daniel needed to escape from the car, jump into his truck and take off.

Thanks a lot, brother. "Coward." She muttered the word as she watched her brother drive away, careful not to speed out of the parking lot, but probably wanting to all the same. The diner owner watched the car leave but switched back to stare at Donna.

Taber's hand passed through the open window and nudged her shoulder. "Don't be so hard on your brother." He glanced back at the diner. "What did you do to get the owner so riled?"

"Who knows? I think this time it was actually Daniel. She called him a pretty boy. I guess that made me his floozy. I'd say she's a bitter divorcee who caught her handsome husband cheating. Now, she's suspicious of all handsome men. The break is rather recent, which explains her attitude, or she keeps the pain alive by reliving his betrayal."

A long whistle punctuated the air. "You're good at this. None of the new detectives would have summed up the woman so concisely, with her only uttering a few sentences. I'm betting you're right, a regular Sherlock Holmes."

An unaccustomed sense of pride swelled up in her chest. Most everything she did was right, professional and to the letter, but people seldom praised her for it. Instead, they expected it rather like the sun coming up every morning. They'd be upset when it didn't happen. "I have a knack for observation that serves me in my work."

His hand moved over his face, lingering on his beard stubble. "I can see that. Apparently, you've been talking the case to death. Remember anything else?"

"I did." She volunteered quickly, sounding a bit like the girl detective from the Saturday morning children's show that honed her observational skills. "Smells actually."

"Smells?" His lips pursed, then relaxed. "Like what?"

"Not any obvious poisons."

He held up a hand, stopping her. "How do you know so much about poison and should you be confessing it to me."

"Seriously." She wrinkled her nose and caught herself smiling. "I'm a nurse. It's my job. I did two years in the trauma unit and we had our share of poisonings, accidental and intentional. I realize some don't leave a scent. I didn't notice any of the obvious ones or skin mottling. A high-end cologne aroma hit me went I bent to check his airway. Still robust, it hadn't faded yet. The scent of mouthwash or just brushed teeth, the smell of a fastidious man or one whose plans centered on more than conversation. Knife-sharp crease lines remained in his khakis. He looked more like a man expecting a romantic assignation. He may have just showered too. I was freaking out a little and could have miss some details."

Taber had pulled out his pad. His pen poised over the tablet, he asked, "Could you name the cologne?"

"Not off hand. I could go to a department store and sniff what they have and maybe come up with a name. If you know who he is, then it's a moot point."

"You're right. Still call me impressed. Well, you're free to go. Remember to call me if you think of anything else. Your observations are gold. I need to go talk to the owner. Lucky for me, I'm no handsome face." He flipped his tablet shut and shoved it back into his inner jacket pocket.

The desire to correct his statement stalled before it could take shape in her mouth. Good thing because he'd know it to be false and would consider it fictionalized flattery. She didn't want that.

The engine turned over with a slight cough. Didn't need car problems when every dime she had in the bank had gone into purchasing the inn. A loan for rehabbing the property would be easy to obtain, but not as long as it was a crime scene. Supposedly, people's memories for sensationalized stories were short. This factoid she needed to be true.

Chapter Five

THE STRIDENT ALARM announced 5 a.m., vibrating with vicious vigor on the bedside table. Its annoying shriek would pierce the heaviest stupor sleep could produce. Her eyes blinked slowly, focusing on the red numerals. It continued its wail until she slapped it into silence. Daniel gifted her with the clock on her last birthday, joking it could wake the dead.

The murdered man took shape in the predawn darkness. He was standing beside her bed, looking just as lifeless, but standing. His bowed head straightened, his eyes opened, and he stretched out his open hands toward her. His lips moved. A whispery voice choked out the words, "Find my killer."

Fear strapped her to the bed, keeping her in place better than a dozen bungee cords. The specter's pale blue eyes held hers, imploring her, although she felt there was some imperiousness about his attitude. Definitely had to be a doctor in his previous life or some other profession where he ordered people around and they all scurried to do his bidding.

An honest-to-goodness ghost, a real live spirit—she paused to consider if spirits merited the adjective *live* or whatever—stood by her bed issuing commands. Her fingers gripped the covers, slowly pulling them up her chest, then over her head, cutting off her view of the glowing ghost. He had to be glowing. How else would she see him in the dark or the color of his eyes? Of course, it could all be the tail end of a dream brought on by a very stressful day. There might have never been a murdered man in her inn either. Her lips pursed as she considered the possibilities. What if she never had purchased the old Victorian? Of course, there'd be no Detective Taber and she'd still be welcome at The Good Egg restaurant.

The alarm grumbled again, starting weak and growing in irritating intensity. Work remained a constant. It also demanded she lower the covers. It had taken years to rate the primo first shift rotation. Unfortunately, it started early in the morning. Technically, it started at seven, but she had to be there at six-thirty to get the shift change information along with enough time for a cup of coffee.

Her mattress depressed somewhere near her leg, freezing her heart in mid-beat. A gentle snuffling sound started it again. Jasper, her dog, often took it upon himself to be the second alarm system. With closed eyes, she dropped the covers, afraid if she opened them, her unwelcome visitor would still be there. Jasper's tongue bathed her face while encasing her in a cloud of smelly dog breath. *Ack*, he really needed breath mints. Her eyelids flickered open, taking in the shape of her dog illuminated only by the glowing clock and the power lights from various chargers. Her hand reached blindly behind her, finding the clock and turning it off.

No ghost anywhere in the dark room, but just to be sure, she announced, "I'll find your killer. Not for you, mind you, but for me. I don't want that kind of thing attached to my inn." No reason to have some dead man bossing her around. She had enough of that in real life.

Jasper stopped licking her face and cocked his head. Unable to see his eyes, she still had no doubt he'd have that expression he often donned, the one with a slight angle of his head that somehow managed to question her sanity. Sure, she gave the poodle mix human qualities, but hey, that's what happened when you live alone. You ended up talking to yourself, being analyzed by your dog and apparently smart mouthing off to ghosts. Could have been a dream, she reminded herself as she half sleepwalked to the bathroom with a canine escort.

Jasper would literally dog her steps until he received his morning can of dog food. The bathroom's astonishing bright light served as another assault on her waking body. Most of the stores no longer stocked 100-watt fluorescent bulbs since they'd all switched over to those curly energy types. Energy saving was all good, but she didn't want to take a shower in a dim cave. Lucky for her, she'd stocked up on the high-wattage bulbs. The bulb's unforgiving glare served as a plus, she reminded herself, as she winced in the sudden burst of illumination.

She managed all her business in the bathroom without looking in the mirror once. Her early morning appearance would be enough to frighten small children with her hair mussed and often raccoon eyes from not removing her makeup completely from the night before. Good chance she'd see a little something else in the mirror, too. She saw enough horror movies as a kid where ghosts ended up in mirrors often talking to the main character. Didn't need that. She smoothed on her foundation by touch alone and decided to forego eye makeup, which would require a mirror.

Her coffee maker gurgled as she unwrapped her breakfast, a granola bar. Already dressed in her uniform, but still wearing slippers, she shuffled outside for the morning paper. She tucked it under her arm and turned as Jasper barked his demand for service. No one liked a barking dog at five-thirty in the morning.

Dog back inside, coffee made, she opened the paper. A full-color photo of her house graced the front page. The inn didn't really look her best against the strong morning light that never flattered an aging lady, even if she wasn't flesh and blood.

The peeling paint created texture, but also shouted ramshackle. Even the slight sway in the front porch showed in the paper. As much as Donna hated to admit it, the photographer had talent, even if most people wouldn't look at the photo as intently as she did. Her guests would be people who wanted to visit the quaint town, not people who already lived here.

The bold headline caught her eye when she finally looked up from the photo. UNKNOWN MAN MURDERED IN ABANDONED BUILD-ING. Abandoned sounded awful. They might as well have called it a crack house. The subtitle underneath spiked her blood pressure. IS THIS THE WORK OF A SERIAL KILLER? Whatever happened to truth in reporting? She shoved the paper away from her. It might as well be a grocery tabloid. No more of that for her. Besides, work awaited her.

The radio came on as the car engine turned over. Daniel warned her about the drain on her battery having everything left on, but she did it anyhow. Just call her a wild woman. The local news came on at the top of the hour. "Police have been handed a real-life mystery. A dead stranger showed up in a vacant home yesterday."

Vacant? That didn't sound much better. It implied neglect. Didn't they have anything else to report on? She knew better, considering the usual news involved the barbecue at the VFW and the Community Chorus Car Wash. George Pippin's steer escaping the stockyard pens monopolized the news for a week as sightings of the freedom-loving bovine came from various witnesses. In the end, the steer had to be retired to the farm after earning the nickname Liberty.

No one at work even realized she had innkeeper aspirations. All she had to do was keep mum about the entire situation until it blew over and her inn opened.

Her car nosed into her parking place. No name denoted it was hers or even for the staff, but most knew it was her place. She parked there every day. It suited her because it was close to the back entrance and she'd maintained the same spot for the last ten years. A phlebotomist, who she jokingly nicknamed The Vampire because of her blood-gathering techniques, started hijacking her place a couple of years ago when the technician first started. Someone, *okay that someone was she*, mentioned that it was the unofficial parking space of the first shift post-op surgery head nurse. You didn't get many perks as head nurse, more headaches than anything else, but her parking place was sacred, even if she enforced its sacredness with what a few might label bullying. The new hire apologized and never parked there again. Close, but never in Donna's unofficial spot.

The guard nodded at her as she swung into the building. She made a quick stop in the lounge for coffee and stowed her purse in her locker. Her cell phone slipped into her smock pocket. Phones were the only sure communication when seconds counted. Her speed dial contained a series of medical personnel as opposed to family. Nan, the shift leader, bent over a newspaper. Not too surprising at this time in the morning since most of the post-op patients still snored away in a drug-induced slumber. Once all her aids and nurses clocked in, the waking-up process would begin by checking vitals, restrooming and then breakfast.

The counter gate clicked as she pushed into the station, bringing Nan's head up. "Lookee, it's our local celebrity. I bet you had an eventful weekend." The nurse Donna often considered her work friend glanced back at the paper, then up at her with a smile.

Great. Was her name in the newspaper as the owner of the house? If so, the newspaper staff showed more journalistic diligence than the sensational headlines hinted at. She peered over Nan's shoulder. On the second page the article continued. Not too surprising, considering it was front-page news and probably the only thing that happened yesterday unless Liberty had made another escape.

A small photo showed her and Detective Taber in the car. Their heads turned toward each other indicated an intimacy she hadn't felt at the time. The words underneath the photo were even worse than *abandon* and *vacant*. **Police question suspect.** C'mon, they never even asked her name. She could sue for slander.

"I'm not a suspect!"

Nan patted her arm. "Of course you aren't. If you were, you wouldn't be here." Gwendolyn, another evening shift nurse, circled the counter, smiling at Donna before she sat and typed patient info using a keyboard. Having everything typed into computers was a lifesaver, except when the system went down. There was a backup system of handwritten notes, but most new nurses never learned the art of deciphering gibberish.

The smile was because of the ending shift or Gwendolyn had heard about the train wreck Donna's life had become was difficult to say. It shouldn't have happened in her house. Murdered folks ended up in the river or in someone's trunk in long-term parking at the airport, a grisly welcome-back present.

A red light buzzed on the patient board. Nan glanced at it. "Mrs. McDermott is up."

Gwendolyn stood without her asking. "I'll handle it. She likes me. I remind her of her beloved granddaughter back in Scotland."

Donna watched the woman leave without complaint. "Did that quarrelsome McDermott actually say that?"

"Nope." Nan winked. "I said she said that, but the end result is Gwen happily deals with the woman. It all works out."

Nan had some techniques Donna might borrow. The night shift was the crap shift. No one really wanted it if married or even in a relationship. They existed in different time zones than their loved ones and seldom saw them. Most nurses dreamed of escaping night shift, except for Nan, who enjoyed working nights because it was time spent away from her spouse. Donna didn't understand why they stayed married if neither one of them particularly enjoyed the other's company, but Nan explained it was too much work to do otherwise.

Her friend folded the paper in half so the photo of her and Taber was on top and handed it to her. "The man isn't bad looking. He has a careworn look. I'm sure the right woman could smooth out his rough edges."

"Yeah, right. Not exactly, a romantic rendezvous, Nan. He's asking me about the dead man I found in my inn." She shook her head, always surprised at a woman, too lazy to divorce her own lackluster spouse, yet found romance in the smallest things. Nan believed it into existence.

The other nurse looked thoughtful for a minute before reaching for the paper. She held it out at arm's length and brought it in slowly. "People have to meet somehow. I guess discussing why a guy up and died in your—" She stopped and looked at Donna with a shocked expression. "Did you say inn?"

Her friend's baffled expression almost made her laugh. Finding a dead man or even meeting an eligible male didn't merit as much surprise, but the idea of her doing something other than nursing stopped everything. "It's not an inn yet, but my goal is to turn the Victorian into a B and B." It wasn't how she wanted to announce her project, but it was better than being a suspect.

★

THE REST OF the day went pretty much the same. The hospital administrator called her in for a chat to make sure he didn't have a homicidal nurse on staff. Charlie, relieved it was a newspaper issue, muttered about it being bad for business otherwise. Never mind that she might go on a killing spree helping patients out of this world sooner than expected. Forget the immorality of murder. It was all about the bottom line. Charlie readily accepted the paper made crap up because they often did. The hospital had their own run-in with the newspaper when it claimed a retired teaching surgeon was a terrorist as opposed to emeritus.

By lunchtime, her minor celebrity status as possible murderer and finder of dead bodies had gotten old. It grew tiresome five seconds after she found the victim. All she needed now was for the police to name the corpse and find the killer—with a strong emphasis on *finding the killer*. She and Daniel had a lot to do to get the house ready in time for the tourist season.

Several festivals in neighboring towns brought visitors looking for a quaint place to stay with added local color. The community's reenactment of Columbus wrecking on their shore on a foggy Christmas night brought crowds too. Usually, the people broke into two camps as far as believers went. A few saw Columbus as a noble figure who did step foot on the North Carolina banks. Another group devoutly asserted he never ever step foot in America and it was inaccurate to say he did. In general, most people didn't care. They used the festival as a time to dress up in loosely based historical costumes from striped pirate pants to tightly laced corsets that had the girls on prominent display. The costumed revelers drank heavily and punctuated every other word with *argh*. Not an expression Columbus ever employed, she'd willingly bet.

Last year, she made the mistake of pointing out to a visitor that as an Italian, Columbus would not have talked like a cartoon pirate. This year she'd keep her remarks to herself. Guests didn't pay good money for history corrections by the innkeeper. The hardest job wouldn't be laundry, bookkeeping, or cooking. It would be playing nice with others, never her strong point. No one would call her a bully, but she didn't suffer fools gladly. She usually called them out in regards to their erroneous speech or actions. It never did much good. No one apologized for their ignorance and promised to do better. No, they just glared at her as if she were the one with the issue.

Her nostrils flared as she inhaled deeply. Hard job, but she could do it. She should start now in little steps. That way it wouldn't be as hard when the Painted Lady Inn opened for business. Yes, today she'd tried to be less abrupt, opinionated and confident of her rightness. On the way back from lunch, she could see a male patient, complete with an oxygen tank, smoking in the courtyard. *Really.* Her mouth dropped open. Talk about a recipe for disaster. Her rapid gait carried her out into the courtyard where she plucked the cigarette out of the startled patient's mouth.

"Were you trying to kill yourself?"

The patient flushed, but it was hard to tell if it was due to embarrassment or anger. It didn't matter. Stupid was stupid. "Are you unaware oxygen will make the flame higher? Singed nose hairs would be the least of your troubles."

Before the man could put together an answer, she pointed to a large green sign adhered to the door. "It says no smoking. Smoking is not allowed within eight feet of the hospital. The courtyard is part of the hospital."

The man nodded, his head slightly bowed. He grasped the handle of his oxygen tank and pulled it behind him as he mumbled. "My deceased wife sent you. I know she did. She promised to keep an eye on me from her place in eternity."

He thought his wife sent her. Well, she'd let him go on thinking that. Obviously, he was not going to be the person she tried out her gentler, kinder personality on. C'mon, the man was a fool. No way could she allow him to kill himself on her watch. Surely, there'd be another practice opportunity today.

To Donna's surprise, it arrived much sooner than she expected when she reentered the hospital entryway. Nora from personnel waved frantically. Donna glanced at her to see whose attention the petite redhead wanted. No one was there except for the water delivery man walking in the opposite direction in the deserted corridor. Her hand went up to her chest as she mouthed, "*Me?*"

A quick bob asserted she was it. Donna slowed her pace, considering why Nora wanted to talk to her. The hospital would be foolish to fire her. As a single, childless, experienced nurse, she epitomized the perfect worker. In other words, too old for pregnancy leave, no family-related excuses for leaving early and always able to come in when needed. With her luck, someone in the administration may have actually read the newspaper and connected the murder mansion with her. Weird considering her name was never in the paper, but the photo did resemble her. *What the fresh hell now?*

The grinning woman confused her. Only the truly evil would smile when firing someone. What did she really know about Nora besides she dressed in jewel tones and used emoticons in her memos? Not the type to engage in emotional abuse as far as she could tell. *Get it over with.* She straightened her spine and pushed back her shoulders. Yesterday, she had worked on attempting to revive an unknown dead man, whose very presence jeopardized her dreams. Could Nora throw anything worse at her?

A blue envelope appeared in Nora's hand by the time she reached her. Probably there all along and she was hiding it in her full skirt. She'd heard of a layoff notice, but never the blue envelope treatment.

"I'm so glad I saw you." Nora talked rapidly afraid someone

would cut her off. Using her hands to gesture, the envelope fanned past Donna's face several times. "Everything is happening so fast. It stresses me to get the job done."

She's stressed. Disbelief hoisted Donna's eyebrows. Seriously, did Nora actually expect some sympathy? Sorry, you have to can one of the best nurses in the building. It would be hard working up any empathy for the woman.

"It all happened at once. Everything. Kaput." She waved her hands, indicating a bomb going off. Donna couldn't take it any longer and plucked the blue envelope from Nora's fingers. A rip revealed a card of some sort. *Peculiar.* She shook the stiff card out. The thick stock featured detailed white scrolls, flowers and doves. She had heard of people getting divorce cards, but this looked more like an invitation.

Nora babbled in a breathy, babyish voice that should belong to some 1940s gangster's girlfriend instead of a grandmother of nine. Everyone knew Nora's nine grandchildren were her favorite conversational topic. It was also the main reason she avoided the woman. If she saw her first with no great desire to hear about how little Josiah started his own search engine for toddlers or that Eliza won a blue ribbon with her miniature horse team, she hid. The fact that the woman's lips still moved meant the conversation wasn't over. *Pretend she's a paying guest.* The words took form but made no sense, rather like a badly dubbed movie.

"Well, you know Dr. Emory's fellowship is over at the end of the week."

Donna grunted her acknowledgment, which is all Nora needed to continue. Donna had nothing against the woman. She rather liked Dr. Emory since she treated the nurses like people as opposed to machines, possibly because she was a woman herself and no youngster, either. The younger residents' expectations involved worship and genuflection. She had to admire a surgeon who had put herself through school and pursued her own dreams.

"She's going back to her home state, Connecticut."

Not too surprising. That's what doctors did when their fellowships ended. A farewell party, the conversation made more sense now. The hospital usually ordered lunch in for the staff, put up a few balloons; people threw in a few bucks and bought a gift card. A formal invitation never happened before today. It could be the personnel staff appreciated Emory as much as she did or even more.

Her thumb rubbed across the raised embossing. *Fancy.* Her shoulders relaxed as she half listened to Nora while planning her escape back to her station. Even though she'd left the cafeteria early, she didn't have all day to stroll the halls. Melanie's lunch break came after hers. The heavily pregnant nurse needed a break more than most. "Sorry to see her go." She liked the way her words sounded. It was a good phrase. She could change it to bid her future guests goodbye, especially the difficult ones.

"Me too," Nora declared enthusiastically, which was weird since personnel did not interact with the general or visiting staff. Employees often joked about human resources running a backroom casino. It seemed the only viable explanation for what they did behind closed doors and why they were so difficult to contact.

"I know you'll be at the party."

"Sure, I'll drop in." Everyone would show for a chance at free food. She hoped they didn't have pizza this time. The tension that had coalesced into a ball in her chest loosened, unwinding, leaving a sense of relief behind. She still had a job. It would be crazy to fire her. All the same, people lost jobs every day. Usually being a murder suspect would be enough. Never mind her remarks at The Good Egg, which could be misconstrued if anyone connected her with the hospital.

"It's this Wednesday, not much time for you to get to the mall and check out the gift registry."

"What?" She'd heard about there being a medical tool registry, but never a gift registry at the mall. Why would she get someone a gift she didn't know that well and had to be making more money than she was? Emory didn't strike her as a person who would make a gift grab from co-workers. Her thumb flipped open the invitation. *Bridal Shower* jumped out at her in bold flowing script. "I didn't know the doctor was getting married."

"Neither did she." Nora tittered, holding be-ringed fingers up to her mouth, her eyes sparkling with mirth at what she considered a funny.

Here comes a long-winded explanation. *Think paying guest. Treat her like a paying guest.*

The chatty grandmother needed no encouragement from her to continue talking. "Happened just this weekend. Her fiancé flew in and proposed. I guess he was waiting for her to finish her fellowship before popping the question." Nora clapped her hands together lightly while grinning. "I love weddings. Bridal showers, wedding dress shopping, picking the venue, planning the honeymoon. Anything about the big event."

The woman's face beamed with delight. People liked weddings. Well, at least women did. The marriage didn't carry the promise or pageantry that a wedding did with everyone spiffed up and polished and on their very best behavior. Hearts aflutter and flowers everywhere. *The wedding cake.* Something clicked in Donna's head. She could host weddings at the inn. *Brilliant.* All she needed were details. "Wow, Nora, you pulled together a bridal shower at a moment's notice."

"I did." Her chin bobbed. "Not that much trouble. I went with

Easy Go Catering, who does a light, inexpensive, but elegant lunch. Then I'm going to pick up floral arrangements at the grocery. They do good work. I used them for my nephew's wedding. Did all the flowers for half the price of a regular florist.

The visible clock over Nora's shoulder announced her lunch break's completion with audible ticks. Talk about an antique, but it still worked and served its purpose. Mercy Hospital didn't replace stuff because of age, which explained the orange vinyl furniture in the lounge, which arrived in the seventies and had stayed. "Sounds great, but my break is over. Got to go."

She tied her actions to her words by walking away. Nora called after her. "Don't forget to check the registry."

If the intended shower was a surprise, then discretion might be helpful as opposed to yelling about it in the hospital corridors. Bypassing the elevator, her long legs propelled her up the stairs. The elevator took forever and was crowded with sick people. No surprise there. She could use the exercise, too.

Melanie greeted her with a grateful smile as she rounded the corner, making her feel a twinge of guilt. She glanced at her watch. Three minutes late. "Take an extra five." The woman murmured her appreciation before heading for the restroom at a fast walk, which increased the guilt Donna felt at making the young nurse wait.

She glanced at the room board. No lights on. *Unusual.* Most of the time lunch served as a time of infinite requests. Those on liquid diets wanted solid food. Most were on bland foods and tried to broker deals with both aides and nurses for a bottle of hot sauce or even a touch more salt. If they wanted tasty food, then their best bet would be to get better or have relatives smuggle it in as they often did.

Grabbing a notepad and pen, she flopped down in her rolling chair, making it scoot across the floor in reaction. Her foot worked as an anchor as she tugged the chair back under the counter. The scent of men's cologne lingered near her keyboard. Her nostrils flared as she sniffed the air like a bloodhound picking up a scent. A sophisticated aroma, familiar, she inhaled again, trying to identify it. Ah yes, Dr. Weiss. *Figures.*

The bearded doctor reminded her of a Biblical movie extra with his deep, resonant voice and grey-streaked hair. His lavish use of cologne started before the ink on the divorce paperwork from wife four dried. She'd made the mistake of asking the name of the cologne one day. It must have sounded as if she said, "*I hear you're free again. How about you and me try hooking up,*" from the way he acted. He'd placed one arm on the counter ledge and leaned over her, boxing her in with his body as he murmured close to her ear using his gorgeous voice. "*Seductive* by Guess."

She would bet good money he'd practiced that line in the mirror a couple of times. A quick push of her foot sent her the other way as she stood. She smiled, thanked him for the info since she wanted to buy a gentleman friend a bottle. That started the rumor she had a beau. If she'd made an effort to squelch the rumor, then Weiss would know she had lied. Occasionally, the other nurses would ask about her boyfriend although she did her best to deflect those inquiries. Let them consider her reticent in her romantic dealings.

That was before. Her pen flew across the paper as she listed what she needed to research as far as wedding chapel services for her business. The front parlor with all the windows would serve as a small chapel. She would have it set up as a chapel all the time. Bring in a podium, some white chairs, a flowered arch and *voila!* Wedding Time. She would have to stage the wedding scene. Surely, she could get Maria and Daniel as her bride and groom models. Most people who wanted a small wedding had one previously. No reason to expect the whole clan to show up for a follow-up wedding. Yes, a little chapel in a B and B would fit the bill. With that in mind, there'd need to be a bridal suite.

Chloe, an aide, pushed the lunch tray cart to the service elevator where the dietary staff would pick it up. If she remembered correctly, the mother of two teenagers had a wedding planned in the future. "Chloe." She motioned the heavyset woman nearer.

The woman cast her a suspicious glance but continued toward the desk. "Yes?" Her tone implied that she knew she wouldn't like whatever new job Donna had for her.

"You're getting married," Donna said, her eyes rolling upward as she wracked her memory for a date, "in a couple of months?"

The usually genial woman narrowed her eyes as she placed her hands on her hips. "I've had my vacation request in for over eight weeks and it's approved."

Donna's nose wrinkled a little at the woman's attitude. Weren't brides supposed to float on a euphoric, pink-tinged cloud of love? "What type of room would you like for your honeymoon?"

The woman blinked. The annoyed look slid from her face as she answered. "One on the beach. I want my room facing the ocean. Why do you want to know? You're not paying for it."

Of course not. Asking personal questions merited other inquiries. How did Taber manage it? She sucked in her lips, wondering if she could solicit the information she wanted without talking about the inn. "I imagine you and your fiancé," she substituted the term since she wasn't sure of the man's name, "looked at hotels, trying to decide. What made you pick a particular place besides being on the beach?"

Chloe looked thoughtful as she held up a closed hand. "Location." She raised her index finger. "All inclusive." The middle finger went up. All-inclusive had merit. People want to know exactly what they were going to pay. A wedding package could work along with a basic one and a deluxe one. Chloe's ring finger went up. "A Jacuzzi big enough for two. None of those whirlpool baths where only one of you fits. Has to be for two. If you know what I mean." She winked broadly.

"I do," she agreed. She scribbled down the items.

1) *Chapel*

2) *Seating*

3) *Justice of the Peace*

4) *Flowers*

5) *Music*

6) *Cake & Food*

7) *Bridal Suite*

8) *Hot tub for two.*

A shadow fell over her paper as Chloe leaned over the counter.

"Love is in the air I see. Are you planning a wedding with your enigmatic gentleman friend?"

"Of course not!" She almost added what a preposterous thought it was, but didn't. Chloe's impending marriage indicated anyone could fall in love and marry. Dr. Weiss was a good twelve years older than she was and the man appeared to be on the hunt for wife number five. Why should the thought of her falling in love and marrying be so unthinkable?

The joy, lacking in Chloe's countenance, made a re-appearance, lighting up her face as if a candle glowed under her skin. "Deny it all you want, but I think you got something going on."

The woman had no clue how close she came to a bull's-eye. However, it wasn't romance.

Chapter Six

T HE MALL SKYLIGHTS cast weak rectangles of light from the fading winter sun. A tinny version of a pop holiday tune played in the background. The frantic pace of the music had Donna striding faster than she normally would have. Get in, pick the first thing on the registry under fifty dollars and get out. Odd that Emory and her fiancé had already registered. They must have set up a gift registry before a champagne toast or a frolic between the sheets. It didn't sound right.

Most people breezed through life never giving it much thought. Too many considered bad things happened to them for no reason at all without realizing they were consequences, not random accidents. Her promotion to first shift came when the constant moaning of a couple of night shift nurses had her almost resorting to duct tape to prevent another edition of being *left by love-and-leave-him* types. Their refusal to listen to her sound advice not to date the bad boys went unheeded. The actions of people continually mystified her. More than once, she caught herself trying to unravel the reason for a co-worker's idiosyncrasy. Figuring out the why of things made her great at solving mysteries.

One of her co-workers had a keychain attached to her purse with no keys. Finally, she had to ask. It turned out the woman rode the bus but displaying the keychain her youngest made her in summer camp kept harmony in the family since her house key resided on a keychain her oldest made the previous year. Whatever summer camp the kids attended needed variety in their crafts.

Her index and middle fingers rested on her lips as she considered the registry dilemma. She had heard Emory never married. Could be she knew the proposal was coming along and already registered. All that was missing was the date. It could also be the result of a failed engagement; her taste hadn't changed; only the name of a bridegroom had. Still, her nose wrinkled; it would be odd to use the same stuff picked out with another man.

The department store squatted at the end of the mall walkway with red sale signs covering most of the display windows. Mannequin heads peeked above the signs, some with, she'd swear, affronted expressions. They only had one job and a sign prevented them from doing it.

Cosmetic and perfume counters crowded the front of the store. A couple of lab-coated consultants paced the area between the cases waiting for a likely victim to talk into buying hundreds of dollars of expensive cosmetics. Been there, done that. She ignored their siren cries about the new mineral makeup and designer clutch with purchase. A wider berth sent her directly into perfume land crowded with bottles of all shapes and sizes.

The profile of a man sniffing a cologne atomizer stroked a responsive chord. Something about him seemed familiar. He turned, caught sight of her staring and put down the atomizer with a clunk that made the attendant behind the counter wince.

The man pivoted, revealing why he looked so familiar and placed both hands together in a prayer-like and pleading position. "Mary, Joseph and Blessed Jesus. You're an answer to prayer."

Detective Taber's eyes sparkled. The man actually looked happy to see her. Her hand went up to her hair, fingering a tendril. By this time of day, there'd be a shine on her nose and creases in the foundation around her eyes. Caught in her work clothes, which were only a step up from her ball cap and cargo pants, she mentally slapped herself. *What are you doing? He's the man who questioned you about a murdered guy in your inn, not a contestant on a dating program.*

"Oh, how are you?" What did one say to the man who grilled her on the details of the dead stranger? *Find any other dead bodies?*

His cheeks tightened as a grin bloomed across his face. "You're just the person I need." He angled his head back toward the perfume bottles.

Typically those words came with a request to work an extra shift, fill in on her off day, or forgo a planned vacation due to the emergency staffing shortage. Her brother started using a similar line on her whenever he conflicted with his new wife. Even though she pointed out not all women thought the same, he still delivered his problems to his big sister, expecting her to solve them. "Uhm, why?"

He pointed to his own prominent blade of a nose, then to hers. Her fingers went up to her nose. Did his gesture infer they both possessed big noses? She felt the familiar proboscis, the only characteristic that she and Daniel shared, the dominant nose as her father liked to call it. He went on to refer to it as a nose for news, a nose for dirty doings and a nose for a business deal gone wrong. Yeah, it worked on the male members of her family, giving a masculine edge to their faces. On her, it looked like she hid behind the door when God passed out the small, cute, feminine versions and showed up late when he'd moved on to the masculine styles. Usually, she didn't really think about it until someone mentioned it, like now.

Taber continued speaking, taking no notice of her nose awkwardness. "Remember how you smelled the man's cologne? Thought you'd be able to identify it if you were in a department store. Here we are." Both of his hands went out with palms up, gesturing to the stacks of fragrance testers and gift sets.

"So, here we are." Her top teeth worried her bottom lip. Should she tell him she had only buzzed into the store to get a gift? No time to help solve crimes. Her stomach gave a rumble, suggesting the less than satisfactory lunch functioned only as a memory. Nope, she had to do it. She wanted the stigma of an unknown dead man removed from her house. Besides, helping in a police case provided more stimulation than eating in front of the television. "I can help."

"Great." He rubbed his hands together as she stepped closer to the counter. Taber held a bottle of women's cologne out to her. She took it and replaced it back on the counter.

"That's the female version of the scent." Apparently, when it came to cologne he really could use her help.

His brows lowered as he considered the oddly shaped bottle. "How do you know? They both have the same name."

She nodded, pushing the bottle toward its male counterpart. "Designers tend to do that. Make two separate versions of the cologne for different genders, but keep the name the same. You may notice the bottles fit together."

"Oh." He angled his head to stare at the pair. "I see. They fit together like a puzzle. You can decipher which one is the male because it…" His voice trailed off as his face flushed. "Never mind. I got it. Could cause some trouble at Christmas though."

Cute. The man blushed when he realized the male bottle included an appendage that went into the female cylinder. Bottle designers must be thirteen-year-old boys. "Okay." Her tone turned business-like to minimize his discomfort. "Let's go with what we know. The man wears expensive clothes and a mucho dinero Rolex."

"Mucho dinero?" Taber's eyebrows went up again. The man could do sign language with his eyebrows alone. It might work the same as whiskers did for cats, enabling them ease in moving through the darkness.

"Sue me, already. Let's not waste time on the cheap stuff." She gestured to the attendant who stood a few feet away from the counter, neck bent, reading her text messages. "Miss, miss, could you show me the higher end male fragrances?"

The request stopped the female in mid-scroll. Her head went up, eyes alert, as her long strides brought her to the counter indicating a commissioned employee. "Glad to." The sales clerk gestured to her right where an opening occurred in the strategically arranged testers.

Ah yes, the good stuff. No testers allowed the cheap romeos to resort to a quick spray before their coffee date. Only those who already owned the cologne or willing to ask for a sample would be able to dabble in the pricey stuff.

The attendant gestured to the bottles under the glass shaped like tiny muscular male torsos. Using her index finger, she pointed to a black decanter. "Aventus by Creed. We have a small bottle starting at $325. Perhaps you'd like to register for a store credit card." A sly look came over the woman's face. "A fragrance that incorporates the male dominance that made Napoleon a leader, but the charisma that won Josephine's heart."

Sounded like a sales tagline to her. She was willing to bet the young chick had no clue who Napoleon and Josephine were. "Sounds possible." She lingered on the last word, making it appear that she found the cologne somewhat dubious. "I want to smell it first."

"As you know," the clerk continued, as she pawed through a box of tiny sample vials, "a cologne mixes with the natural smell of a man, creating an entirely original scent."

"Yes, I do know," Donna, replied in a slightly bored manner calling on her inner diva, finding the girl easier to deal with than she would have thought. "Still, a superior cologne will always provide the recognizable top note of the mixed aromas emanating from the male." In other words, don't try palming off that cheap stuff on me.

Taber muttered near her ear. "Sounds like an excellent way to overcharge for scented water."

The attendant held out a black card with a tiny spray vial inside it. Donna took it. Sprayed it in the air. Sniffed the air, caught a scent, but it fell fast, too soon. She picked up the slender aroma sticks on the counter and sprayed one. She waved the card in the air.

Taber watched her with a curious expression. "Why are you waving that in the air? Shouldn't you be sniffing it?"

"Not yet. The sprays use an alcohol propellant to get the scent out of the bottle. If you smell it immediately, all you get is the noticeable alcohol scent." She waved it a few more times before sniffing it. *Complex combination.* She could detect the musk over a vanilla base, citrus splurge and a hint of bergamot. Yes, this was it.

She shoved the scented cardboard under the detective's nose and announced, "This is it!"

Taber took a good sniff. "Seems familiar, but how can you be sure?"

"I have a great nose and better memory." She felt like adding she didn't know anyone, doctors included, who would spend that much on fragrance. It had to be someone with so much money they treated money like toilet paper or someone who wanted to give the appearance of being wealthy.

Taber nodded, took the sample away from her and pocketed it.

His hand cupped Donna's elbow, turning her away from the counter. The attendant's voice flowed over their shoulders. "Don't you want to buy it?"

The poor thing actually thought she'd buy vastly overpriced cologne. Glancing back over her shoulder, she noted the female's nametag. "Not today, Brendi, but I will consider it for a future purchase. I'll make sure to ask for you." The attendant, who had been on her toes, suddenly rocked back, her height diminished along with her forced smile.

The two of them walked away from the counter into the glove and sock section before speaking. Donna glanced around her looking for any shoppers who might also serve as eavesdroppers. *Nada.* "Are you going to subpoena the records of all those who bought that cologne?"

"No."

She blinked. Must not have heard him right. "How are you going to discover who the man is without going through the sales records?"

"Local store records won't help that much. Too many variables. The man could have bought the cologne on the Internet. It could have been a gift. He could have bought it elsewhere, even another county. Then again, he could have breezed through the store and asked for a sample. We'd waste time checking sales records."

Why was he even bothering to sniff cologne? Why did he waste her time then? Her mouth dropped open as she realized she'd put her much vaunted olfactory skills to work for absolutely no reason.

"I didn't say we wouldn't use the information. It helps create a profile of the unknown man and places he may have frequented and better yet, people who may be able to identify him."

She nodded. "Why didn't you say that in the first place?" Her tone sounded a touch harsh even though she tried to hide her disgruntlement.

Taber laughed. "My goodness. You're a breath of fresh air. A woman who says exactly what she means."

"Not really. About 85 percent of the stuff I think I don't say." *If he only knew.* Her eyes skimmed over the laughing man, miffed that he found her hilarious when she had no intention of being so.

Inside the overheated mall, he'd discarded his suit jacket and loosened his tie. He carried a little weight around his middle, but not too much. Not unexpected, considering his work consisted mainly of sitting behind a desk or a steering wheel. The very opposite of nursing, which consisted of reacting, continually putting out small fires and the occasional mad dash with the crash unit when someone went into cardiac arrest.

His laughter died as he gulped for air. His merriment clearly showed in his eyes, despite his gasping. Her smile tugged at her lips, despite her natural desire not to laugh at herself. "Yeah, yeah, I'm a laugh riot. That's what they keep telling me at work." Actually, they never did. Except for Karen, on second shift, who usually made a joke out of everything and often couldn't differentiate that others weren't kidding. When Donna warned her, the patient in room 412 was meaner than a bee-stung jackass, that's exactly what she meant.

Taber ran his hand over his face a couple times, rubbing way the laughter. He blinked, composed his face into a reasonably somber countenance, although amusement showed in the way the skin around his eyes crinkled. "You must be a delight to work with."

Delight. She inhaled deeply to prevent a bark of spontaneous laughter that threatened. "Ah, yes. Delight is not often a word associated with me. Efficient. Punctual. Responsible. Makes me sound more like a Boy Scout."

"Not a bad deal, either." He shrugged his shoulders. "So what brings you to the mall? I'm betting you didn't come to sniff men's cologne."

They fell in step together as they moved out of toiletries and passed lingerie. Donna lengthened her step, determined not to continue their conversation by a mannequin attired in a tiny black corset and fishnet hose. *Ah, yes, why she was here.* "There's a bridal shower at work and I need to pick something up from the gift registry."

"Makes sense." His gaze dropped below her chin briefly, returning to her eyes. "See you came right from work."

"No wonder you made detective with such astute observations skills." As soon as the words were out of her mouth, she wanted to recall them. It bordered on being sarcastic and unfortunately, she often was. Not smart to mouth off to a cop. The man didn't make her tense up the way flashing lights in her rearview mirror did. Guilt settled on her, similar to a gargantuan pigeon, pressing her down into her car seat, even when she motored along at the set speed limit. Somehow, Taber did just the opposite, relaxed her when she should be nervous. What was it about him?

His mussed hair gave him an absent-minded professor mien. His features settled into a pleasant expression as if he could break into song or laughter at any time. His folded plaid sports coat rested on one arm, his remaining hand settled in his pocket, where he jingled change and keys from the sound of it. Interesting, a telltale sign displaying nervousness.

"You're a pistol. Can't decide if you're a smart-ass or a flatterer."

Before she could clarify, she was neither, Taber continued. "Probably the first, since you're not one to give false praise."

"You're right about that, but that doesn't mean I'm a smart aleck either. Sometimes a donut is just a donut."

Merciful Heavens, did she just say donut? You couldn't get any more stereotypical than that. A location sign hung from the ceiling directing her to the bridal registry with a stylized arrow and lettering. Rescue in the form of a sign, she could peel off before any other jewel of stupidity tumbled from her mouth.

"Donut. Ha ha!" His brows bounced up and down with his laugh. He withdrew his hand from his pocket to slap his thigh. "Donna Tollhouse, you are a sharp one. I might have to linger around to see what you'll say or do next."

What? No one had ever wanted to hang about in case she made another brilliant remark. "Might let you." She murmured low, not even meaning for him to hear, but he did.

He touched her elbow briefly, guiding her in the direction of the registry. A small desk with two chairs and a diminutive silver-haired woman dressed in a pastel suit sat behind it. She looked up at their approach. "Oh, another happy couple, I can tell." Before Donna could correct the woman's erroneous assumption, she continued. "So unusual to see two mature individuals shot by Cupid's arrow. A second chance at love, heh?"

What second chance? She didn't even get the first opportunity. *Mature individual.* Her nose wrinkled at the euphemism, another word for old. "I'm here to purchase a gift from the registry."

The woman's enthusiasm dimmed. No doubt realizing she'd only sell one gift as oppose to making a list of endless gifts from pickle forks to electric blankets. "I need the list for Courtney Emory." What was the fiancé's name? She had only heard it once. "I think the groom's name is Kevin."

The woman's fingers flew across the computer keyboard. "I know which one you mean. A half dozen people have already come by today."

A hearty sigh escaped Donna's lips, causing the man beside her to give a curious look. She stood closer as the registry printed out and then spoke in a low tone. "That means all the inexpensive presents may be gone, leaving only vacuum cleaners and stand-up mixers."

"You don't know that."

"Yeah, but it's how my luck's been."

The woman stapled the list and handed it to Donna. "Make sure you tell them at checkout that your gift is on the registry. That way it can be checked off to prevent someone else buying it again."

Donna nodded, anxious to be away from the desk and all it represented. The clients would come in holding hands. Two love-saturated people oozing affection all over the floor would prance through the store with a label gun of sorts, pointing it at everything they wanted on their list. In the china section, they'd linger, discussing what pattern would best represent the two of them, planning dinner parties, deciding how many plate settings would be best. Her gait picked up as she gritted her teeth, crumpling the paper in her hand, irritated that memories she thought long buried would resurrect similar to zombies. A few sharp turns brought her into the brightly colored world of kitchen supplies.

Taber lifted a neon green metal teakettle and turned it around. He whistled. "Never even knew these came in this color. Easy to find in the morning while still half asleep."

"Yeah." She acknowledged his comment while searching the list for the cheapest unpurchased item. A shadow fell across the paper indicating Taber reading over her shoulder. The behavior typically solicited an annoyed comment, but she chose to let it go.

His index finger tapped at the paper. "The plastic storage bowls are a good bet. Practical."

"Thank you, Detective. I considered that one and the handheld vacuum too." Strange that they would come to the almost same decision. Then again, there wasn't a large selection of items under fifty dollars.

"Detective." He spoke with a touch of scorn right into her ear. "I hope you can call me Mark. After all, we did sample cologne together."

"Mark." The name had a good, solid feel, traditional name. Daniel's comment about Mark being interested came back. She shook her head. *Ridiculous.* At the grand age of fifty, she didn't expect any casual flirtation. She wasn't a young babe in yoga pants and a revealing belly shirt.

"It sounds different when you say it, Donna." He lingered on her name, making the derivative of her father's name all soft and lovely. Her brother at the young age of seven barked her name several times, trying to illustrate how it resembled a canine utterance. Her mother put an end to that behavior, but it didn't stop the barking imagery from attaching to her name. No wonder doctors calling her by her first name got on her nerves. She preferred her last name, Tollhouse, even though she had endured multiple snide comments about being a cookie expert.

A nervous giggle escaped as she shoved the list into her scrubs pocket. *Okay.* That did sound flirty. *Get ahold of yourself.* Rubbermaid set purchased, and then she'd make her departure. A banner guided her to storage. She plucked up the nearest box, compared it to the ID number on the list. Satisfied, she tucked it under her arm. A quick glance confirmed Mark stood where she left him. Stuck between a display of boxed pots and pans and table linens, awkwardness wafted off the man. His discomfort touched something deep inside of Donna. Just a tweak, but still a touch.

Her firm plan to make her goodbyes and head out softened a bit. Box in hand, she sauntered up to Mark, displaying a bravado she did not feel. "Ready. Now all I have to do is remind the clerk that this is from the gift registry. Whaddya doing for dinner?" She ran the words together; half-hoping he hadn't heard the question.

"Ah." He shoved his hand back into his pocket. "There's my dilemma. There's a certain nurse I'd love to ask out, but because I'm still on a case, I can't."

"Oh." She hadn't considered that angle. She should have since it came up in enough police dramas. "Don't think she's guilty of wrongdoing, do you?"

The smile, which was becoming familiar, stretched across his face again. "Oh, she's guilty all right."

Donna's breath caught in a gasp. He knew good and well she had nothing to do with that man in her inn. Before she could protest, Mark continued, catching her attention with a wink.

"Guilty of a smart mouth, equally keen nose and a very observant eye."

"Ha, ha." She forced the words since she didn't feel like laughing, just yet. Her heart had to slow down to a normal rhythm. "I can see that's a problem. Too bad, I had some grilled sirloin meatloaf I wanted your opinion on. I was considering it as an offering for the inn."

A frozen loaf of sirloin meatloaf sat in her freezer. Along with many other items she had created, trying to decide what recipes would work best for the impending B and B. Of course, she expected to vary them with the season. It had never crossed her mind to invite Mark over to sample some of the food until she did. His comment about not associating because of the case meant he'd refuse.

"Sounds like a great idea. I do love a homemade meatloaf. You almost never see it in restaurants anymore." His expression reminded her of her brother's when he spied the wished-for bicycle underneath the Christmas tree.

"Okey dokey, then." *Sure.* She had just muttered her grandpa's standard agreement and pivoted in the direction of the sales counter. What fresh hell did she just create? Didn't the man realize he should have refused? Who knew meatloaf would exert a siren call?

Chapter Seven

T HE SALES CLERK handed her a receipt with a sunny smile. Donna attempted a return one, but her jaws felt frozen. The clerk's smile dropped as she stumbled back a step. Her lifting of her lips must have resembled a snarl. The urge to growl, at least grimace at the situation, pressed on her, similar to the waiting crowd on a Black Friday shopping day.

Not ready for company, especially of the male variety. Her evening plans would include shoving her purchase in one of the floral gift bags she kept in stock, convinced they suited a variety of occasions, followed by a stiff drink. The closest she came to a stiff drink was a small glass of sherry, but tonight she'd unearth the Hennessey brandy. A nervous, cardiac patient who ran a liquor distribution warehouse gave it to her after he had survived open-heart surgery, convinced she held the key to his recovery. Donna would generally refuse such an expensive gift, but the heart surgeon voiced his contempt, remarking that a plebian nurse wouldn't appreciate aged cognac. Yeah, she might be a plebian, but she got the bottle.

Now everything changed. Instead of slapping on her comfortable pajamas and kicking off her shoes, clothes would be a requirement. Not too many worries about the state of the house. If her mother taught her nothing else, it was to keep the bathroom and living room reasonably tidy. No real reason for guests to wander into any other rooms. The kitchen she kept spotless, ironically because she spent the most time there. The stainless steel appliances and granite countertop crowded with an array of culinary devices retained the place in her heart that many women reserved for shoes or celebrity crushes. A particular skillet or powerful blender carried more punch than a strappy pair of Jimmy Choo sandals.

Bag on her arm, she nodded at Mark, prepared to take her leave and speed home as fast as legally possible. His forehead wrinkled as his brow lowered, he moved his lips. Nothing. Finally, he shook his head and let out a shuddering sigh.

"Ah, Donna, you don't have to invite me over because you think I'm some lonely old man who eats takeout over the sink while watching television in the next room. Even though you offered the invitation in a generous moment, it is clear that you have doubts." He shook his head again as if surprised at himself for even accepting.

There it was. A lovely way of backing out and being able to go back to the night she'd previously planned. Mark shrugged into his sports jacket, fiddled with the buttons as he waited for her reply. An artist could use him as a subject if his theme were loneliness. *Lost Man in the Mall* could serve as a title. Everyone knew women ruled the mall. Occasionally couples showed up early in their dating relationship and non-custodial fathers appeared on the weekend, tasked with updating their child's wardrobe or treating them to a current movie.

A small violinist set up shop in her brain and played the most melancholy music possible. What type of monster would she be if she waved a delicious dinner in front of a lonely man only to yank it back? "Um, that man watching television from over the sink. That wasn't you, was it?"

Mark put one hand up to his chest and winked. "Would it matter if it was?"

Oh mercy. It was him. No hope, no chance to weasel out, but suddenly when given an opportunity she didn't want to. Inhaling deeply, she decided what she'd do. *Be herself.* Yeah, what a concept. "Nope, the invite is still good. Give me about an hour. Nothing fancy now. I might want to go home and slap on some sweat pants."

Two teenaged girls with earbuds trailing over their shoulders slowed as they walked by. One of the girls elbowed the other. "Did you see that? I think they're making a date."

Apparently, daily music blasting compromised their hearing. Mark waggled his eyebrows at the remark. Donna almost laughed, but the friend's reply stopped the chuckle before it even worked its way up and out of her throat.

"No way, Lauren. They're old. No romance ever rocks their world. They do well to get up off the sofa."

Sofa. Might as well have said an assist lift chair that all the medical device stores always advertised. The commercial had the chair not only lifting the people to a standing position, but also doing everything else, except giving them a little push to get them started. Her eyes cut to Mark, who appeared undisturbed by the remark, even amused. His hand cupped her elbow as he urged her to the exit door.

Aware of his intentions, she fell into step beside him. They strolled silently for a few minutes. He glanced back over his shoulder before chuckling. "Goodness, those two would have us dead and buried already."

"I'm not sure about you, but I'm a little insulted that they would consider us so old." She gave a little sniff but realized her behavior would be exactly what the girls would expect from an older adult. When did she get old? The invitation from the AARP could have been her first indication.

"Donna, don't you remember when you were their age and convinced anyone over thirty wasn't worth your time?"

At the time, malls weren't that trendy, but she could remember her best friend Portia and her yucking it up because two of their teachers were dating. The idea that adults might desire romance and companionship kept them amused over the very public courtship of their teachers. Their every shared glance, remark and casual touch became fodder for lunchtime conversation. Eventually, the two of them quit seeing each other, proving only the young should engage in the provocative dance of attraction.

"Yeah, you're right. I remember a couple teachers dating at my junior high. We gave the two of them such a hard time they broke up."

Mark half jogged to get in front of her to open the exterior door. "My lady," he murmured as she passed through.

"Thanks, kind sir." She teased him back with a slight jump in her pulse. It didn't mean anything besides being grateful. He didn't think she was the murderer, or did he? Plenty of television detectives played the suspect, lulling the person into a sense of false security where the criminal inadvertently confessed to the crime.

The cold air rushed at her like a linebacker, causing her to fold her arms as she walked into the blustery wind. She pointed in the direction of her car and gave a small wave. "See you later."

Taber grinned and shook his head, pointing in a similar direction. "I'll see you to your car first." He moved up closer to her, but didn't touch as they walked. His open sports coat whipped out behind him, creating dark wool sails that might suddenly float him up into the sky like a kite. The dropping temperature dictated their fast pace across the hole-pocked asphalt.

Her burgundy sub-compact sat near a parking light, her usual place. She chose it not because she worried about safety, but more about the inconvenience of not finding her car. Although the handful of cars at this time of day made such an occurrence dubious. Key fob in hand, she aimed it at the car, unlocking it.

"Donna, you should really wait until you get closer to do that." Mark remarked, gesturing at the distance between her and the car. She was five feet, maybe six feet from the car door. "Why?"

Instead of answering, he looked around and gestured with his right hand to a half dozen cars. "Thugs wanting to rob, assault, or steal your car could be lurking nearby. The beep alerted them, along with your car flashing its headlights, which one was yours. Someone could come from behind, slam into you, take your keys and drive off." His head bobbed up and down vigorously at the wisdom of his pronouncement.

"Ah, thanks." Not what she wanted to say, but his comment made her feel unsafe in the mall she visited countless times. They'd reached her car and she made a show of peering into the backseat. No one, not that she expected anyone, but she hadn't expected her keys stolen along with her car, either.

Mark opened her car door before she could. Gentlemen were scarce in the area. Plenty of women, both co-workers and patients, made various comments about the lack of such a commodity. The remarks usually occurred after a run-in with an abrupt doctor, rude technician, or a boorish specialist. She smiled up at him as she sat in her seat, reminding herself it was a detective trick to fool her. *Yeah buddy, not buying it. You'll find I'm not an easy nut to crack.*

He stood near the open door, leaning into it while talking, creating a small pocket of intimacy. "As for those teachers, I bet they kept seeing each other outside of school. They only pretended to stop because of all the attention the students gave them. As a detective, you learn to look past the obvious and expect the unexpected. See ya at seven." Mark slammed the door and strolled off before she could reply.

Just as well, she didn't have any great comeback. She could have remarked it sounded like he stole the last bit from a Sherlock Holmes novel. Didn't make it less true. Any dedicated mystery looked past the obvious. Clear clues led people to suspect an underpaid domestic or a disenchanted spouse at the start of the story. Some authors felt it important to make the person so disliked that everyone had a motive.

The motor purred, but the temperature gauge hung at cold, which meant a chilly ride home. With her luck, it wouldn't warm up until she pulled into her garage. Not much, she could do about it, especially with a guest on his way.

Her tires squealed as she accelerated out of the parking lot a little faster than needed. The rearview mirror showed a minivan behind her. Good, it wasn't Taber. He probably went out a different exit. Just as well, she didn't need any comments about her driving. She had enough to deal with finding an unknown dead man in her house wearing a watch that could have served as a down payment on the inn. Robbery couldn't be a motive. Maybe a rendezvous. A known empty house served as a point hidden away from prying eyes because his lover or he, or both, were married. It would make sense that the woman lived nearby. All of it worked. The suspicious husband could have followed and killed the stranger after his wife left.

Unaware of his wife's infidelity, the husband didn't bother to pack a pistol. He didn't even own one. In the end, he resorted to his hands as a murder weapon. *Ah ha*, she had just solved the crime. A self-satisfied smile graced her face as she pulled into her neighborhood. Wait until the good detective arrived. He'd be so pleased.

There was the issue of not knowing who the killer was, but all she needed was nearby neighbors with a shaky marriage. Her smug expression dropped as she realized that could describe a good number of people. She had heard on some radio talk show that over forty percent of people cheated while married. Her head moved side to side in disbelief at the figure. It was just as well that she didn't marry. Any husband of hers who decided to cheat would end up with a sizeable crease in his skull from her cast iron skillet. One of the benefits of singlehood is that it kept her out of prison.

The car bumped up the driveway and idled as she hopped out to get the mail. In the garage, she scampered out of the car mumbling, "Why did I invite that man to dinner?" An abrupt snort answered her question. The same reason she had picked up her pup, she felt sorry for him. The man practically salivated when she mentioned the grilled Angus meatloaf and it wasn't even one of her best dishes.

As a future B and B operator, she concentrated her recipe repertoire on crepes, frittatas, challah French toast and gingerbread waffles. She'd pair the breakfasts with superior coffee or tea with a glass of fresh squeezed juice.

Jasper's excited barking made her walk faster, knowing the dog had spent a few extra hours alone in the house. The last thing she needed was an accident before Taber arrived. Jasper danced around her feet as she squeezed sideways through the tight laundry room with her purse and mall sack. Baskets of clean laundry teetered on the dryer. She should have put away the laundry Sunday, but after finding the dead man her schedule had derailed. Another reason she didn't need guests over. Her dog buffeted against her legs like a furry, excited tide and she a cruise liner.

She steamed into the kitchen with the dog following her. First things first, she opened the back door for the dog, who ran out and immediately turned back and stared at her. He never quite understood that after his fulsome welcome, she always stuck him outside, but his loyalty to her always outweighed his limited comprehension.

The frozen block of meatloaf went into the microwave defrost cycle. What should she wear for a casual evening at home? Typically, she changed, especially if she had no reason to go out. Her polar bear decorated PJs certainly were more comfortable than her work clothes, but probably might err on the side of being too casual. A pair of jeans and a checked shirt would give her the right balance between normal and not trying too hard.

A brush smoothed out a few of her windswept tendrils, while a cosmetic sponge eliminated the creases in her makeup. No reason to redo her makeup, the man had already seen her at her worst on a Sunday. Anything other than her hair sticking out of a ball cap and her face white with shock would be an improvement.

Not a date, but more of a fact-finding mission. He thought he'd dig up stuff on her and she'd eek out info about the case from him. Only difference would be he'd think she was clueless about his intentions. It served her purposes to let him keep on believing that. A spritz of perfume at her neck might help. A chirp from her microwave reminded her the ultimate aroma still needed to go in the oven.

A sharp bark denoted the dog's whereabouts. "Oh, I forgot to let Jasper back in. Where is my head?" Her bare feet smacked the hardwood floor as she sprinted for the door. Her pooch marched in on stiff legs and gave her an imperious glare. How a rescue dog managed such a high and mighty attitude both amused and puzzled her. A person would think he'd be in a constant, grateful mode. If there was a thought bubble over his head, it should be sentiments like *Thank you wonderful human for rescuing me from certain death* or *I'm so lucky to have a happy home*. Nope, Jasper's thought bubble contained phrases, not sentences: *want in, want out, cold, hungry, food giver, bacon!* Strangers, not that many ever came to the house, fell in either the category bacon giver or serial killer.

The doorbell chimed, setting off her canine alarm. Startled howls worthy of a sighting of pillaging Vikings echoed down the hall as she padded to the entrance. The good detective fell into the mass murderer designation as her dog bumped against her legs, trying to hide behind her while investigating the visitor. Her hand gripped the doorknob, but she hesitated opening it. In the intervening seconds, she reminded herself that entertaining Taber would be excellent practice for hostessing a B and B. People she didn't know would come through the doors of The Painted Lady Inn and her job would be to not only welcome them, but also draw them out, make them comfortable, relaxed with an underlying desire to come back.

Her brother could do it in his sleep. Donna sucked in her lips, considering the lacking skill set. "Good practice," she mumbled to herself as more of a reminder than mantra as she opened the door.

Chapter Eight

DETECTIVE TABER STOOD on her porch clutching a green tissue-wrapped bouquet of flowers and a bottle of wine. He grinned, holding up the flowers and the bottle. "It's been so long since anyone invited me over for dinner I wasn't sure what the proper hostess gift was, so I brought both."

Her misgivings fell away like broken Mardi Gras beads when she realized no one ever invited the man over. How could she have even regretted her impulsive invite? Another part of her, the one that usually frightened the newbie nurses, pointed out there may be a reason people didn't invite him over. Possibly, she'd have a hint of that before the evening ended.

At her silence, Taber wiggled both items. "Maybe things have changed. Wine and flowers are no longer acceptable gifts?"

"Oh, they are. Sorry." She backed up, bumping into her dog, who peered around her legs checking out the visitor. "Back, Jasper."

"Ah, I see you have a guard dog. Good." He stepped into the foyer, handed her the flowers and closed the door with a single push.

Typically, she locked the door, but Taber stood in her way. If she turned the lock would it seem as if she were locking him in? Before she could decide what to do, the detective turned and shot the deadbolt into place. "Always keep your door locked. Keeps out opportunistic robbers who simply try doors as opposed to breaking in."

"Thanks." It wasn't what she wanted to say, but exactly what a polite B and B host would. Would she lock the inn eventually? How would the visitors get in after a long day of antiquing or wine tasting?

Taber laughed as he followed her into the kitchen. "Ah, that's not what you really meant. Might as well have grumbled something about you know enough to lock your doors. I know you do. Guess it's habit more than anything else. I walk into residences where doors and windows are unlocked and they're unsure how the intruder gained access to their home."

She pivoted as she entered the kitchen, catching the detective looking confounded at the stupidity of people. A point they both could agree on. "I do lock my doors and windows. Plus, I have this excellent guard dog." The canine protector trembled by her legs, unsure of how to act around a man who had managed to gain entrance to the house. Fed Ex, UPS, mail carrier, even the neighbors she greeted at the door but never allowed them to come into the house.

Instead of laughter, silence greeted her remark as the man squatted on the floor, placing the wine bottle on the floor and holding out his hand. Jasper left the shelter of her legs and cautiously sniffed at the hand. "You're a good boy watching out for your owner. Dogs are always an excellent deterrent since they not only alert the owners of a possible intrusion but their unpredictability to a potential intruder."

Donna watched the man and dog together, unsure if he was talking to her or the canine. Jasper's tail flicked side to side rapidly, indicating Taber passed the smell test. "What's up with their unpredictability?"

"Oh, that..." Taber grimaced as he used a nearby chair to pull himself up. "The unpredictability I mean is a burglar would never know if a dog would bark or attack. Even small dogs attack out of fear as opposed to bravery." He turned to reach for the wine, but Donna grabbed it before he could.

"I could get the wine you know. I'm not decrepit. Just a little stiff since I took a spill on my motorcycle in loose gravel this past weekend."

"You have a motorcycle?" Her eyebrows went up with her voice.

Before answering, he unbuttoned his jacket and hung it over the chair. *He had on a different shirt.* "Do you live close by?"

He angled his head, giving her a narrowed eye glance. "Are you asking because you want a ride on a motorcycle or some other reason?"

"No, of course not." Her refusal dried up in her mouth as she considered the idea. Apparently, he didn't think he was too old to ride. She'd wondered about older couples on Honda Goldwings when she idled at traffic stops and caught sight of them. Were they touring the country, fulfilling some lifelong dream or just out for a bit of fun? "I figured you bought flowers, changed your shirt and arrived shortly after me, which means you either shamelessly used your police privilege to speed or you live close by."

"Excellent work, Sherlock. You're observant. I do live close by. Off Moontown Road in the Calumet subdivision. I went back into the mall, which has a flower shop. I may have driven faster than I should, but I didn't use a siren. I changed shirts at home and grabbed a bottle of wine from my wine rack. I figured a red would go with meatloaf."

Should she consider his proximity a plus or a minus? The flowers needed water so she scoured her cabinets in search of a vase. Donna liked fresh flowers, but hadn't had any in a while and couldn't remember where she had put her one and only vase. While filling an oversized glass instead of using the missing vase, she answered the wine question. "Any wine works as a hostess gift. The wine is usually not served with the meal since the hostess has already decided on the wine beforehand."

She pivoted with the impromptu flower vase in hand and noticed Taber's slightly open mouth. He'd expected the wine on the table tonight. Donna chuckled. "Well, that's normal. I had no big plans about wine tonight or otherwise. In fact, you'll have to wait a little for dinner to cook, but we could open your wine."

His mouth closed and his lips tugged up at her suggestion. "Yeah, that sounds good. I'll need a corkscrew. You get the glasses."

"It's in the top drawer by the sink."

Her frustration at her impulsive invite faded away as she reached for the crystal goblets. It had been awhile since she had a man in the house. It was hard to say when the last time was, not counting when she had asked the UPS man to bring in her Royal Doulton China for twelve she'd bought online. No men ever mysteriously materialized inside her house. Not too surprising since she didn't invite anyone over. She never had any reason to. Donna avoided romantic relationships and all the troublesome consequences they represented. Her last brush with romance left her with a non-returnable designer dress, a four-tier cake and two hundred guests who RSVP'd to a wedding that never happened.

Ancient history. No reason to go there and it wasn't exactly as if they were on a date. Taber filled the glasses she sat on the table. After setting the bottle down, he lifted a glass. "A toast to an enjoyable meal."

"I'll toast to that. I'll also guarantee it will be delicious." The glasses hit with a delicate clink. A silence hung between the two of them as they drank. The full-bodied red slid across her tongue, unveiling layers of velvety flavor in its wake, reminiscent of sunlit days, early morning mists and oaken barrels stored in a cool, dark cellar. "Excellent choice."

"Hmm." He took another sip before answering. "Yeah, I'm surprised myself. Not sure where I picked it up."

The microwave timer pinged, stopping her reply. The meal Mark expected had her pivoting in the direction of the oven. Her stove chirped as she set the temperature. "How do you feel about a baked potato and salad?"

"I would feel euphoric." His countenance mirrored his words.

"Glad to hear it." Two freshly scrubbed potatoes went into the microwave. She preferred a conventional oven for baking potatoes, but the already cooked meatloaf only needed some warming up. The ingredients for a salad landed next to her cutting board. A whim to use her newly purchased china nibbled at her as she diced a red bell pepper for the salad. After all, she planned the china for everyday use at her inn. It deserved a test run if only to see how the food looked on it. She hoped it looked delicious since the set was non-returnable.

Okay. She had exhausted the potential dinner conversation. *What now?* The provocative questions dealt with her house. When would she get back into it and what about the identity of the stranger? *Be casual.* "Hmm, heard anything else about the stiff found on my property?"

A masculine chuckle sounded closer than she expected. "Wondered when you'd asked. You lasted longer than I thought you would. Can I give you a hand with those?" He motioned to the filled salad plates.

"Sure." Was she so transparent that he had anticipated her actions? Her mouth twisted to one side as she realized he hadn't answered her question. She gathered the remnants of her salad makings and stored them in the fridge, which gave her an opportunity for pinpointing his position. Salad plates sat on the table across from one another while Taber leaned against the wall with his arms crossed and a slightly mischievous expression. It reminded her of the one the Cheshire cat had in her childhood edition of *Alice in Wonderland.*

With the fridge door opened, she bent, putting away veggies, but very aware of his eyes possibly on her backside. The thought had her straightening abruptly and quickly grabbing a couple of bottles of salad dressing, she whirled around only to discover the detective fingering paint chips. Why did she think for a moment that he had ogled her rear?

Crazy. "Those exterior colors are period authentic for the inn. I'm trying to decide what to go with, whether I should be subtly traditional or flamboyant."

"Are you trying to decide how much you can rile your neighbors after jumpstarting a crime wave in the neighborhood?"

That thought had occurred to her. Initially, she wanted the color to pop. She'd be able to describe the house as the lavender Victorian with the lemon and ecru trim. There'd be no doubt which one was the inn and it'd look great in photos, especially if she enhanced them. Not too much though, or her potential guests would never find her. In her research, she had visited her share of B and B's in the tristate area. Most had great websites featuring majestic manors with rooms that appeared huge. A fish eye lens gave the tiny rooms width they didn't possess, even turning a full-size bed into a king. As for the exteriors, none of the inns looked as good as their ads. The pics were more like online dating profile photos for inns in the building's younger, firmer years.

"I haven't decided yet. I didn't lure the man into the house and kill him. They can't possibly blame me for that. It wouldn't be logical."

"Now, Donna."

He remembered her name. *How nice.* The thought pleased her for the briefest second before another thought rushed up and stomped the joy out of the moment. Of course, he knew her name due to working the case. Her insistence on calling him by his last name would sound stupid now.

Mark kept talking, unaware of the mental dialogue going on in her head. "You've been around people enough to know logic seldom occurs in the real world."

That sounded like a crack about her age. If she had feathers, they'd be puffed up by now, alerting him of the offense. Instead, she returned to the fridge for a canister of ready-made crescent rolls. Maybe he didn't deserve buttery, soft bread, but then again, she sure deserved some. Another lull in conversation; she should say something.

"You never told me about the inn. Skipped over it entirely."

"Ah, yes, I did."

Was that a smirk on his face? Crescent rolls in hand, she placed a cookie sheet on the stove, sprayed it and unwrapped the cylinder. She slammed the edge of the container on the curve of her counter, releasing the dough and relieving her frustration.

"Okay, no reason to get violent about it."

Donna composed her face into what she regarded as her serene look before glancing back at Mark. "I'm not upset, just making dinner."

"Yeah, yeah and I'm the Pope. Don't think I'm unaware you

invited me over just to get facts out of me about the case. Didn't think for a moment that you had any interest in my humble self." His opened hand landed on his chest dramatizing his statement.

Not true. The information angle would come later. "No, no, not really." The protestation came readily to her lips, but she stopped just in time. *Getting information out of him.* Let him think that was her reason. It was certainly better than admitting he inspired pity from her. A silent glee rushed through her veins knowing she wasn't as transparent as he insisted she was. No one would refer to her as a con artist, but she could apparently keep some secrets to herself.

An errant thought pierced her balloon of smug contemplation. So far, he had read her fairly well. What if he understood her motives and his question was actually a decoy? She'd not give him the confirmation he wanted. Her fingers pressed into the soft triangle of dough, rolling it into a crescent form. Ideally, she'd make these on her own, adding rosemary or cheese. Impromptu guests had to take what they got. Perhaps her detective friend might be more forthcoming with information after he ate.

Most women thought men became all warm and loving after sex. Could be they did, when the demand exceeded the supply. Nowadays, with so many single females on the prowl, knocking boots was easy, too easy in her opinion. A delicious home-cooked meal ranked up there with a billionaire girlfriend. Well, maybe not that high, but close to it. Dessert would be the crowning touch.

In her freezer, she had blonde brownies with macadamia nuts, fig bars, bourbon balls and a praline cheesecake. Her lips twisted to one side as she considered her options. Both the brownies and fig bars would create a casual effect. The bourbon balls would melt if she tried to defrost them in the microwave. The cheesecake would warm well enough as they ate. Still, the man could be lactose intolerant.

"Um, Mark," she said, hesitating on the name. It felt odd on her tongue. A cross between spitting it out as if it were something that didn't belong in her mouth or wanting to hold it on her tongue, similar to one of her prime bourbon balls. Good solid name, one she hadn't heard in quite a while. "Do you like cheesecake?"

"Do I like cheesecake?" He pushed off the wall with a huge grin that answered the question. His smile slipped as his forehead beetled and he slowly shook his head. "You fight dirty, bringing out the heavy artillery in the form of cream cheese and sugar."

It was as she thought. Sly like a fox, the man knew her intentions. *Distract.* Being honest to the point of abruptness, distraction didn't come easy. Instead, she channeled Suzanne, the lazy nurse on second shift. Thank goodness, she never had to work with the woman much, but vacations, sick children and the occasional weather emergency threw them together. Less than ten minutes together allowed Donna to discover that the woman managed as little work as possible. She never impaired the health of the patients in an immediate way, but definitely let the record keeping slip.

When doctors asked about the lack of records or the status of a particular task, she'd looked up at them with widened eyes and ask in whispery little girl voice, "Oh, did you mean today?" Her expression mirrored an apologetic puppy so well none of the male doctors called her on it. Her double D cups didn't hurt, either. If a female doctor were on the case, especially Dr. Stedman, she disappeared aware her standard methods had no effect on the woman.

Facing toward the wall, Donna composed her face. Eyes wide and surprised, but not terrified. Okay, she had it. She pivoted on her heel, striking a pose with one hip jutting out. She went with hips since she didn't have Suzanne's girls to do the work. She fluttered her eyelashes once before purring in a husky timber. "Mercy, you'd think I'd do such a dastardly deed as preparing mouth-watering dishes to lure you into a sense of complacency? Where you'd then babble out any information you may have gained regarding the unknown deceased?"

Mark's intense gaze stayed on her face, not her hips. Her hands landed dramatically on her chest. Did it take? Did he believe her? A silence lengthened between them as she evaluated her performance. Finally, the man winked at her. *Winked.*

"You're an excellent nurse," he started, his expression giving nothing away.

Yes, she was. "How would you know?"

He lifted his bushy eyebrows, questioning her need to ask. Oh yeah, he was a detective and all that. The man had investigated her. Donna continued, "Hmft. I told you I never saw the man before. I certainly didn't murder him. That would be asinine, even if I did know him and heartily disliked him. I wouldn't be so stupid as to leave a body in a building I owned, then call the police and try to brazen it out. Oh no, I would."

Mark put up his flat palm. "Stop now. I don't want to know how you'd kill someone and dispose of the body. I'm sure you'd have a foolproof plan. Currently, I like my image of a hardworking nurse who'd like to try her hand at innkeeping. I'd prefer no murderous possibilities attached to you."

Goodness. Her mouth ran off as if skipping school on a near-summer day leaving her common sense behind. "Uh, what were you saying?"

His long legs stretched out in front of him as he settled into a chair. He folded his arms without speaking, once again falling silent.

Familiar with the method, she remained speechless too. Finally, he grinned. "The gist of my conversation is you'd never make a good actress."

Her brother Daniel had shared similar sentiments on more than one occasion. Still the remark rankled. Shouldn't she be able to do anything she set her mind out to do? "Why?"

His fingers stroked his chin as he contemplated his answer. Could be the man might even be searching for a tactful reply to guarantee he still received his dinner. Her opinion of his intelligence doubled. No wonder he saw through her pitiful acting attempt. Most men would rush in with their answer in a bid to prove their superiority.

"Ah." He hesitated on the word, drawing it out. "We haven't spent more than an hour or two together at the most. Still, you struck me as a strong, motivated woman who believed in hard work and plain speaking. No way you'd resort to a bimbo act."

She opened her mouth ready to respond, but the man held up a finger as he spoke.

"If you were a bimbo, you would have acted the part when you found the body. Instead, you started CPR and called the police. When you were hustled out of the house, you went over and questioned the nosy neighbors." He angled his head slightly as if inviting her rebuttal.

Stall. She stepped over to the freezer and opened it. After a few seconds of moving around finger-numbing packages, she unearthed a circular plastic container deep enough to hold a pie. Grabbing it, she hip-checked her side-by-side freezer door close. A beautiful swirl of color across the creamy cheesecake's frozen surface greeted her as she pulled off the lid. The dessert gently smoked in the heated kitchen. She carried it over to Mark and held it at chest level for inspection.

"Looks delicious. My stomach will think it's died and gone to food heaven."

His words appeased her somewhat. The microwave chimed, indicating the potatoes were ready. She positioned the cheesecake on top of the stove after removing it from its plastic container. The residual warmth from the oven would warm it. After the meatloaf finished, she'd turn off the oven and place the sweet in the still toasty oven. "By the way, I was only getting to know my neighbors. Not the best circumstances, but I wanted them to know my intentions of being an excellent neighbor. A few were probably already miffed; unaware their neighborhood was zoned for both residence and business."

"Zoned for business." He echoed her words, reached into his suit coat and retrieved his notebook and pen. "Okay, you obviously looked into this. What were the specific guidelines as far as running a business?"

Before she'd considered houses, she went to the courthouse and looked up all the zoning restrictions. Better locations existed, which she had to abandon since they were residential only. "Well, it was zoned for small businesses employing fewer than five people. The employer would provide parking and bathroom facilities. Initially, I think it was for more home-based businesses such as daycare, accounting, or even alterations. As the neighborhood grew higher in the instep, those home businesses faded away, although there's probably a few who still work from home."

Mark's pen flew across the paper as she spoke, making her wonder if he were even listening. He glanced up feeling her stare. "Yep, some of those folks would be as mad as a wet hen to have an actual business in the neighborhood."

"Mad enough to kill?" Surprise colored her voice. She could understand someone not wanting a car chassis on cement blocks, but what harm could an inn do? "It will be a classy place, not your budget motel. Folks with money will stay there. I'll improve the exterior of the building, landscape the yard and even provide an afternoon tea every other Sunday. What's not to like?"

A snort punctuated her statement. Mark stopped writing and glanced up. "Sorry. It's change. People don't like change, even if it's positive. Probably didn't like the building standing empty either. Now, they'll have the discomfort of workmen hogging the best parking spots, then the construction noise and finally strangers entering their neighborhood with nefarious intentions and evil plans."

Donna lifted the meatloaf pan out of the oven, holding it high in her hot padded hands. "What evil plans?" She placed the meatloaf on a waiting trivet and slipped the cake into the oven. "These are people who come for a romantic getaway. At most, they take in a street festival, do a little antiquing, take advantage of the two wineries right outside of town."

"Yeah." Mark's head bobbed in agreement. "It makes sense when you say it, but we have a dead stranger disproving your theory of everything being safe and ordinary."

Not this again. She had nothing to do with the man. Why couldn't he have died somewhere else? Even outside her house on the lawn. The dinner plates rattled as she slapped them on the counter, harder than she intended. "You know, I don't know the man. I have no clue why he was in my house. The way I see it is one of my neighbors or even the real estate agent could be implicit in this matter." She faced Mark, whose pen flew across the pad. Was he writing down what she had just said?

"Go on." His hand, holding the pen, gestured for her to continue.

"Who would know the house was empty, except for someone in the neighborhood? Not like people go cruising through the neighborhoods looking for empty houses for clandestine meetings. It also had to be someone who could get in and out without making a fuss." An image of a man slipping through the bedraggled backyard formed, a secret smile tugging at his lips as he tried the back door.

"No sign of forced entry. Do you think he came through the window?"

The image of the man continued in her mind, peering up at the windows, which sat a good five feet out of reach due to the foundation. "No, he could have had a key, someone inside had a key, or the agent forgot to lock the door once she took off the lock box. Or better yet—"

Mark interrupted her before she could finish. "Someone took the key from the lockbox."

Donna slapped her hands together. "Exactly. Whoever took the key knew the house was vacant."

"The agent should have mentioned a missing key." He murmured the words as he scratched in his notebook.

"Yes, she should have." An odd phone call after the finalized sale suddenly made sense to her. "She called me almost immediately after the sale and talked about the importance of changing the locks, especially because of the foreclosure and missing former owner."

An indecipherable comment that sounded more like a grunt with a few muttered expletives came from the table.

Donna prompted, "What did you say?"

"Real estate agents, the bottom feeders of the construction cycle. They would never tell you outright someone had your key. You could have been killed in your sleep. All she cared about was her commission. What's her name?"

"Julie Lawless."

A long whistle rent the air. "Rather appropriate. Think I just might stop in and say, 'Hello.'"

The agent's antics had rubbed Donna the wrong way from the very beginning. She got double commission since she also represented the bank as the last owners of the foreclosed home. The woman would have thrown in her own grandmother as a cook and maid if it'd sealed the sale. "If something isn't disclosed it can invalidate the sale."

A metallic click indicated the note taking had ended as Mark pocketed the pen. "Oh, I don't disagree that Ms. Lawless has some serious ethical issues, but the invalidation deals more with wood rot, sinking foundation, not a missing key."

It would be the easiest way of getting a key. "Yes, it could have been. I agree with that, but someone could have left the door unlocked. I'm assuming whoever it was came in the back door. Herman, the nosey parker neighbor, pointed out where he lived provided an excellent view of the Painted Lady, which meant he would have noticed someone entering through the front door."

"Painted who?" His furrowed forehead announced his confusion along with his words.

Donna arranged the slices of meatloaf and baked potatoes on the delicate china plates. She had considered a bolder pattern, but didn't feel it would complement the Victorian architecture. "The Painted Lady, my inn. I mentioned that." His head bobbed in agreement, but she had her doubts he'd even heard her, or worse yet she may have only thought she had mentioned it. *Oh, my stars, another senior moment.*

The detective cleared his throat. "Um yeah, the inn. I knew that. So you think a real estate agent left it unlocked?"

"Could be. I insisted on a final walkthrough. Julie was already at the lawyer's and sent her son, a young man named Oliver. He showed some anxiety about getting me out of the building after the walkthrough." The tall, slender man with round wire frames had reminded her of a doctoral student. He couldn't be too old. Certainly didn't look the real estate type with his Shetland sweater splitting under the arm. An agent would never don such a shabby outfit. Real estate might be about location, but agents had to radiate success through their appearance and their car. The practice didn't make sense to Donna since it would suggest overcharging.

"Do you think he might have something to do with the murder?" Mark's hand went inside his sports coat and withdrew the pen once again.

"No, just a kid, really. Probably forced to show me the house. His mother struck me as a real ball buster." Her eyes cut to Mark, who pondered something in his notebook. "No offense intended."

"None was taken. Why do you discount the kid? Youngsters kill more than you might think. Usually, it's an impulsive action, which was probably the case with your uninvited visitor."

Donna centered a plate in front of Mark and sat the other directly across from him. "Need silverware." She grabbed two salad forks, knives and two regular forks. "Well, he didn't have the right feel," she answered as she slid into a chair.

A throat clearing caught her attention as Mark lifted his glass. Her glass rose to meet his, clinking lightly together. "To a delicious, unexpected dinner."

His lips tugged up as she touched his glass again. "To an excellent partnership."

His brows went down as a pained expression crossed his face. "Now don't go doing that. We're not some television cop show. I'll get you in your house as soon as safely possible." He put the wine glass to his lips.

"You need me." A choking sound greeted her statement as a sudden realization of what he may have thought she meant colored her cheeks. "You need my mystery solving skills."

"Uh, no." He put down his glass, threw her a warning glance, before picking up his fork. A chunk of meatloaf went into his mouth. An approving murmur punctuated his chewing as his eyes rolled upward. *Great.* Her own cooking served as her competition.

"Wait. I'm good at this. Solving mysteries. Whenever there is a murder mystery on television I know who the killer is before the police do."

He continued chewing as if he'd never heard her. "Great meatloaf. Sure to be a hit if you decide to serve anything else besides breakfast." His potato-laden fork lifted to his mouth, ignoring the daggers her eyes threw in his direction.

"Why can't I help? You can tell me no, but it won't stop me from starting my own research mission."

A chunk of potato flew across the table as Mark coughed. Donna jumped up, ready for the Heimlich maneuver as she worked her way over to his chair, but he held up a restraining hand.

"Don't. Making wild statements while I'm eating is enough to almost kill me." His voice sounded strained, making Donna retrieve a water bottle from the fridge. She poured the cold liquid into a glass tumbler. "Here."

Mark's fingers wrapped around hers as he took the glass. His bloodshot eyes peered into hers. A question lingered there, one she couldn't decipher. As a nurse, she wanted to point out he wouldn't have choked so easily if he didn't smoke. Not a good time to bring that up. Besides, the broken capillaries could have resulted from choking, an activity he asserted she had caused.

Mark took a large gulp, then a deep breath, before he looked at her. No wink, no twinkle in his eyes, his lips pulled into a grim line. "You do realize one person is dead from whatever went on. You could be next if you got in the way."

Her fisted hand found purchase on her hip. Her jaw shifted side to side as she digested his words, not liking the taste of them at all. "Okay, a valid point. I'm not going out, guns a-blazing. Just a few questions here and there. I'm a woman, people expect me to be nosey. Might even open up easier to me than you."

"Might." He agreed and returned to eating with gusto.

No promises to let her help or anything. Two could play that game. Wielding her fork, she returned to her dinner, chewing methodically, allowing the flavors to register in a less busy part of her brain. How long could he hold out?

A cherry tomato evaded his effort until he finally speared it on the tines of his fork. He gestured with the tomato-topped utensil. "You must be the oldest child. Parents must have given you a great deal of responsibility."

Just maybe he was considering it. "Yes, yes, they did. I was very responsible."

"Hmft, I bet you were. Did they ever tell you no, or if they did, was it a word that even registered with you?"

Odd question. Her eyes flicked to his salad plate smeared with the remnants of too much dressing. Almost done, except the praline cheesecake would only extend his time for annoying comments about her childhood, even if some of them were true. "Would you like some coffee with your dessert?"

"Is the Pope Catholic?" A broad grin graced his face, signaling he was over his snit, even if she wasn't.

She made a move to stand, but he grabbed her hand. "Stay seated. Eat your meal. It won't hurt me to wait."

"Okay." Her chin dipped in acknowledgment as her mind suggested delaying tactics, which would allow her a few more minutes of information extraction even if it did include a few slams on her upbringing. The man considered himself a good detective, but it was nothing compared to an emergency room nurse on triage duty. Most people who showed up at the emergency room had no insurance, a condition that worsened past office hours or suspicious injuries that required immediate assistance. Those situations took investigative skills. The patient couldn't be treated appropriately unless he or she confessed to what combination of drugs they ingested or dangerous activity they had attempted. Occasionally, a friend or relative came along, eager to tell all without any shame or embarrassment. The reticent ones were often victims of abuse. Her duty required her to get a statement before she could document it and contact the proper authorities.

Donna noticed the man staring at his empty plate with a forlorn expression. Eventually, he'd start to suspect her turtle-like pace. What was it he mentioned about her parents? Oh yeah, she remembered now. "I don't think my parents told me no much because—"

"Ah ha, I knew it." He slapped the table hard, which was the same reaction Daniel had whenever he bested her at cards.

What did she think was attractive about this man again? "You didn't let me finish. I never asked my parents for dangerous toys or engaged in questionable activities. Why should they tell me no?" Her parents had stressed how important hard work and diligence were so much that she never spent too much time on childish behavior. With both parents working, she had fallen into the role of being her mother's helper. Her natural desire to please her parents and practical personality made her the perfect older sister.

Half of a crescent roll worked as a broom, sweeping up any crumbs of meatloaf left before Mark popped it into his mouth. Another appreciative murmur followed the bite. At least the man had excellent taste when it came to food. Wouldn't hurt to have a travel writer with Mark's enthusiasm for her cooking. It would be difficult to be mad at a man who appreciated her culinary creations.

"Of course they didn't tell you no. You were the template of the responsible older sister, probably made five-year plans when you were in your teens." The man hoisted one eyebrow as an unrepentant smile broke over his face. "So how about that cheesecake?" His hands rubbed together gleefully.

It was as if he had some dossier on her with photos of her painstakingly writing out her junior high expectations in a college-ruled notebook. Graduating with honors, winning a full scholarship, she did that. Went into medicine, she did that too. She had considered being a doctor once, but her school counselor didn't encourage her. At the time, she expected adults to have all the answers. It never occurred to her that their thwarted dreams would squeeze the life out of her own aspirations.

Her hot pad-encased hand opened the oven door, releasing the subtle scent of cheesecake with the higher sweet note of praline riding along. The pan shouldn't be hot since the cheesecake had only slightly thawed from the time spent in the off oven, but why take chances? It served as her life motive, especially after her life took a severe right turn when Thomas decided the two of them wouldn't live happily ever after. Thomas had been her step into unknown territory. Inadvertently, he had taught her a lesson. No one ever accused her of being stupid so one single experience served her well.

"It's done. All I have to do is plate it." Ah, she liked the terminology. It made her feel like a cooking show participant or the owner of a celebrated B and B. The knife slipped through the soft contents, creating eight perfect wedges since the cake still had enough firmness from not being totally thawed. All the better, she liked her cheesecake cool. She lifted a wedge with her cake server and centered it on the china dessert plate. Should she add a drizzle of raspberry or caramel syrup? It would give it a fancy look, but the cake itself would already be sweet enough.

The detective's phone chirped as she debated. His one-sided conversation attracted her attention.

"Really? I'm on my way."

It didn't sound like a casual conversation, especially when the kitchen chair skittered backward as Mark stood.

"Hey, work calls. Can I take a rain check on that coffee?" He gave her a forced smile as his gaze dipped to the cheesecake on the counter.

Her pride took a hit since his regret in leaving centered on the cheesecake and not conversing with her. She'd already accepted years ago that her athletic build and no-nonsense nature did not drive men wild with desire. "I could box up the cheesecake for you."

His car keys in hand, he stopped on his way and turned with a delighted expression. "You can?"

He resembled a kid who just found out Christmas wasn't canceled this year after hearing it was.

"It will only take a second." Flipping open a cabinet, she reached for a small bakery box she folded into a wedge shape. She had bought a dozen of them as a trial before she had the inn's name printed on them. Box completed, she inserted a paper doily inside before placing the cake on top of it. Despite Mark's rush, she gazed at the cheesecake surrounded by the three cardboard walls. Her first official boxed creation if she discounted everything she'd carried to work previously.

Enough. She closed the box and handed it to Mark as a suspicious thought popped into her brain. "Not rushing off to my inn, are you?" Local crime wave consisted more of burglaries, speeding and the occasional trespasser call.

The detective hesitated with his palm on her exterior door. The white edge of the bakery box stuck out of his sports coat pocket. The man had mangled her dessert in his hurry to leave. Her inward cringe almost made her miss his parting sally, but not quite.

"I wouldn't tell you that because if I did you'd hotfoot it over there and get in the way."

The door slammed, ending the need to reply before she could.

Chapter Nine

THE CLOSED DOOR mocked Donna. It ended the conversation before she even poked at Mark's pronouncement that he wouldn't tell her if it were her inn that drew him away. Probably because she'd just go sticking her nose in police matters. Her lips pursed as she considered the possibilities. If the good detective were off duty as he mentioned, then why would he tear off unless whatever happened involved a case? Her case.

The iconic lightbulb practically glowed over her head before she reached for her purse and car keys. "Sorry, bud," she murmured to her dog who stood close to the garage door with his tail whipping side to side like a flag caught in gale force winds. "You're not going. Mama has a case."

No need to look at her dog who would have melted onto the floor, casting forlorn gazes worthy of a rescue pet commercial. *Be strong.* She admonished herself as she slipped into her car and started it. Of course, she needed to investigate what was happening, especially if it occurred on her property. Detective Taber, *Mark,* she corrected herself, could be closemouthed even when bribed with mouthwatering delicacies.

No one cared about the inn the way she did. Most likely, the neighbors saw it as a harbinger of bad things to come. Anyone who read about it in a newspaper probably forgot about it within forty-eight hours. A few might remember it, those who watched crime dramas religiously and in turn expected a series of bizarre murders. The police saw it as a case. Nothing more, something that needed solving, the sooner, the better, which resulted in many murders pinned on surviving spouses, children, or exes. Quicker to find someone close by with a motive than do any deep research.

Her car reversed down the driveway as she mulled over the possibility of a nearby person slapped with a murder rap in the name of expediency. Her head swiveled as she checked the street for traffic as she pulled out. The most expedient person to blame would be her since she called in the murder. No one suspected her, or did they?

It could be the detective played a deep game, allowing her to think she wasn't guilty and then pretended to like her just a little. The casual meeting in the mall could have been a set-up. For all she knew there could be a tracker on her car. Her foot depressed the accelerator, pushing the speed too fast for her residential neighborhood. *Watch it.* Her anger occasionally got the best of her. In that case, everyone took cover. Mount Vesuvius had nothing on her when she exploded.

The route to the inn she could almost drive blindfolded considering the number of times she had driven by the place. A freight train's whistle alerted her of the possibility of delay. Three engines chugged by as the safety arms went down, preventing any daredevils from sprinting across the tracks. Visual inspection of the cars ahead of her assured her that Mark had missed the holdup. He'd already be at the inn and possibly gone by the time she arrived. Her flat palm pounded against the steering wheel. Unfortunately, her impatience wouldn't hurry the train along any faster.

Typically, she counted the cars or admired the graffiti. The detailed artwork done in the dead of night surprised her. Why anyone worked that hard for something they couldn't even claim amazed her. Today, she did neither. Instead, she replayed famous murder cases highlighted in the newspapers. For the most part, someone close did murder the victim. Usually the spouse or the soon-to-be-ex-spouse, which would make sense if the victim were hooking up with someone else.

The image of the dead man shimmered and faded as she tried to recall it. It was becoming more like a dream upon awakening. "Really?" Her voice echoed in the car. The picture should stay burned into her memory forever. Sure, she could see him stretched out on the wood floor in his expensive clothes and flashy watch. What she couldn't see was his left hand or his ring finger. Even married men knew enough to pocket their wedding ring when going to an assignation. Police never mentioned it, but they didn't report to her, either. A thorough search may have discovered it tucked in his pants pocket.

The train wheels clattering faded away as the crossing arms went up. The red digital numbers on her dashboard clock informed that a long twelve minutes had passed. Time enough to turn off her engine, although she hadn't. The cars in front of her were hesitant to cross the tracks, afraid a speeding engine might appear with an ominous bright eye directed their way.

"C'mon, folks." Her muttering didn't increase the other motorists' speed. Finally, her turn came as she bumped over the crossing. Her foot tapped the gas only to move a grand two hundred yards before a traffic light blinked red. Everything conspired against her speedy checkout of her property.

She seethed silently at the light until it turned green and she stomped the accelerator. Tires squealed near her as her car jumped into the intersection. Her head swiveled, looking for the offender until she realized by the other drivers' expressions that it was her.

Goodness, she sucked in her lips and used her burst of speed to get away from her silent accusers. After two blocks, she dropped to the speed limit well aware the section served as a speed trap.

Her inn came into view along with a police car and the detective's sedan. *Great.* What would she say? Mark leaned against his car with his arms folded, talking to a police officer. She slowed, wondering if she should drive on by. A wave in her direction signaled recognition, which meant she should stop. No help for it, she nosed her car in front of Mark's.

"What took you so long?" His question greeted her as she exited the car.

"Train." Might as well go with the truth since the man knew her intentions.

"I knew you were coming so I stayed." He winked.

The man winked at her, or did he? It could be a facial tic that would be embarrassing if misinterpreted. He motioned to the house. "I had an officer watching the house when he spotted a possible break-in."

"Again? It's like Grand Central Station and I haven't even opened for business."

The young officer spoke up. "Looks like teenagers to me. They ran back home." He angled his head to the surrounding houses. "Teens can be on the macabre side wanting to see where someone died and all."

Teens. Her eyes narrowed as she regarded the young officer. How well did he follow up on the intruders? Did he actually see them? Probably too busy texting since he was little more than a teen himself. Before she could even form her question, the detective held up an open palm in her direction, halting any inquiry.

A nearby slamming door caught her attention as a large poodle, trailed by its well-dressed male owners, left for a walk. Her gaze remained on the three. Didn't they realize how obvious they were walking the dog whenever a police car appeared in the neighborhood? Then again, dogs needed to be walked, especially an oversized one. Her lips pulled to one side as she considered the dog walkers. Ideal people to question if they were out all hours walking Miss Prissy, the name she christened the dog with since it seemed to fit.

A slight awareness danced across her skin, which always came when watched. A backward glance caught Mark's brown eyes focused on her while his expression didn't reflect a trace of lust, but rather a weariness akin to dealing with a tiresome child or a wayward puppy. He shook his head slowly side to side, acting like he knew. How could he? Oh yeah, her lack of a poker face or the ability to fabricate. *Need to work on those qualities.*

"Donna, if you promise not to hound your neighbors with impertinent questions, I'll tell you about the attempted break-in." The officer beside him made a distressed sound that he tried to muffle as a cough. Mark cupped her elbow and directed her away from the listening police officer and closer to her car.

She'd listen since she hadn't thought of an appropriate way to bump into her dog-walking neighbors yet. Next time, she'd load up Jasper. This would allow her a casual saunter through the neighborhood, where she could greet the dog lovers with a smile and a compliment for their dog since people loved it when you complimented their pet. It served as an accolade for the owner without the suspicion that usually accompanied the unmerited flattery. Somehow, she'd insert a remark about if they'd seen anything strange. Even with her dog as a prop, she couldn't see the conversation flowing naturally to unknown dead men unless they brought it up. It could happen, though.

"Here's far enough."

The masculine voice interrupted her rehearsal of how she could lead the possible witness into confessing what he knew. Her eyebrows lifted as she considered Mark's words, which sounded more like a command, causing an eyebrow lift.

Sensing her mood or at least guessing at her unspoken question, he angled his head in the direction of the officer, then the dog walkers. "It seems fair to me you should know details about who tried to break into your inn. Better to hear from me than go into all sorts of speculation that might have you camped out in the building trying to catch someone entering without a key."

The stranger had entered with a key or through an unlocked door. *Camped out in the inn waiting for a possible follow-up visit.* The thought had merit; except for whoever returned would be a murderer. What was the saying? Murderers always returned to the scene of the crime, which she always found a stupid action, rather like waving a red cape at a bull. *Camp out,* she'd have to remember that tidbit, even though the idea unnerved her as much as wading through a creek with water snakes in it.

Feeling his gaze, she stumbled for an appropriate response. "Yeah, yeah, crazy. Who would do such a thing? Not me, that's for sure. Have to be a wacko." Her rambling denial stopped as his expression changed, causing his eyes to sharpen and his lips to tighten. He suspected her or her police drama addiction made her paranoid.

"Donna," he started and then let out a long sigh. "I like you. You're a smart, capable, strong woman and a hell of a cook. There's a great deal to admire about you." A twinkle appeared in his eyes, causing the crow's feet to deepen. One of his hands went into his pants pocket and rattled his change and keys.

Talk about unexpected. Her shoulders went back and her head up as she preened under his flattery. Could be she had misread the man entirely. Never thought of herself as a femme fatale, but her brother reminded her on several occasions she still had her looks. Sometimes, she felt the mention served as a backhanded compliment to his own handsome appearance.

"You're also one of the most headstrong, bullheaded females I've ever encountered and I've met a few in my profession."

Her smile disappeared as her gaze latched onto Mark's unconcerned demeanor. Was the man unaware he'd just uttered fighting words? Sure, she wouldn't wrestle a police officer over a variation of a comment she'd heard more than a half dozen times from different lips. Of course, in the past she mentally had called it a compliment before blacklisting the speakers as people to avoid.

The dog walkers drew closer; making her wonder if, she should somehow signal Mark not to say anything. Bad enough a crime wave started when she took possession of the inn, but no reason for everyone to know the details. Without her saying a word, he stopped his litany on her stubbornness. "I do not see why you couldn't start renovation work on the inn. You should be inside painting walls and buffing floors within twenty-four hours."

"That's great!" Not as great as she liked since she worked twelve-hour shifts most of the week, leaving her little daylight in which to work. The thought of working alone in the house in full dark unnerved her. No use asking her brother since he had his own job and a new wife. Even having him drop by on weekends was a huge concession on Maria's part. Still, if she hoped to be on schedule, work had to be done. Her mind raced as she weighed the prospect of being alone in a large, empty house that apparently wasn't too hard to enter.

The dog walkers sauntered by with a nod that Donna countered with an enthusiastic, "Good evening." Her overly bright greeting made her wince as she realized she sounded more like a car salesperson running for political office. Yep, desperation and need had colored the two words. Right now, what she needed was for everyone to believe the inn posed no threat.

One of the dog walkers gave her a startled glance and murmured "Evening" back. The other fussed with the dog's ornate collar, which probably weighed down the canine's neck. The price the dog paid for his owners' need for excessive attention. Four steps carried them out of hearing range as Donna considered their observation skills. Did they see anything out of the ordinary? People analyzed everything in relation to themselves. A handsome man would garner notice from the two if only nudging them down the neighborhood hotness ladder. The stranger's possible plan was not to attract notice by slipping in through the backyard, hiding in the shadow of the overgrown hedges. If nothing else, the neighbors should be thankful she'd step up the landscaping. The real estate agent's curb appeal service included regular lawn mowing, but apparently nothing else.

"I said that for our nosy friends, not you. It's your house, but I don't expect you to work alone or at night, especially alone at night."

Even though she'd agreed with his words as the skies darkened, her eyes still rolled upward. "It's my house." She felt the need to protest his high-handed manner. Who was he giving her orders? Her hands balled at her side as she shuffled her feet restlessly.

"Yep," he agreed, peering at something over her shoulder. "Wonderful, another inquisitive neighbor making a beeline to you."

The detective's phone chirped at the same time silver-haired Herman reached her. Mark stepped back to take the call. Part of her medical training insisted she use the patient's name in conversation.

Studies showed it relaxed the patient and gave confidence in the care providers, all good. It also allowed to a certainty that the right person would get the appropriate medical procedure. No tabloid headlines for her hospital about amputations of the wrong limb or unexpected sexual reassignment surgery.

"Herman, so nice to see you."

A huge grin stretched across his face. "Good to see you, too. I knew things were looking up with the possibility of a beautiful woman moving into the jewel thief hostel."

Her skin flushed at his substantial praise, a curse of the fair-skinned. Flattery served as the much-used tool of the elderly male, but the remark pleased her nonetheless, almost making her miss the rest of the sentence. "Jewel thief hostel?"

"You mean you never heard the story?" he asked, playfully wiggling his eyebrows. A significant pause, along with the gleam in his eyes, evidenced his enjoyment of being a holder of such a tale.

A quick look revealed Mark engaged in a phone conversation with much gesturing and grumbling, usually indicative of family or an ex. Just as well, there was no doubt the man would pooh-pooh the tale. Turning back to Herman, she nodded. "Do tell," she urged with an avid look and placed her hands in front of her in a prayer-like position. She dropped them immediately, afraid it might be overkill.

Herman chuckled, rubbing his hands together reminding her of a silent film star villain. "Back when your house was built another crime happened in the area. No one associated it with the house, which was under construction."

"What happened?" she prompted, wanting him to get on with his tale before Mark returned with his police protocol and debunked the whole thing. Even urban legends started for a reason.

"Well, I may be old, but I wasn't around when the house was built, but my grandfather and father were." He stopped, apparently waiting for a commentary on his age.

Yeah, people did that. She usually ignored it because it wasn't pertinent to anything. *Okay, think, what would Daniel say in such a situation.* "Good heavens, a handsome gentleman like yourself couldn't be more than sixty." Warmth seeped up her neck, always a tell when she lied.

Herman's eyes twinkled; making her wonder if, he actually believed the words or enjoyed the comment no matter how brazen. A wheezing chuckle escaped as he shook his head. "Sixty is but a distant memory."

She tamped down an impulse to yell *Get on with it* by breathing in hard and holding her breath for a few seconds. Herman gave her a bewildered look but thankfully continued his story.

"Around that time, there was an exhibition of precious gemstones and the Lowery diamonds."

Lowery diamonds, never heard of them, but part of her brain went on high alert similar to the way she responded to the various medical codes when at work. Whatever would follow merited her attention as opposed to humoring an elderly resident.

Herman's eyes drifted over her shoulder; making her wonder if, he'd stop his tale if the law showed up in the form of Mark Taber. "The Lowerys were some type of British aristocracy I think. Anyhow, they were showing off their collection of precious gemstones in Charlotte when a daring jewel heist happened. The stones were stolen in a caper worthy of an action movie."

This is probably where the house tied in, but she wasn't 100 percent sure. "Did they ever recover the jewels or find the thief?"

"No and yes. That's part of the mystery. The jewels were never found. A known jewel thief by the name of Corky Barnstable was the police's primary suspect, but he didn't have the jewels on him. Under extensive interrogation," Herman paused to nod in the direction of the police car, "their methods might have been a tad extreme due to the theft being an international incident. Corky admitted he didn't have the jewels but heard rumors that an unknown thief stole them and had headed in the direction of our small town."

"Why did he do that?" Whatever happened to the no-squeal rule among thieves? It didn't sound right unless Corky had been in the deal originally and eliminated later.

"Several reasons including not ending up in jail. Jail would have resulted from some trumped-up charges. Most people thought he was in on the crime, especially with what happened later."

"What happened?" She knew her response was as predictable as any child's, but she wanted to know.

"Nothing." Herman shrugged.

That couldn't be the end of the story. A gleam appeared in Herman's eyes, demonstrating he knew he'd left her on tenterhooks.

Her hands balled into fists, which she perched on her hips. Her resolution to be softer, gentler and more understanding dissolved under the non-delivery of promised information. "That's not all of it."

Herman half chuckled, but it turned into a cough. After clearing his throat several times, he continued. "Oh, that's what the public thought. Even though my father was a youngster at that time he had a different theory. The newspaper story caught his imagination and he cut it out as he did with all remarkable news stories. Re-reading the stories helped him develop writing skills."

Donna never had a chance to protest against the side trip into

Herman father's journalistic aspirations because he held up one finger signaling her to wait.

"The next day with police crawling everywhere in search of the jewels," Herman paused until she gestured for him to finish, "they discovered the bullet-ridden body of James Bancroft."

Okay. Dramatic, but it didn't make any sense yet. "Did they find him in the house? Was he a jewel thief?"

"Ah." Herman stopped, rubbing his hand across his face. "That's where it goes astray some. Newspapers just reported the man murdered, which was a huge scandal at the time. People assumed it was an organized crime hit because no one wanted the possibility of a rampant killer on the loose. Bancroft fits in because his sister was married to the original owner of the house."

The whole story resembled a puzzle with significant pieces missing. "Do you think he was visiting his sister?"

"No one knows. My grandparents tried to shield my father from it, but people still talked and he listened since his goal was to be an investigative reporter. Bancroft hadn't contacted his sister in years. Regular black sheep. He traveled the world sponging off wealthy, lonely women. My dad theorized he hid the jewels in his house for his sister. Corky shot him when he refused to tell him where the diamonds were."

Herman grinned at her as if he'd given her a precious gift instead of a mishmash of news stories, ancient history gossip and the conjectures of a would-be teen journalist. Of course, the young kid would have a great imagination. "A jealous lover or even irate family member could have filled Bancroft with lead as he left one of his wealthy widows."

"True." Herman agreed without any resistance. "The widow could have shot him herself. People often underestimate the female need for vengeance."

"Men often underestimate a woman's ability for violence. Women never do. They work hard to keep up the façade of being the delicate feminine flower."

Herman's eyebrows shot up at her words. A throat clearing behind her indicated he wasn't the only one to hear her frank summation of her gender.

Mark stepped up beside her, putting out his hand to the elderly man. "Detective Mark Taber."

Herman grabbed the hand and shook it for all he was worth. Had to give Mark credit since he allowed the man to win the handshake contest, even wincing, acting like the octogenarian had hurt him.

"Herman Fremont. I live catty-cornered to Donna's house."

His comment made her blink. She couldn't remember saying her name today. She had when they first met. The old codger was more mentally alert than she gave him credit for, but it didn't mean his father's story had any merit. Just one of those fabrications people made up trying to connect with someone or something in history. They retold the story so often, adding more detail with each telling, that they started believing it. Rather like a dream that felt so lifelike it became confused with reality. Yeah, that's all it was.

"Oh. Really. I bet you see a great deal from your vantage point." Exactly what she thought too. Herman would probably tell him the diamond heist story, but the man remained strangely silent on the subject.

Mark prompted him. "See anything unusual lately?"

An unreadable expression settled on his features. "I see a great deal. Most isn't worth mentioning. Teenagers talking loudly as they jostle their way down the sidewalk. Young mothers full of too much wine staggering to their cars after the latest party, which featured the hawking of overpriced candles, costume jewelry, or marital aids. Carpet cleaners, landscaping services and exterminator trucks roam the neighborhood rather like feral cats, stopping at various houses for an influx of cash. Is that what you want to know?"

Odd. Herman had many facets. Instead of being the friendly, chatty neighbor, he turned all laconic and uncooperative when Mark questioned him. His behavior puzzled her. What could be his motivation?

"That's good. You have excellent observational skills." The detective wielded his compliments carefully, better than she had. "Sure could use someone like you with your talents. It would make the neighborhood a safer place."

The elderly man's frail shoulders went back with the praise. The front of his coat rippled as he tried to pull up his sunken chest without success. "Yep, what can I do for you?"

"On January 29, did you see a man sneaking around the house?" He pointed to the inn as if there might be some question what house he meant.

"If a man were sneaking about, then he wouldn't want anyone to see him. I didn't see anything." Herman's left hand landed on his coat zipper. His fingers played with the tab, unzipping a half an inch, then zipping it back and repeating the action. He could have seen something.

Even though Mark's face didn't display any real emotion, his posture sagged slightly as if he had developed a slow leak somewhere and all the air that held him upright had bled away.

"Did you see any women that night?"

Herman's behavior indicated he considered himself a ladies' man and would notice an attractive woman before he did a man.

Besides, men didn't have the corner on crime.

Herman's eyes lit up as he launched into his description. "Boy, did I. Must have been two hen parties on the block that night. The women around here are always meeting about something from book clubs, arts and the inevitable stuff parties. Lenora, an older woman who must have been a looker in her prime, has a book club."

Did the man have a personal calendar of the neighborhood events? There might even be a website. A few of the pricier communities did that. Before she could ask, Taber did.

"How do you know it was a book club?" His pen hovered over his notebook page. The older technology suited the man. Certainly better than sticking a recorder in someone's face.

"Simple." Herman tapped his head. "The women parade in clutching a book, a bottle of wine, or some other covered platter. One of those modern novels that no one really reads but pretends they have. Something with a cover blurb about it being life changing and all that."

It made sense. She nodded, encouraging the man to elaborate, which he did.

He gestured in the direction of a brick Federalist house that appeared out of place surrounded by restored Victorians or newer reproductions that resembled the grand dames. "The real action usually happens over there."

The three of them stared at the red brick home with the green shutters. The sharp-edged blocks didn't sport the softness of faded quality of an older home. Taber whistled before commenting, "Looks like a fox among the chickens."

The elegant houses could hardly be compared to farm animals. Donna added, "I don't know, I think it is more of the fox among the peacocks. Being mean birds, the peacocks would set upon the fox."

Herman gave her a hearty slap on the back for her remark, propelling her forward a step. "Good one," he chortled. "Pretty much what happened, too. Dr. Winston bought the property about twenty or so years ago. There was an aging Victorian on the property that he had demolished with much outcry from the historical society. He bulldozed the whole place to the ground, which explains the lack of mature trees."

The green lawn unfurled around the red brick shoebox-shaped house spotted with a few slender magnolias and a weeping mulberry close to the house. Not exactly brand new trees, but they didn't even compare to the majestic oaks and maples shading the other residences. "Neighbors snubbed him?" Part of her expected similar treatment.

Herman glanced up at a tree where a crow lighted. His hand went up toward it. "Crows are considered a sign of impending death. This one must be late."

Crows. Apparently, Herman needed help staying focused.

"What happened to the doctor?"

The man regarded her with a bewildered expression until something clicked. "Ah, Dr. Winston didn't care what the neighbors thought. Not exactly a social butterfly, besides he pulled down major money nipping and tucking the aging affluent set. Good chance he did a few of his neighbors, too. May not have liked his house, but they left him alone pretty much until he married." Herman grinned broadly as if the idea of marriage amused him.

"They didn't want him to marry?" The neighbors appeared invested in the doctor's personal affairs. She hardly saw her own neighbors, except in the summer when the roar of lawnmowers brought everyone out of hiding.

"Don't know if they cared if he married, but they didn't like who he married. A woman more than half his age whose last job required hanging upside down from a pole. There's nothing old money about Bambi."

Her eyebrows went up at the name, thinking anyone with sense would create a name a little more traditional such as Barbara or even Stella.

"Yep," Herman rubbed his hands together. "The good matrons do not like Bambi at all. I felt sorry for her at first. The women rebuffed her friendly overtures. Dr. Winston never attempted to be friendly or liked. At best, if I see him out, he'll give me a short nod. For the most part, I think people preferred it that way as opposed to Bambi dashing out of the house to greet anyone she saw strolling by."

Mental note to self. Be standoffish to neighbors. Apparently, Bambi had plenty of parties, which made her wonder where the guests came from.

Mark inadvertently inquired for her. "So where did all the women come from who attended her parties?"

"Not from around here, that's for sure. They arrived in modest cars and the occasional pickup truck. The big hair, heavy makeup and revealing clothes indicated they could be former co-workers. The constant parties with endless parades of females in sequined tops, skirts tight enough to be painted on and clear Lucite heels enraged the local female populace. The men probably enjoyed the show, which would have made the wives angrier. Have to give Bambi credit. If she wanted to upset her snooty neighbors, she did exactly the right thing." A door slammed, causing Herman to glance down the street. A diminutive white-haired elderly lady stared in their direction.

The fragile woman reminded her of her grandmother a little,

except for the bright fluorescent orange object in her hand. "What's she holding?"

"The tape measure. She's off to measure her parking area. Anyone parked too close merits a call to the police. Don't say I didn't warn you." Herman waved in the direction of the woman, but she turned her back as if she didn't see him. *How rude.* Apparently, the neighbors were every bit as snobby as indicated.

"Do you think anyone would be upset enough to kill over Bambi's parties?"

Donna threw a sharp glance at the detective. Sounded like a stupid question, not one worth asking.

Herman's brows knitted together. "Hmm, good question. Not the parties themselves, but a few people felt Bambi was ruining the neighborhood." He angled his head to the elderly woman who squatted at the curb measuring the edge of a car bumper to the area in front of her house. "She might, but why kill a stranger?"

An icy chill whipped down her coat collar at his words. The man had to be exaggerating as people did to make a point. No way could the frail woman have murdered a large man. A strong wind could have blown the would-be parking inspector over.

"Yeah," Taber agreed. "Doesn't matter how angry your neighbor is, I wouldn't label her a killer for a second."

"You're right." Herman agreed with a long sigh punctuating his comment. "Loretta used to be nicer than she is now, but something bad happened to her, which soured her on life."

What could it be? Could it be pertinent to the case? "Do you know what happened?"

A weariness swept over the elderly man's face, rearranging the easy grin into a melted frown sliding down his chin. "I do. Guess you could say she didn't marry well."

Anyone living in the neighborhood married well enough. Her first instinct was to probe deeper when a suspicion she'd be treading into a personal area stopped her. People had secrets buried deep in the past they'd not like to see paraded around similar to a moldering corpse on display for public inspection. Yeah, she could identify.

The wind pushed the lilac coat around the elderly woman as she hurried up the walk. The temperature sped up her steps. The two men beside Donna both considered the elderly woman a nuisance, reporting petty grievances and starting frivolous lawsuits. Good heavens, could she ever turn out like that because she failed to marry well? A shiver racked her body as she considered the possibility. No way, she shook her head trying to shake off the image of her older shelf running outside in a plaid robe to measure the distance of cars from her curb.

Another image of her yelling at her neighbor to pick up after his dog after his pet crapped in her yard replaced the last picture. Wait a minute! That happened last week. Her mouth dropped open. Mark nudged her with his elbow, drawing her back to the present.

"Hey, if you're trying to catch flies with that open mouth, you're out of luck in this weather."

Her mouth snapped shut with a bone-rattling jar. Her eyes stayed on the tiny lilac-garbed woman as she disappeared into her home. To think she worried about turning into the crotchety old lady of the neighborhood when she was already there. Okay, the younger version, but still there.

The rasp of whiskers under a dry hand meant the detective must be running his hand over his chin again. Funny how she already recognized that trait about him. He tended to do it when he mulled things over. The two men could be discussing something pertinent to the case, which she needed to hear as opposed to becoming the cranky biddy everyone whispered about. Pay attention, she mentally reminded herself, this could be significant.

Herman's face reddened as he choked out the words between guffaws. "Bambi's proportions, never tiny to start with, have swelled since she married the doctor, probably two cups sizes."

This is what they were discussing? Donna didn't bother to hide an eye roll, which Taber noticed and addressed with a smirk. Obviously, no great clues dropped from Herman's mouth. Why would anyone care if the plastic surgeon inflated his wife's measurements?

A mechanical chirp had both Donna and Mark reaching for their phones while Herman pointed to his beeping watch. "It's time for me to take my pills." He waved at them before heading off to his home.

Donna watched the man, waiting until he reached his steps before speaking. "Any clues in all his neighborhood gossip?"

"Yes and no." His hand returned to his chin, giving it a good stroke but dropping when he noticed her gaze fixed on his actions.

Personally, she didn't see merit in the comings and goings of the members of the book club or the former stripper club either. "I can guess the no. What about the yes?"

Mark gestured to the houses near hers. "Lots of movement in the neighborhood the night the murder took place. People trotting back and forth to their cars."

Donna's head swiveled, measuring the distance from the houses to hers. Someone could have taken a turn on the way out and slid around to her house, taking advantage of the shadows. Her lips pursed as she considered the possible scenario, but she had an issue with it. "Only women went to these parties. Did you think the murder could be the work of a woman?"

Mark's fingers moved across his chest, searching for the pocket that hid the cigarettes. The outside lights winked on, creating blossoms of light in the approaching twilight. A dark shroud of shadows surrounded her house. No wonder it had become rendez-vous central. That and being empty. Did the clandestine visitors know the house would soon no longer be vacant? Had to, since the real estate agent stuck a large SOLD sign onto the regular wooden post sale sign. The woman even asked to keep the sign planted for another month.

Rock bottom prices sold the house. Location sold it. The fact it had eight bedrooms and bathrooms sold it. A real estate agent who wore enough jewelry to set off airport security had nothing to do with it. It was more of a case of buying the house despite the agent.

Instead of pulling out the smokes, as he wanted, his hand flat-tened on his chest with the pack resting under his fingertips. He cut a slightly chagrinned look at her. Was she that bad? A regular dragon?

"Go ahead and smoke if you want." That made her sound more tolerant. Her shoulders went back with a sense of pride. She could do empathy if she tried.

Mark's eyebrows suggested his surprise as his fingers delved into his sports jacket in a hurry to shorten his lifespan.

"Go ahead and complicate health issues already compromised by your age, gender and occupation."

His eager expression dropped as did his hand.

She hurriedly added on. "It's your life, isn't it?"

Her tone should have sounded conciliatory, but instead it sounded sarcastic. Might as well said, "Go ahead and kill yourself."

"Never mind." He grumbled the words as he thrust his hands into his pants pockets. "Could a woman have murdered our victim?"

"Yes. She'd have to be strong to overpower the man though."

"True," she agreed, thinking of some oversized female wrestler type. Surely, Herman would have noticed such a woman. Not the kind of woman to escape scrutiny. *Too easy.* Had to be something else. "A woman could have surprised him. What if he were on the floor and she came up behind him and strangled him using her full body weight?"

"I never mentioned he was strangled."

"Ah-ha, you did now."

The cigarette pack appeared in his hand as he shook out one. "Your fault with all your smart answers." She kept her lips sealed as he lit the smoke and inhaled, getting a glowing tip for his effort. Using the cigarette as an extension of his hand, he waved it in her direction. "Tell me, how did you know?"

Her shoulders went up with a shrug. "Well, I knew it wasn't poison. No signs. Definitely not bludgeoned or shot. No signs of electrocution, either. There were no visible signs I could see and you kept going on about someone being as big as he was to kill him. Strangulation is the only thing that made sense. The mock turtle-neck he had on would have covered the marks."

Taber exhaled a long smoke stream. "You'd make a hell of a detective."

"Wouldn't get paid as well," she countered the remark before realizing it was a compliment.

"True," he agreed without any rancor. "The idea of you toting a gun is a scary one."

Her brother had bought her a gun for safety and now Mark didn't want her to have one. "Why shouldn't I have a gun?"

Mark chuckled. "That attitude for one. You might not shoot people who irritate you, but there's a good chance you'd intimidate them."

Her arms folded under her breasts as she huffed her disbelief. "You make me sound like a bully."

"Not a bully." He paused, causing Donna to lean closer to avoid missing the pronouncement of what she was. "A driven individual. A woman on a mission."

It sounded like code for bully. A sinking feeling sucked at her emotions, pulling at her, dragging her into a dark place she didn't want to be. It never occurred to her before today that she was well on her way to being the grouchy old woman who lived down the street. The realization lodged in her throat like an unchewed piece of meat. Lifting her hand in a wave, she turned toward her car. "I need to go."

Taber called after her. "I'll call you once we know when you can get back into the house."

Chapter Ten

TABER'S WORDS TOOK form the way smoke does, hanging in the air before vanishing. Donna would usually answer, but not now, as she half-jogged to her car. The image of her walking around with an oversized tape measure flickered at the edge of her consciousness. Why were grumpy old men amusing? There were even several movies about the subject. Double standards, that's what it was. An opinionated older woman develops a reputation as a nag, hag, or whatever unflattering term implied crotchety female. Old men could be wise, gentle and a mentor. Only older women who had married and had children received any of the pleasanter descriptions.

She shifted her car into gear as she silently fumed. Her hands tightened on the steering wheel as she drove at a circumspect speed, although she wanted to stomp on the gas. "Spinster, nag, dried-up old prune, sexless biddy," she half-growled, glad no one was in the car to hear. Plenty of terms for women who never married, all derogatory. "Makes it sound like marriage is some grand prize that all women aspire to."

The bridal industry worked that angle, making the bride feel like a sweepstakes winner who had thousands of dollars to throw away on her fairy tale wedding. "*Hmpft.*" She snorted her contempt. Anyone who didn't marry became a pariah of sorts. Most people had good enough manners not to mention it, but it happened just the same.

In her twenties and part of her thirties, friends tried to match-make, often without her permission. She wasn't totally against it, but her long hours, tallness and opinionated attitude worked against her. Still, seriously, why would she be interested in a man who couldn't stand up to her? Daniel was the only male who'd faced her down. He told her once she was an eight on the attractiveness scale. Of course, he added, she had more balls than most men did. At the time, she considered it a compliment. What if it wasn't? Her vision got foggy. Stupid defroster, it should work better than this. Her finger pushed the fan lever to high, blasting warm air on the windows. It didn't help much.

She blinked, sending tears cascading down her face. Her right hand touched her cheek in disbelief. *Tears.* That couldn't be right. *Sissies cried.* She could remember her father's words as if it were yesterday. Tears rolled down her face then too as she lay on the grass after tumbling from a stone wall she'd been walking on. It didn't matter she'd been told numerous times not to walk on the wall. All her father saw was weakness. He also probably saw the boy he didn't have and was determined to make her tougher, less girlish. By the time Daniel came along, most of the softer, gentler emotions had vanished from her personality. At least she thought they had. Maybe they had only been hiding.

A bent knuckle wiped away the tears. Why was she crying? She'd accepted a while back that marriage, the picket fence enclosed yard and a home with 2.5 children was not her dream. Her life hadn't been horrible. Other nurses, weighed down with financial responsibilities of motherhood, envied her ability to travel. However, her single travel life was not the one featured in movies. Solitary Sojourner Tours sounded much cooler than they were. Women comprised 80 percent of the group, mostly widowed or divorced with a few never marrieds. The men who chose the tour were a handful of lonely widowers and the scum who preyed on lonely wealthy widows. While she did manage to travel the world with other people, the experience often left her feeling even more alone.

A final sniff accompanied by a deep inhale stopped the water-works. No time for such nonsense. Besides, she might be getting into her inn soon. For that, she needed paint. Primer first since the half dozen viewings of the house revealed damaged walls from the various tenants. A little digging in the newspaper archives at the local library revealed the grand home had passed through several hands including a stint as a VFW when they covered the plaster walls with paneling and had installed pool tables. The image of aged veterans sitting on bar stools swapping war stories as they sipped beer caused a physical cringe.

Spilled beer and cigar ashes rubbed into the wooden floors made refinishing a must. The last owner did nothing to the place as far as she could tell. The papers reported the VFW moved to a new location with better parking while a foreign interest bought the residence. If nothing else, the owner had removed the paneling, the pool tables and bar. Too bad about the bar, that may have been useful, but probably wouldn't suit the atmosphere. Standing unused for years dissipated the cigar smell but allowed the market price to plummet.

Vacant buildings resembled unemployed people in the regard they were both undesirable. Rather like unmarried women, people assumed some horrible affliction troubled the older single woman from nagging to hoarding. No one ever believed a woman chose not to marry. Whenever her marital status would come in an introduc-tion, people stumbled over Miss or Ms. She'd end their quandary by asking them to call her Donna. She didn't care for the titles and they invited probing such as asking if she were divorced. When she confessed she wasn't, people managed a sympathetic expression and then whispered *widowed*. Apparently, all those who lost a spouse were addressed in hushed funeral home voices.

Once the busybodies went through their repertoire of nosy questions and discovered she never married, little antennae emerged from their skulls and waved wildly as they processed the information. The antennae might not be visible, but she could hear the crackle of their thoughts. The next foray into no-boundaries inquisitiveness would be if she had a significant other. The end goal would be to decide if she were lesbian by the name of her beloved. Sometimes to befuddle the nosey parkers she'd mention a sweetheart by a sexually ambiguous name such as Taylor or Morgan. Occasionally, she mentioned her dog, Jasper, to stop the questioning.

A request to call her by her first name made her sound much more laid back than she actually was. Housekeepers of the last century or more often referred to themselves as widows. A never-married woman wouldn't have been able to land a plum domestic assignment such as housekeeper. The mantle of marriage, no matter how brief, bestowed both respectability and competence on the Victorian woman. It may have stopped unwanted inquiries too. No one questioned a widow because it could trigger tragic memories.

The idea of posing as a widow had merit. She could even scatter photos of her beloved around the house. Some of the dishes she'd call her late husband's favorites. Something like Josiah's Best Loved Scalloped Potatoes. Definite promise. Her dear husband's benign ghost could haunt the place; he would have more a tendency to turn down the lights as opposed to scaring guests. Josiah believed in saving energy. A grin worked its way across her face as she created the personality of her late husband.

The only problem with the mythical spouse was if someone mentioned she had never married. "Daniel." The word came out as a snarl. Her brother figured prominently into her restoration plans and part of the day-to-day services, although she hadn't approached him about it yet. Daniel would never remember she had a deceased husband, making her a somewhat tragic figure. Even his wife Maria might accidentally mention it. If she wanted a friendly ghost, she'd have to look elsewhere.

A long soak in the tub with a mystery novel she'd started beckoned with a siren call as appealing as any dark chocolate ganache. Odd, she found herself turning into the oversized parking lot of the home and garden store. Tired, a part of her dared whimper, while the other part, the one that didn't cry, decided now would be a perfect time to load up on primer. The good stuff that didn't allow colors to melt through the paint. Some stains and colors had the same tenacity as bloodstains in a haunted house that continued to appear no matter how often they were scrubbed.

Donna forced herself out of the car, reining in the emotional side that decided to emerge after all these years. Weariness pressed down on her as she strode toward the entry doors. Plenty of times, she worked back-to-back shifts, not because she wanted to, but because there was no one else to do them. After being on her feet for twenty-four hours, she insisted on driving home as opposed to using a hospital bed. It didn't matter if the linen was fresh. Hospitals bred super germs, not the thing she wanted to inhale into her vulnerable lungs as she slept. It didn't matter if her feet were barely moving or her driving suffered in her fatigued state. She often was unaware if she was stopped at the light or if she still moved. In the end, she made it home where the worst issue was inhaling dog hair as she slept.

A haphazard collection of carts awaited her at the door. Her hands landed on a standard oversized shopping cart, which she pushed into the brightly lit warehouse store. The shelves shot up to the ceiling, holding everything from glass-fronted security doors to power washers. An indistinct voice mumbled something about help being needed somewhere. Her experience with the place was you had to find stuff on your own. She made a hard left toward the paint section. The cart pulled to the right while making an ominous thumping sound. Defective, no wonder it was on the edge of the carts, rejected.

Instead of returning for a new cart, she wrestled her current one into compliance. At least into some semblance of making it down the center of the aisle without hitting any of the tired-looking people pushing their own recalcitrant buggies. Half dozen gallons of primer should weigh the cart down too.

Cardboard banners proclaimed the abilities of each primer. One declared that it dried in thirty minutes. Good deal since she didn't have all that much time. Six gallon cans sat in her cart as she calculated how much she would need. The tiny print font stated it covered 450 square feet. That referred to a perfect wall with no dips or gouges. Her lips twisted to one side as she considered the can. It might not be the right kind.

"Look who's here." A familiar masculine voice had her looking over her shoulder where Daniel and Maria stood with a loaded cart.

"Come here," she remarked, waving her brother closer. He abandoned the full cart along with his wife, whose lips pursed. Donna noted the expression and surmised she might not be the first person Daniel had recognized in the store. Maria, while typically a kind, giving woman, had issues with sharing her husband. Construction workers worked long hours during peak season, but Daniel's time waster tended to be socializing. The man had never met a stranger.

Holding up a can of primer, she asked, "Is this the type that fills in the holes?"

Her brother's hand wrapped around the can handle, turning the front label to face him. "Nope. This is just primer. What you need is a primer that's a sealer too. Should have been suspicious since this is only $28."

Maria pushed their cart up to hers and laughed before Donna could respond. "He makes dollars sound more like pennies." The exotic-looking woman continued talking before Donna could hazard a response. "He assumes everyone knows the different types of paint."

Donna's brows lowered as she realized her sister-in-law lumped her in with all the other clueless people. "It's not paint. It's primer."

Maria shrugged her shoulders. "What's the difference?"

Before she could enlighten her that primer was only the start of a job while paint indicated a finished product, Daniel elbowed her, inadvertently causing her to bite her tongue. A dark look and a short stare acknowledged her brother's warning.

Ah yes, the beautiful woman syndrome. She forgot. No one corrected beautiful women no matter how stupid their comments might be. If they did, they came off looking petty. Besides, Maria loved her brother and might be Donna's only hope of having nieces and nephews. It would do her well not to alienate the woman. If her brother had to choose between her and Maria, she knew she'd end up with the short end of the stick.

Daniel put the cans of primer back on the shelf before answering his wife. "It's more like the moisturizer you put on before the foundation. It prepares the walls to accept the paint. Otherwise, it can be splotchy in spots."

Donna's head swiveled between her brother and Maria nodding in understanding. Her brother had managed a relevant comparison without sounding superior. He loaded her cart with the more expensive primer sealant as she considered the changes love had made in her brother. Yep, it could work for some people. Mentally she tabulated the cost as he added each can. This would cost a fortune.

"Don't forget the rollers and drop cloths," he reminded her.

From birth to teen years, she had supervised her brother, reminding him of common sense safety precautions that he probably already knew. As a result, he took every opportunity to do the same now. The roles were not reversed. He just liked to annoy her.

"Got it." A pair of rollers and assorted drop cloths landed in the cart. She picked them at random, not even paying that close of attention. Her brother picked up the drop cloth and eyed it with disdain, his nose crinkling.

"Okay." She grabbed it before he could comment, placing it back on the hook. "I meant to get this one." Her fingers landed on the most expensive, heavy drop cloth. Her eyebrows shot up at the price. Old sheets could work just as well.

"Seriously, Donna do you have money to throw away?" Daniel cut her a knowing look at the same time Maria's hand landed on her brother's shoulder.

"I'm exhausted, sweetheart. Why don't we go home? We could stop by the Chinese place."

Thank goodness, Maria had saved her from an unwelcome lecture about money. "Yeah, you kids should get home and get something for dinner. Why are you here anyhow?"

Daniel directed a loving look at his wife before answering. "We're remodeling the guest bathroom."

Their cart held bathroom fixtures, a heated towel rack and an ornate bathroom light. Yeah, she wanted to say good luck with that but didn't. Maria would find out soon enough that the construction boss's family would be the last to get anything done on their own house.

Maria waved and pushed the heavy cart forward on her own, causing her brother to leap into action to wrestle it from her. His actions amused her. She'd bet Maria was as strong, or stronger, than she was. No man jostled for the opportunity to push her cart. Oh well, she needed to get home and pacify her dog anyway.

The cart proved to be even more cantankerous when weighed down. The third wheel froze in place, preventing forward movement. Pushing on the cart offered no results. A good tug backward could snap the wheel in place. She gave it a hard tug that released the buggy from its initial position and sent her windmilling into a display of metal paint trays that hit the floor in a crescendo of metallic clangs.

Several trays bounced off her arm as they fell. The pain shooting up her humerus bone had her sucking in her lips. A roll of blue painter's tape bounced off her head. Her fingers wrapped around it before it escaped.

A couple stared at her as they strolled by with a cart loaded with indoor tropical plants. No offer to help, no inquiry if she were all right. She could hear muffled laughter drifting out behind the couple.

It would be nice to abandon the mess, stroll out the front doors and head home. The trays scattered around her feet earned a glare. Typically, she'd pick them up. Not today. Her purse lay open on its side among the paint pans. She reached for her bag just as she heard a voice.

"I thought I heard something."

The words held her in place. They had found her before she had the opportunity to escape. A white-haired man trailed by a slender youth both turned the corner at the end of the aisle before she could knock the stubborn cart into motion. Their matching blue vests identified them as employees. *Great.*

Vanishing into the next aisle, leaving her cart abandoned in the aisle tempted her, especially the way the man rushed up the aisle. Would he insist she pay for all the paint trays or perhaps some legal release he would coerce her into signing, leaving the store clear of any legal ramifications?

"Ma'am, ma'am, are you all right?"

The man placed a large hand on her arm. Generally, she'd give the hand a pointed look, which served as message enough.

His concerned expression along with his anxious hazel eyes stopped her action. "Ma'am, are you okay?"

The fact she hadn't said anything might worry the man that she'd slapped the store with a liability suit for some outlandish reason. "Uhm, I'm all right." Probably have a huge bruise on her elbow, but other than that, no damage.

The younger man hung back. He could have viewed her as dangerous. *Smart.* "My cart." She gestured to the problem buggy that somehow managed to make it halfway down the aisle as if distancing itself from her. "It has a frozen wheel and I was trying to get it to work when it spiraled out of control, sending me into the paint pan display.

The older man, with *Marvin* stenciled on his vest front, nodded, not even cracking a smile at the ridiculousness of her explanation.

Instead, he gave the cart a censorious glance before turning back to look at the boy who was in the process of soundlessly drifting away.

"Brent, go get another cart. One that works." The youth took off on his errand, but not before grimacing first. The thought of having to work while on the job upset him.

No easy way to vanish, especially when a new cart was on its way. "Thanks." She almost added there was no need when she caught the man staring at her with a goofy smile. Marvin acted thrilled to see her. A middle-aged woman whose hair had to be ruffled due to the collision.

Her lips tilted up without any conscious thought. Brent arrived with a rattling cart that she suspected wasn't much better than her previous one. "Thanks." The acknowledgment came out soft, making her into a simpering, helpless female who expected men to buzz around her as if they were bees and she was a newly opened flower. Her teeth ground together at the dated image.

Before she could counter the simple word that evoked such attractive associations, Brent disappeared, demonstrating she wasn't a fresh flower at all. Not too surprising, she shook off the errant thought and readied herself to move the primer gallons. The primer and painting paraphernalia already filled the new cart that came complete with a grinning Marvin behind it.

His eyes lit up as he asked, "Need anything else tonight?"

Her glance dropped to the full cart, then back to the man. "No, not this evening. I'm just getting started. I'll need more stuff in the future." His overwhelming brand of customer service was something she'd never encountered before. Part of her wondered if it portended something more than a high rating on a client satisfaction survey. *Nonsense.*

The heavy cart moved forward with her helpful paint man behind it. *This was weird.* "Uhm, I can handle it. Thanks, Marvin."

She thought the mention of his name would be the trick that freed her cart from his capable hands. It didn't. He kept pushing the cart and talking.

"I usually work every Tuesday, Thursday and Saturday evenings from six to closing. I teach construction at a vocational school during the day."

Small talk wasn't her strong point. Think, what response could she make? "That must keep you very busy."

"It does." He nodded his head while his grin slid off his face, turning his expression serious. "I prefer to stay active. It's much better than roaming around my big house all alone."

A too-much-information warning, she recognized the introductory volley. She'd heard enough from her post-op patients, especially those still heavily drugged. They felt the need to confess life regrets to a total stranger. Luckily, most never remembered anything mentioned while under anesthesia.

"Good thing you have this job to keep you busy." She matched her steps with his long strides, edging closer in hopes of taking control of her merchandise. The towering gunmetal gray shelves loaded with lights and ceiling fan boxes created an unfortunate tunnel of intimacy. An occasional mumbled request came over the PA system indicating that other potential customers needed help. They'd probably never receive it based on the announcer's lack of articulation.

Her outstretched hand reached for the cart handle, brushing against Marvin's, which resulted in him beaming broadly at her. Oh no, bad move, wrong message. He moved his hand to brush against hers.

"I can run you through the checkout and use my employee discount."

The cart slowed, giving her a chance to walk instead of her awkward trot as she analyzed her next move. *Employee discount. How much was it? If it were around forty percent, it would save her almost two hundred dollars. Get a grip, girl. You're not seriously considering it.* She jerked her hand away from Marvin's.

"Um, no thank you. That wouldn't be ethical." Not a stellar comeback, but the best she could come up with. She'd long since closed the door on romance. Sure, co-workers close to her age were already on marriage two or three. Becca in the phlebotomy unit hit husband four at forty-nine. Work made her privy to all the issues dealing with the current man in Becca's life from unexpected big-ticket expenditures to leaving the toilet seat up.

Marvin chuckled at her reply while sending her a slightly lecherous glance. "Ah a good girl, they're so much more fun to break."

Her eyebrows went up with his last word and her mouth dropped open before she could snap it shut. *Fun to break?* No one broke Donna Tollhouse. Straightening her spine, she assumed her best steel nurse demeanor. "Get your hands off my cart!"

Marvin's hands released the cart, which rolled a few feet on its own. Enough space for Donna to swoop in and take over. She wrestled the awkward buggy into a checkout lane where a bored middle-aged woman stood. The woman glanced past her to where Marvin stood with a dumbfounded expression.

The cashier picked up her scan gun and ran it over the primer cans. "Looks like Marvin tried to chat you up."

Her words made the man's over-the-top actions seem innocent and playful. Donna grunted her acknowledgment, unwilling to talk about it. Her response didn't deter the woman from speaking.

"Yeah, we all feel sorry for him. Married thirty years, then his wife died in a freak accident while they were on vacation. I may have suggested he should try dating since it's been a year. The only problem is I'm not sure if Marvin was ever good at flirting."

Donna felt a twinge of regret at her barked command, not enough, however, to apologize to the man. She watched the cashier bag her drop cloths and painter's tape, wondering if she could do it any faster and not prolong the conversation. Apparently not because she continued talking.

"I think he may have read one of those online advice columns that try to get guys to act like some bad boy from the movies. You're not the first woman to run up to the counter with Marvin straggling behind."

She didn't need a lonesome hardware man and a chatty clerk. *Mental note to self,* Daniel would get all the needed construction supplies or she'd have to drive to the next town.

The cash register finally spit out her receipt, releasing her from the familiar store that had somehow morphed itself into a carnival house of mirrors. Each image spooked her more than the last. The outside parking lot provided more resistance than the inside floors did. A side-to-side glance revealed an almost empty parking lot. No would-be construction-oriented robbers hanging near the edge of the building ready to dash out and grab her cart. Even if they did, they'd need help moving it.

Grabbing her bag and purse, she jogged to her car with the intention of driving it to the cart. She drove the car back to the buggy, alert to any would-be robbers. No one approached, saving her the need for laying on her horn or accelerating toward the thief. Primer must not hold the same attraction cement mix did. A local news article reported recently that someone's pickup truck had been relieved of six bags.

A quick push of her fob popped her trunk as she exited the car. By can number five, she could see the merit of having a man's help, especially knowing she'd have to do this all again once she reached the inn. The good news was it wouldn't be tonight. Trunk loaded, she slapped the lid down, anxious to get home to her bubble bath.

Car lights cut through the dark as she headed through the wooded neighborhood. An occasional porch light created a tiny orb of light and every now and then, a street light would throw out a pool of illumination. Thank goodness, she knew the neighborhood. Otherwise, it would be easy to get lost in the dimly lit rabbit warren of streets.

Her own outside lights gleamed due to the fact they were light sensor lights. They flickered on at twilight or on stormy days. Their cheery glow made her feel welcome, even expected despite the fact only Jasper waited for her. A four-legged male with a voracious appetite was better than some other options.

Her mind immediately went back to Marvin's leer and threat to break her. Before that strange statement, he seemed okay, even possibly someone she wouldn't mind dating. The thought surprised her almost as much as the man's repulsive comment about breaking her.

"Forget about it, chick. Romance passed you by a long time ago. Besides, you have a mystery to solve and an inn to refurbish."

Chapter Eleven

TWO NURSES ON vacation had shrunk her normal three days off to two. Donna's typical reaction would be to grumble about it as she lugged the cans of paint to the back stoop of the old Victorian. A remnant of yellow police tape tied to the back banister fluttered in the frigid wind. Her energy centered on getting her courage up to go back to her house as opposed to her griping about her schedule.

The fact it was no longer a crime scene should give her some reassurance. It didn't. It meant the forensic team tabled the case. Detective Taber described it as an impulsive act of passion, which suggested the killer wouldn't be hiding in her inn's stairway waiting for his next victim.

Donna hefted another can onto the porch before she shielded her eyes, looking in the direction of the street. No sign of Daniel, which wasn't too surprising since promptness wasn't in her brother's skill set. The last thing she wanted was a repeat of last week's entrance into the deserted inn and stumbling across an anonymous man. The victim's fingerprints had yielded nothing. That no clear identification came from the man's prints could mean the man had never been fingerprinted, which meant no trouble with the law or jobs in finance, security, or banking since almost all their employees required fingerprinting.

The last can of primer joined the others with a clunk. After shutting her trunk, Donna decided to sit on the porch and wait.

Her talkative neighbor slowed down on his morning walk and waved at her. The man wanted to talk. She didn't. All the same, the man watched the neighborhood better than a paranoid mercenary. She should talk to him. *Yeah, yeah, be nice. An excellent chance to work on her friendly small talk skills.*

Herman stood in one place as she ambled across the frozen grass. He greeted her with a hearty, "Howdy, neighbor" and a smile.

"Howdy yourself." Donna mumbled the words, wondering if she sounded friendly enough. Technically, Herman was the first person she'd talked to today. Mornings weren't her best time even though she trained herself to get up at obscenely early times to be ahead of schedule for her twelve-hour shift. Most nurses tolerated the long shifts in favor of the three days off.

"See you're back at work, painting the old lady, eh?" He angled his head in the direction of the inn.

Apparently Herman had noticed the paint cans, which meant it wasn't worthy of an answer. Why repeat what he already knew? Her pause lengthened into an awkward silence before she remembered her goal to be better at small talk. Small talk consisted of remarking on the ordinary and the known.

"Yes, I am. My brother, Daniel, is coming to help me primer the walls."

"Good deal." Herman nodded and chafed his arms a bit, chilled from standing. "Guess the police solved the mystery of the dead stranger then. Didn't see anything in the paper about who it was."

The paper. She hadn't given it any thought. The police must be more successful at circumventing the annoying reporters than she thought. Her shoulders went up with a shrug. "Nothing to report. No name came up with the fingerprints."

She didn't bother to tack on that it had to be a crime of passion.

The neighbors were already upset enough at having a dead stranger in their midst. No reason to alert them that one of them might be wearing a mask of respectability that hid the heart of a reactionary killer.

"Couldn't find any fingerprints for him, or he didn't have any fingerprints?"

Small talk really was redundant. Her first instinct was to assert the man had no fingerprints on file, but her first interaction with her neighbor had determined that he took in more than most. The question probably meant more. She repeated the last part of his question more to herself. "Didn't have any fingerprints?"

"That's right." Herman's eyebrows shot up in a speculative fashion. "He probably sanded them off with sandpaper. All the safecrackers do."

"Safecrackers?" All she knew about safe cracking she had gleaned from reruns from *It Takes a Thief* and couldn't remember if the main character sanded his fingertips. An image of him donning black leather gloves was the best she could recall. "Wouldn't he be recognizable by his face or dental records?"

"As for his face, he could have been photographed at one time for a passport or driver's license. It would also depend on our town running the photo in the right system to even get a hit. Probably just ran his picture through the known offenders' registry."

"There are different registries?" She didn't mean to ask, but the surprise of a cache of photos, perfect for identifying that an unknown person existed, prompted her response.

"All sorts. You're probably in a few yourself such as the BMV since you have a driver's license. National security can tie into any of them to trace a suspicious person."

Her neighbor might even be a better armchair sleuth than she was. A grudging respect grew for the man. Her eyes darted up and down the street, noting the presence of the dog-walking couple who always seemed to be out along with the measuring tape woman. Too far away to overhear anything, but possibly working on getting nearer.

"Strange. They didn't come up with an ID then."

"Maybe," Herman replied but somehow managed to sound the opposite of the word's meaning. It contained doubt and a slight suspicion of accepted order of police protocol.

Ah, she knew this game. Dr. Lennon played it well enough with her, giving her symptoms and expecting her to diagnose the patient. "Okay. You think the police tabled the case because the person was an unknown and not a local?"

"I do believe that, but it could also be too hard to ID the man." He used his bent knuckle to rub at the furrow between his eyes.

"Couldn't they use dental records?" They did it all the time in crime shows when the victim was too badly burned to be recognizable.

Herman shook his head slowly, acting disappointed in her. "Smart gal like you should know better than to believe a television show."

Donna hurried to acknowledge she didn't. Although, most of her forensic knowledge did come from television.

"That's only good if you know who the victim is. You also have to know the victim's dentist, who also has current records. If someone had come forward and mentioned knowledge of the deceased, then dental records could be used."

It all depended on knowing the victim. "The man was handsome, mid-thirties and tall. The type most women would remember."

Herman's mouth twisted to one side as he pondered her words. "I'd have to agree with you. He could have had plastic surgery. Something like those makeover shows where the unpopular girl returns as a beauty queen."

Plastic surgery, why did everything lead to another trail? "Plastic surgery, why?"

"Who knows?" Herman shrugged his shoulders this time. A chime on his watch drew his attention. "Time for another pill."

Her time with her chatty neighbor was almost at an end and she had more questions than ever.

Herman glanced at his watch, then back at her. "Change his identity, of course. I hear those in the witness protection program do it all the time."

Donna fought back a snort and a retort about his gullibility. Enough books and movies used the plot twist of someone assuming a different identity with the help of a new face. Her neighbor unaware of her doubt, continued with his far-fetched theories.

"Could be the murderer sandpapered his fingerprints off. If he is local and no one recognizes him, then he altered his features." Herman turned sharply, reminiscent of a military pivot and headed for his house.

How many pills did the man take anyhow? She hoped he lived long enough to explain his various theories. Donna swung her head in both directions, looking for Daniel's truck. The wind kicked up, pushing a few forgotten leaves across the sidewalk. No sight of her brother, no real excuse for staying outside, except maybe she should pick up the leaves.

Even though it was the dead of winter, *a rather gruesome expression*, her neighbors' manicured lawns waited in a state of dormancy. The evergreen hedges sported clean lines while mulch covered the empty flowerbeds. Even the leafless trees bore more resemblance to impressionistic paintings as opposed to the stark, winter survivors they were. None of the other homes had dead leaves in their yard. She chased after the crumpled emblems of yard maintenance neglect. An eddy caught the leaves, flinging them out of her grasp. A sudden surge of speed had her almost on top of the leaves before the wind teased her again, sending them off in another direction.

The measuring tape woman stood with her hands on her hips, staring in Donna's direction. Her scrutiny stopped the leaf-catching game, initiated by the frigid air. *Great, the neighborhood critic will think I'm bonkers.*

Donna smiled and waved to her neighbor. Instead of waving back, the woman turned away as if she hadn't seen. Ah, in Regency novels they'd refer to the action as the *cut direct*, a simple expression that she didn't belong. Her eyes narrowed as she stared at the woman while her shoulders stiffened.

She did belong. Donna didn't need anyone's approval, certainly not Grandmother Crochety's. It was a perfect name. She applauded her choice as she marched up to the back stoop. The key fit into the lock without any problem. The inside of the house bore a slight chemical smell along with the odor of disuse. The pine-scented room deodorizers the real estate agent had placed in every room could only do so much.

A few taps on the thermostat set the furnace humming. A twist of the radio dial located her favorite oldies station, filling the kitchen area with an old ballad about sitting on the dock of the bay. Summer would be here before she knew it and so would the guests. She shook out the first throw cloth while analyzing the difficulty of painting around the cabinets. Rows and rows of cabinets, which was great for storage, but the devil to paint.

The throw cloth, still clutched in her right hand, trailed behind her like a bridal train as she surveyed the ground level rooms. The dining room, while being cabinet free, boasted several full-length windows. Eventually, she'd have to primer it, but something simple first. The long, narrow foyer was free of cabinets and windows, except for two long decorative windows framing the entrance door. She decided to start there.

Cloth spread, blue tape outlined the windows and door and she was ready to start. A device that looked more like a beer bottle opener allowed her to jimmy open the primer lid. "Okay, Donna, you need to do a good job in here. This is the first area guests will see."

"Who are you talking to?"

The masculine voice caused her to freeze in the motion of dipping her brush into the thick white liquid. The hairs on her arms managed an even more erect posture than they already had with the chilly temperature. Ah, she needed to identify her unknown visitor. No one ever called her a coward and there was no reason to now.

Her grip tightened on the brush as she considered the feasibility of using it as a weapon. Already on her knees, she rocked backed into a crouching position, curling her toes under, ready to run out the front door. A live coward could call the police. An angling of her head revealed the deadbolt on the front door, which explained why all her visitors preferred the back door.

A metallic rattle pulled her eyes to her visitor, or at least his giant aluminum ladder he left in the foyer as she saw a jean-clad leg disappear into the dining room. "I know what you're up to." The familiar voice bounced off the walls of the empty room.

Her hand went up to smack herself on the forehead at her stupidity, but instead the bristles of the paintbrush poked her in the eye.

The brush tumbled from her fingers as she flung it against the wall. Her brother returned to the room as she rubbed her assaulted eye.

He clicked his tongue. "Don't think acting inept is going to keep you from painting. You already picked the easiest room and left me with cabinet hell. Don't think I didn't notice."

The adrenaline that had raced through her body only seconds before slowed to a slight dribble. "I jabbed myself in the eye with the paintbrush." A couple of blinks assured her that her vision hadn't suffered. Only one brother stood before her with hands on his hips and a mocking smile on his lips.

"Okay, whatever you say, but you're the smart one in the family so it is a bit hard to believe you could do something so dumb."

Rather than insist she actually did poke herself in the eye with a paintbrush, which would lead to explaining she hadn't recognized his voice, she said nothing. Weird, she hadn't known immediately it was Daniel. Too many other things occupied her mind, from her snobby neighbor to murderers who sandpapered off fingerprints.

Her brother's greeting had startled her, that's all. No murderer comments on the intended victim talking to herself. It would give the person too much time to react. Nope, her fear had made her act irrational. Standing, she glared at the paintbrush, pretending it was the cause of her problems. Her legs, slightly stiff from maintaining her crouched position, forced her to march over to the brush like a tin soldier.

"About time you got here." She refused to dignify his earlier statement with a response. Her brother got the lion's share of desirable traits in her opinion and yet he continually pointed out she did better in school. So what if she had maintained honor roll throughout school, except for the dismal C- in gym her first year and flunking driver's ed in summer school. Graduating college with honors didn't guarantee her happiness or a devoted spouse for that matter.

"Nag, nag." He waggled his eyebrows, knowing the remark would irritate her as it usually did.

Her pursed lips reflected some disgruntlement, but she refused to give into it. *Inn owners had to handle cantankerous guest with velvet gloves.* She shrugged and turned her back to him, just as the neighbor had done her. Bending at the waist, she dipped her brush into the primer.

"Where's your paint tray?" Her brother's voice close to her ear almost caused her to drop the brush into the primer.

"I don't need it. I'm only doing the trim work before I use the roller." Her actions should be apparent, but she sucked in her lips to prevent her from saying as much. *Good job, you're mastering self-control. Before you know it, you'll be a world-class innkeeper.*

A metal paint pan blocked the brush's descent into the primer. "Here's your pan. No need to thank me."

Donna's eyebrows drew down as she contemplated the metal pan finally wrapping her hand around the rim, "Why do I need a paint tray?"

"A remark like that says it all. Less chance of spillage and you can share the can." He confirmed with a head bob.

Her irritation showed in her voice. "A remark like yours," she pointed with her brush in his direction in case he might think she addressed the door or the stairs, "shows monumental arrogance. A regular know-it-all."

"Takes one to know one." He answered with a twinkle in his eye that caused her to chuck the brush at him. It hit him square in the chest as she intended. True, she never scrimmaged well in basketball or climbed the gym rope to the top, but she could throw with accuracy.

"Ah ha! Got you." She gloated with glee.

Daniel picked up the brush and approached her. His grim countenance had her scampering out of the way. His footsteps erupted
into running behind her. His arms wrapped around her before she
could make an evasive move.

"Caught you." He croaked the words into her ear before running
the brush over her face. "Eat brush."

Her hands pushed the brush away as she laughed and choked
out a few words in between breaths. "You win."

He released her and handed the brush over with a grin. "We
both won, especially since you went back to acting normal. Not sure
what that other stuff was."

Her lips twisted to one side with the realization that her good
innkeeper behavior wasn't normal according to her brother. "I was
the congenial B and B owner and you were my demanding guest."

Her brother handed her a rag to remove the paint from her face
as his laughter boomed through the foyer, sliding into the empty
rooms and echoing. It created the eerie effect of the house laughing
at her too. His merriment ended as he placed an open palm against a
nearby wall. "Sister, you better hope I'm the crankiest guest you ever
get, but I won't be."

"Why is that?" One eyebrow lifted on its own, recognizing his
ability to pontificate on almost any subject. She folded her arms,
allowing the brush to rest across her bent forearm. "Illuminate me,
oh great one."

"Glad you used my proper title. Otherwise, I wouldn't." He held
up his free hand, stopping her initial protest. "I've noticed people on
vacations or getaways have expectations."

"Okay, I get that. That's why I'm providing excellent accommodations, superb food and sublime service." She ignored Daniel's cough when she mentioned service. "What's not to like?"

"All those things are good and helpful for people whose expectations are met, but often people want to rekindle the romance, feel important, fall in love and be lifted out of depression. These are things lace-trimmed pillowcases and afternoon tea will not do. They're dependent on the person, the companion or set of mind. When they aren't having fun or relaxing, they blame you as opposed to themselves."

"How do you know so much about this? Can't remember you running an inn." His point was a valid one she had never taken into consideration. In her fantasy, happy smiling people left her inn with promises to return soon with friends.

"Oh," he drew out the word as he rolled his eyes upward, "I think some of those unhappy women were ones I made the mistake of traveling to some romantic B and B with. Apparently, a hotel or even a cruise doesn't rate as high on the relationship scale as a tiny independent inn run by a sweet couple. They expected me to drop three little words on them."

"Will you marry me?" She knew even after she said it. It was four words, not three.

Daniel shook his head, refusing to comment on her mistake. "I love you."

"You never ever loved anyone before Maria?"

"Nope. Loved my dog. My first motorcycle. My family, but never any woman before Maria." He uttered the words with total sincerity.

Her right foot tapped the floor. "No wonder those women were upset. Seriously, you agreed to go off on some romantic getaway they probably planned."

Her brother nodded.

"You knew what they were thinking."

"I did not."

Her toe-tapping increased. "You had to, especially after the first time."

"It was a different woman."

"She was still a woman. Trust me; females who've planned a romantic getaway with a significant other aren't that different. They were already miffed you hadn't planned it. I'm just glad you're married. Don't think I could stand your angry girlfriends stomping around the place."

His face assumed a wounded expression as he pushed off the wall. Daniel's hand landed over his heart. "Somehow, you think I'm at fault here for getting their expectations up too high. I never promised them anything."

"*Men.*" She snorted the word as she picked up the paint pan. "Make sure to thank Maria for me. She saved me from all the angry women I could have encountered in my inn."

The thick primer dripped into the pan as she tilted the can. Her brother came up behind her. "You're a woman. What did I do that made those women think I was serious?"

She placed the weighty paint can on the floor. The thick shielding she put around her heart splintered. Not a noticeable crack, but it was there all the same. Then she remembered a habit her brother had and the crack sealed up as suddenly as it occurred. Her brother couldn't figure it out. No wonder she was the smart one in the family. Holding the tray against her side, she stood and stared at her brother's clueless expression. How did he date so long and still be clueless about women?

"You kept dating them."

"They wanted me to keep dating them."

"Of course, they did, but it wasn't fair unless you intended to make a future with them."

"Is that why you don't date? Afraid of leading someone on?"

Where had that come from? "We're not talking about me. You were warning me about angry women who might come to my inn and wouldn't get their expectations met." Her steps carried her to the front door where she angled her loaded brush between the narrow window and the door.

Daniel followed her unaware the conversation had ended. "You never answered me."

She knew she hadn't answered him because she didn't want to. "Have you thought of any possible suspects?"

Her brother heaved a sigh. "Don't think I don't know what you're doing. No, I haven't thought of anyone. It's a puzzle. Hard to find a motive for a man no one knows. In most mysteries, everyone hates the victim."

"Yes!" She had thought the same thing. "Taber should have a photograph of the dead guy too."

"Heard anything?" The fact she hadn't, made her suspect the detective was holding out on her. "No." Even she heard the petulance in her voice.

Daniel smirked. "Yeah, burns you good too. Who do you suspect?"

There were so many possibilities from neighbors, real estate agents, strangers intent on revenge. "It would be better to say who I don't suspect. I think Grandmother Crochety is off my list."

"Who?"

Oh yeah, she hadn't brought her brother up to speed on the various nicknames she'd assigned her new neighbors. "The grump with the tape measure."

He nodded. "Got it. Too frail anyhow. Any motives?" He strode toward the doorway ready to exit, but glanced back expecting her reply.

"I'm working on it. It could have been impulsive, but I think it is more of a lover's spat." Saying the words aloud solidified it. Had to be, they could have been meeting in her inn for a while. Cold, hard floors didn't conjure romantic images, but illicit affairs took advantage of opportunity and secrecy. Hard to be more out of sight than a vacant house.

"That's good." Her brother saluted her then headed to the kitchen.

She shouted her question. "What's good about it?"

Silence hung in the air, followed by footsteps as Daniel strode back into the foyer. "It's done. Over. Fatal attraction affair ended in its inevitable conclusion. Police might catch the culprit, then again might not. In the end, it has nothing to do with us. No worries."

Yeah, no worries. No wonder people loved her brother since he never engaged in overanalyzing situations.

So far, he hasn't come up with anything.

Chapter Twelve

A WIDE SWATH of primer followed the brush as she moved it downward between the window and door. A metallic thump and rattle of a paint can indicated Daniel setting up in the kitchen as she hoped he would. *Good.* It meant no begging, which was just as well since she sucked at it. Being in charge, seeing the big picture, giving orders came naturally as the older sister. The same skills slimmed down the selection of potential beaus. Probably the reason she had hung onto Thomas, even though she had seen red flags. Couples usually spent time together doing even trivial activities. Thomas spent more time away than with her. He was also a bit more traditional than she liked. Old school because he believed women could have jobs outside the home as long as they kept the house clean, dinner on the table and laundry done.

Just as well, they never tied the knot, since they'd end up untying it after a few years, maybe even a few months. Still, would her outlook be different if she'd married? Her brush stopped in mid-stroke as she considered the ninety-degree turn her life took on that fateful day years ago.

Her brother reminded her once that thousands of other people went on to find fulfilling relationships. Did that make her a quitter? Her back went rigid at the word. Might as well call her a coward. She'd never thought of herself as either until now. Her brush dripped into the pan with a hollow plunking sound. Daniel's voice rattled her self-induced mental reverie as his footsteps came closer.

"You have the easiest job in the place and you're still dragging your feet."

Her glacial stare did not freeze her brother on the spot. Over the years, he'd built up a resistance. It helped that he knew she wasn't as tough as she pretended to be. The insult she planned to hurl at him dried up before she ever made it. Instead, a question she hadn't intended to ask popped out instead. "Did you make up the comment about thousands of people being left at the altar?"

Donna realized the secret to Daniel's popularity was more than a toothpaste commercial-worthy smile and good manners. Early on, he could size up people and tell them what they wanted to hear, which usually only contained a kernel of truth. She knew the answer before she even asked.

The sound of footsteps meant he had come off the ladder to talk to her. Never good when a person felt like they had to be close to talk to someone. In the hospital, she often hovered about a yard from a patient's family when she related that their loved one had taken a turn for the worse.

"Ah, sis. You know no one has that type of data. It's easier to get murder stats. Anyone who has been left at the altar seldom talks about it."

His voice grew closer with each word, which meant he'd proba-bly put an arm around her shoulders to reassure her, treating her like a five-year-old who fell off her bicycle. Placing one foot behind the other, she pivoted before he could. "No one ever mentions it because it makes them sound like a loser. No one wants to be a loser."

Her actions didn't stop Daniel's approach. Upon reaching her, he took the paintbrush from her hand and placed it on the tray. A spray of tiny white dots decorated the floor.

Her brother knelt at her feet, withdrew a bandana from his back pocket and mopped up the primer. "I'd say Thomas was the loser, not you. I've followed the jerk once social media became popular. The idiot even wanted to be my friend. I refused his request because I saw it for what it was."

The idea of her brother cyber stalking her old fiancé and using social media to do it astounded her. "I didn't even know you spent time on the Internet, other than reading construction blogs."

Daniel sat back on his heels and shrugged, then flashed her his famous smile. "Didn't use to, not until Henrietta."

"Who?" The women came and went in her brother's life so often that she needed a spreadsheet to remember them all.

"The feisty redhead with fantasy issues." Daniel gave the floor a final swipe before standing up.

Fantasy issues, not something a sister needed to know about her brother. A brief image of her brother dressed as a pirate and an anonymous redhead as a fairy popped into her head. She shook her head violently, ridding herself of the picture. "Too much information."

"Not that kind of fantasy." He chuckled, before continuing. "I wish you could have seen your face. Anyhow, she was a cousin to someone I went to high school with. Bumped into the man when I picked up a load of shingles. He congratulated me since he'd read on his cousin's social media that we were in a serious long-term relationship."

"Were you?" Odd, she remembered nothing about this female. She should have. It made her an unobservant sister.

"Not you too." His punch buffeted her shoulder. "No. I only went on two dates with her. Actually one and a half. I invented a construction emergency to end the second one early. She'd gone all weird telling me the names of our future children. Apparently, she told everyone else via social media. I decided I needed to be aware of how my name showed up in her media feed."

"What was your construction emergency?" She tried to imagine her brother's shocked face as some sweet young thing revealed the names of their children.

"Shingles. Someone's flew off in the thunderstorm and I needed to nail them back on." He winked at her, proving their momentary tenseness had left.

Her eyes rolled upward as she tried to imagine anyone taken in by such a flimsy excuse. Her brother might be many things, but an inventive liar he wasn't. One hand rested on her hip as she considered the scenario. "Seriously, you mean she believed you'd crawl up on someone's wet roof with an iron hammer in a thunderstorm?"

Her brother's silence served as an answer. "Dodged a major bullet there. Your kids would have been idiots."

Her brother made a rude gesture with his hand she chose to ignore. Even though she hated asking, she still wanted to know. "What did you find out about Thomas?"

"Enough to know you're better off without him. He's stuck in a dead-end job, which he whines about daily and he's bald. Not the cool, deliberate type of bald, but the fringe around the head like someone's uncle."

The news cheered her. Did that make her a petty person? She wasn't sure. "I guess I lucked out being left at the altar."

"Yeah, you did. Your only issue was not seeing it until now." Daniel crammed his handkerchief in his pocket and strode back into the kitchen.

Didn't see it until now. The words flashed through her mind like on a chasing light marquee, the kind the stores and churches employ hoping to catch the attention of motorists. Thomas didn't leave her because she was too bossy or too tall. The man exemplified jerk. At any time, he could have told her, but he didn't have the backbone to do so. A weight she hadn't known she'd been carrying suddenly lifted. Donna continued painting in a better mood.

The slam of the back door indicated her brother had tromped out to his truck for some reason. The easy camaraderie they shared painting the walls disappeared along with his presence. Uneasiness moved into her shoulders she tried to shake off. Seriously, no way she could run a B and B if this creeping apprehension afflicted her every time she was alone in the place. The slender window beside the door displayed a narrow image of her brother standing by his truck with his phone in his hand. He waved at someone and then his lips moved.

Of course, Daniel was outside talking to the neighbors. The same people who managed to look through her had time to chitchat with her brother. Well, except for Herman, who always had a gossipy tidbit to share even if no truth went into the making of it. Perception could be her problem. Daniel assumed everyone was friendly and would like him. It worked out that way, except for the angry server at The Good Egg. Every now and then, he'd bump into someone who remembered someone else with a similar name or face.

It had happened to her more than one. On the other hand, she cared for darling elderly ladies who often confused her with their daughters whom they adored. It could work either way. Assured her brother wasn't leaving, she picked up her paint pan and headed into the room she labeled morning parlor/chapel. More than half dozen floor-to-ceiling windows faced east. The sunlight flooded through the bare windows highlighting the dust on the wooden floors. The window treatments went with the house to keep nosy neighbors from peeking in. Logic would dictate the owner couldn't use the drapes in the next house because the possibility of buying a house with the same size and number of windows would be slim. Whoever owned the place decided they needed the curtains more than she did.

However, it made it easier to paint. The real estate agent could have taken them down because they were horrid. They did things like that. It was the opposite of fluffing where they trotted in items they thought would make the place look homey or chic. She'd heard some good real estate fluffers charged in the thousands. Donna shook her head in disbelief as she strode toward one window. The wood and glass windows possessed a wavy quality that hinted at the original glass. Restoration people would go crazy about it. Her lips twisted as she placed her hand against the glass. *Cold.* Exactly what she expected. At least there wasn't frost inside. Not exactly, double paned, but thicker than the glass currently available.

From her angle, she could see a woman at the end of the side-walk gesturing to someone. The porch support blocked her view, but she'd bet it was her brother. The blonde sported a fur coat, despite the current sentiment against such coats. Apparently, no one told her animal hair belonged on the animal. Of course, the ardent anti-fur supporters never had issues with wearing leather belts or shoes. A woman talking to her brother wasn't new. Still, she glanced at the sidewalk leading up to a brick saltbox house and she knew who the woman was.

Daniel must be talking to the former stripper who had married the doctor. How wonderful! Donna clapped her hands in excite-ment. According to Herman, the blonde was hosting a party when someone had snuck into Donna's house and murdered her unwanted houseguest. Just maybe this woman could give her some info. While waiting for her guests, she would have noticed a man lurking nearby.

Her hand was on the front doorknob twisting it open before even thinking through her actions. The door swung open with a creak, allowing in cold air and enlarging her field of vision. Her brother Daniel stood about two feet from the blonde.

The woman turned with a finger wave as she headed for her house before Donna even had a chance to talk to her. The blonde's feet stepped over one another, exaggerating her swaying prance, the type of walk she'd expect from a stripper. Daniel said something to Donna as she kept her eyes on the woman. The prancing stopped once she realized her male audience wasn't paying attention and morphed into a slow, straight walk similar to a tired shopper wearing shoes that pinched.

Daniel shouldered his way past her, talking while he did so. "Show's over, sis."

"Yeah, I see. Did you get something from the truck?" Her hand, still on the knob, pulled the door shut.

He held up a paint-spattered bit of plastic. "Yeah, the straight edge I needed." He grinned before pivoting and heading for the kitchen.

"Seriously, you're going to play that game with me." A few jogging steps caught up with her brother's long-legged strides. "C'mon what did you learn from my lovely neighbor?" Donna postured similar to the neighbor and batted her eyelashes.

"Ah, you must mean Bambi." Daniel smirked at her, fitting the pad to the plastic edger form. He pressed the edger into the paint tray, scraping off the excess before cutting around the cabinets.

"Not Crystal, Desiree, or Dee Light?" Her glance went over the kitchen at the blue tape outlining the ceiling, cabinets and door-frames. Good thing she had palmed the room off on Daniel.

"She could have changed her name to go upscale with the neighborhood and all. Bambi sounds a bit cutesy. Buffy would have worked better." The wall Daniel faced muffled his voice.

"Okay, makes sense. What did *Bambi* tell you?"

Her brother snorted. "Not much. Nothing really. Just a woman who needs a whole lot of attention."

Donna fisted her hands on her hips. "Here's my big opportunity to find out what happened on the night a man was murdered in my house. She could have seen the man who snuck in here and all you do is discuss the weather?"

The smooth paint line Daniel made stopped as her brother gave her a disbelieving look over one shoulder. "How should I have phrased it? Oh, by the way, did you possibly spot a murder suspect entering the vacant house next door?"

"Vacant, there's no reason to call it vacant. It makes it sound too much like derelict." She placed two fingers up to her mouth, considering the issue. "It wouldn't be too weird to say something. You know everyone is talking about it."

"Hmmm, maybe." Daniel went back to edging around the cabinets. The broad splash of primer hid the scrape marks and covered the gouges. By the time the entire room was done, it would look totally clean and new.

The foyer wasn't getting itself painted. Donna pivoted, but her brother's words froze her in place.

"For someone who had men stuffing dollars in her G-string, she struck me wrong."

A game buzzer went off somewhere in her brain. Not the type that sounded similar to an electronic fart, but the cheery type signaling she had something right. She turned slowly, facing her brother who held up the edger in mid-thought, another trait they shared.

"Why?" Her brief side view had allowed her only to see the big hair, an expensive coat and stylish boots.

"Hmm, yeah, now that I mentioned it, it's hard to explain. She had that huge coat, which prevented me from seeing her rack."

"Sister—female here." She waved her hand and pointed back to herself with her thumb. "You know I tend to think of women as being more than a few body parts."

"Me too, but you're the one who told me she was a former stripper. I wanted to see what got her moved into the good life. Great hair. Face wasn't that great, prominent nose with small eyes."

"Yeah, but as you demonstrated men seldom look at a stripper's face." Her regret about missing a chance to talk to Bambi deepened, though there was a good chance the woman wouldn't have talked to her. She might feel the female neighbors were against her, which could be true. She didn't care. Bambi might have information she needed to solve the crime.

"The way she called out to me and engaged me in conversation struck me as needy. Strippers on the whole have an arrogant attitude."

Arrogant? "I thought they'd be super friendly. Wasn't that the entire idea behind men going to strip clubs?"

His shoulders went up with a shrug. "Yeah. You'd think that, but if they seemed too accommodating there'd be no reason to charge big bucks for lap dances."

Her brother ignored her disgusted gagging sound and continued talking.

"Bambi waved at me when I was walking back to the house. She initiated contact, not me."

Typical. Women were flagging her brother down all the time. Besides having a great profile and a fit form, he had the warmth factor of the boy next door. People automatically sensed he'd help without expecting anything in return. Most women preferred a handsome man helping them than an ordinary fellow. It made for a better retelling.

"That sounds like an everyday occurrence in the world of Daniel." She wrinkled her nose, making her brother laugh. "What did she ask you?"

"Nothing really. Made some inane comment about the weather. Asked me when I was moving in. If there would an open house allowing the neighbors to peek at the restoration?

Did the man even listen to himself talk? She held her hand up similar to a cop stopping traffic. "Stop.

What did you tell her?"

"Nothing really, since neither one of us knows when the place will be done. Months, I think I said a couple of months."

Yeah, that sounded about right. A lot could happen in a couple of months.

Chapter Thirteen

THE RUMBLE OF the overhead PA system bleated about a sale. Most of the distorted words Donna couldn't make out, but she did understand the first word, *Sale.* Apparently, the other shoppers had no such translation problems as they maneuvered their shopping buggies through the narrow aisles road rally style. She glanced at the departing mob, wondering if she should join the max exodus.

Probably a markdown on athletic shoes that lit up when they hit the ground or a gallon can of jelly belly bears, not anything she'd need for camping out at the inn. The jelly belly bears might not be so bad, though.

Her hand rested on a twin-size air mattress. A smiling child clutching a teddy bear decorated the advertising placard on it, which announced it supported up to 220 pounds. Well, she definitely came in under that, but the thought of her own pillow-top queen bed, decorated with a purple paisley comforter and numerous pillows, mocked her. The lavender 500-count sheets managed to be soft and luxurious when she slipped into bed each night. Nothing in her home came under the label of roughing it. Why should the inn be any different?

A few yards down was a king-sized air mattress with a pillow top advertising itself as the apex of airbeds. It would only be a short time. No reason not to move her real bed, if she planned to stay at the inn. First things first, her hands gripped the oversized box and tugged. A few items beside it moved, but not the box. Someone had crammed the mattress into a too-small spot. Another hefty pull moved it a couple of inches forward, but no more. Two red-vested male employees strolled past her without offering any assistance.

Her lips twisted in disgust. Seriously, it had come to that. The dreadful in-between years between hot babe and frail senior likely to file a lawsuit after falling. Her breath pushed out with a long sigh as she placed one foot on the bottom shelf for leverage and used her weight to pull the stubborn box forward.

"You need help, ma'am?" A skinny, teenage male stood at the end of the aisle, regarding her.

Donna inhaled as she silently counted to ten. Not sure what was worse, that she needed help or that the boy called her ma'am as if she were some friend's elderly relative. *Stay calm.* Her initial desire to shout *Of course I need help!* she channeled into a resigned "Yes."

The employee reached for the box, lifting it into her cart. "Thanks," she mumbled with an apologetic smile as she steered the buggy toward the bedding section.

She should have shown more appreciation to the young man. He certainly did more than his fellow workers did. Her back straight, shoulders back, she peeked at a full-length mirror as she moved in front of it. Not too bad, not the old woman she felt like when she fought with the mattress box. Another look confirmed the capable woman who usually stared out from her bathroom mirror still existed. *Shake it off.*

In the linen aisle, she tossed in a cabbage rose sheet set. The price caused her to grimace a little. The store had the nerve to call itself a discount store. All the same, she might as well go with 500-count because she could use it later for a guest bed. Nothing worse than cheap sheets on a bed when engaging in a weekend getaway. She ought to know, she had stayed in enough inns before coming up with the idea of her own.

Patched sheets in an expensive, historic hotel in Cincinnati, cold breakfast in Lexington better suited to a motor lodge and cheap soap that stripped her body of its natural moisture in Savannah. The offenses of what not to do made up a sizable list, convincing her that she'd be able to do a much better job on her own. Her buggy cleared an end cap topped with an orange clearance sign. An asymmetrical-shaped clear bowl caught her eye.

It could work filled with assorted teas, gourmet chocolate mixes and a few instant coffees nestled on a Butler stand tucked into a hall self-serve refreshment station. The machine that served individual cups might be more convenient, but not very attractive. Besides, coffee ran about forty dollars a pound when purchasing it in personal units. Expensive, lukewarm coffee in a paper cup was not the image she wanted for her bed and breakfast either. Classic elegance in china teacups with perfectly steeped tea would serve her better. Small fridges stocked with soda and bottled water would be on each floor.

Plug-in air fresheners joined the air mattress and sheets. Since she turned on the electric, the subzero fridge would work. The thought of a small fridge in her room that would keep her in one place appealed. Certainly better than roaming the dark halls pocketed with empty rooms perfect for a secret rendezvous or a murderer on a return visit. Her lips thinned as she considered the possibility of unwanted visitors. In the end, wandering the house was exactly her whole purpose in staying, that and catching any unwelcome visitors. Jasper, her dog, would go too. It would be difficult to get past the animal who barked when the wind changed directions. Besides, he'd be good company, especially since no one else knew about her plans.

Her trek through the store came to a standstill as her buggy bumped to a stop. The small shove she gave had no effect. Her hands gripped the handle bar a little harder as she examined the recalcitrant device. A sticky patch left over from a gum-chewing child or adult could be the issue. The two front wheels pointed out at opposite angles, explaining the unplanned halt. *Weird.* The cart wasn't that way when she started since she tried to avoid the lame and the thumping carts that had the rubber off one wheel roller. Her grip dropped from the handle as she moved toward the front of the buggy and kicked the wheels into place. The cart gave a tiny jump and then rolled forward a few inches. Her shoulders relaxed after conquering that obstacle. The cart stop could be the universe giving her a jab for either her plan to camp out in the inn or the fact she wasn't telling anyone.

After a careful examination of the three open lines out of the dozen or more that served the store, she opted for the one with only one other customer in it. The other two boasted weary women pushing rounded baskets with enough food to feed dozens of children, which might explain their tired demeanors. Good decision on her part, until the woman in front of her asked specifically for unfiltered cigarettes. The clerk's confused expression didn't bode well as she scurried off to wherever they hid the coffin nails.

Great. Maybe the other lines would be better, but the image of the bulging carts discouraged her from shifting lanes. Unfiltered cigarettes. Seriously, did the woman want to die faster? Perhaps she was unaware how smoking affected the body. Plenty of stage four lung cancer patients ended up in her hospital. The gasping individuals had oxygen leads taped to their noses since their own lungs failed to do the job properly. Her hand paused in the air, preventing her from tapping the woman on the shoulder.

The smoker wouldn't thank her. Might even think she was a nosy busybody. Her hand landed on the nearby magazine stand offering almost every variety of celebrity gossip available along with a few other tabloids. One magazine that promised the secret to dropping twenty pounds in two weeks also featured a decadent chocolate cake on the cover. Did no one else see the cover as counterintuitive besides her? A glossy photo of a celebrity couple caught her eye along with its bold headline.

"She's getting married again," she muttered in surprise, grabbing the attention of the woman in front of her.

The dark-haired woman swung around, glanced at the magazine display. "Yeah, that woman goes through husbands the way I do gum."

A quick head bob acknowledged the comment as Donna marveled at the woman's unlined face and wondered what to say. Her bent knuckle pointed at the man in the photo. "They're all so handsome too."

The other woman shrugged. "Doesn't mean they're any good for her. Just because the chick's famous doesn't mean she isn't taken in by the packaging."

The clerk returned with a carton of cigarettes under her arm that caused Donna to remember commercials showcasing an alpha man smoking while doing manly pursuits back when cigarette ads dominated the airwaves.

The woman continued talking, not aware of the returning clerk. "It's all packaging. People fall for it every time, even when they should know better. I run a service that provides shopping and transportation service for homebound individuals. Kenny, the man

I'm shopping for today, told me he started smoking because it made him feel sophisticated." She shook her head before continuing.

"I have to do his shopping for him because he's too frail to do it himself. Cigarettes are the last thing he needs, but if I don't buy them, someone else will. As a single parent, I need the money he pays me."

The clerk cleared her throat, making her presence known. The woman turned around and paid for her purchases, giving a small hand wave before she left. Donna's hand went up in reply; glad she'd never mentioned the cigarettes. The incident proved her brother right that she tended to judge people too quickly. Still, she kept her opinion to herself longer than usual. It was a start on her way to being an extraordinary innkeeper. Her customers would talk about that as much as the charms of The Painted Lady Inn.

Donna smiled at the clerk, hoping to engage her in a casual conversation the way she would potential guests. The young woman kept her gaze fixed on the scanner as she pushed the items through. *Shy*, that must be it. Her cheeks ached from the smile she pasted on waiting for the girl to look up. Seriously, how did beauty contestants manage the constant grin? What a waste if no one was looking. Her cheeks relaxed as she gave up on her image of geniality. The girl looked up, meeting her eyes briefly and then looked down again. *Figures.*

Who knew being consistently welcoming would be a challenge? Not her, she never considered herself perky or cheerful, but she wasn't exactly the villain either. She went to work, did her job the best she could, treated her fellow humans with respect, occasionally with a side of unsolicited advice. Still, some people needed it, right?

Her silent clerk attempted to wrestle the air mattress into a bag but ended up ripping the thin bag in the process.

"Never mind," Donna called out after the clerk tore another bag. A glare that could have read *Now you tell me* hit Donna as the girl glanced at her. She liked it better when the girl didn't look at her. Debit card in hand, she tried to think of a suitable parting comment. Something that would uplift the clerk and make her feel good about herself.

After paying too much for the convenience of getting something immediately, she smiled again as she pocketed her receipt. "I appreciate how well you checked out my order."

No murmured words of appreciation or even a gracious smile. Instead the girl looked startled, then burst into tears and ran toward the customer service door. Not the reaction she expected. The best thing would be to leave, but her cart turned cantankerous again. Long enough for her to hear her clerk gasp out between sobs that a customer had ridiculed her because she couldn't bag a mattress. Then the same customer went and made a snarky remark about what a great job she'd done.

The heat in Donna's face spread to her ears, no doubt painting them both bright red. A fierce shove pushed the buggy out of the checkout aisle and closer to the crying clerk. The small crowd of fellow employees turned as one and watched Donna as she wrestled the laden cart toward the exit.

Don't you dare stop on me now, you piece of scrap metal.

Telling people that she wasn't getting married after her fiancé found someone he liked better still held the number one awkward moment's position. A discount clerk breaking into tears over a misunderstood remark didn't even break into the top five. Definitely not after finding a dead man in her inn. It fit in nicely between the time she beaned the self-important golf pro on the driving range with an errant ball and the laxative-laced coffee meant for a patient that ended up in the doctors' lounge.

Outside, she continued walking fast, still feeling the condemnation of a dozen pair of eyes. It didn't help that she didn't deserve it. People still ended up in jail when they hadn't committed the crime. The assumption, speculation and the inability to hire a high-price lawyer could get you five to ten.

Packages stowed, car doors locked, she managed to regain her normal sense of anonymity she usually felt when driving. A classic rock station played softly as she steered the car toward home while composing a mental checklist of everything she'd have to bring. Her original intention of hiring a manager to stay at the inn made sense, except for paying the person. Yep, for a while, she'd be it. Owner, manager, cook and possibly maid, although she hoped she could at least get some college student to help clean the rooms.

The garage door moved up after she punched the opener. Jasper accompanied the creaking with his own high-pitched yelps. Most hardened criminals wouldn't be scared, imagining the owner of the not-so-menacing barking as a fluffy poodle or Pomeranian. Although, Donna had run across a vicious poodle or two growing up. Jasper was bigger than his bark. Once when she walked him around the neighborhood, a charge from an unleashed chocolate lab startled her and her pooch defended her by growling at the oncoming dog. An invisible fence brought the lab up short, causing her and probably Jasper to both gasp a sigh of relief. Her pet could be courageous on occasion if the need arose.

The visit home allowed enough time for her to nuke her homemade chicken pot pie. It was stuffed full of fresh veggies and quarter-size chunks of chicken breast embraced by a buttery white sauce and finished off with a crust so light it practically floated above the dish. Usually, she'd heat the already baked pie in the oven, but time counted.

Her goal included getting her and Jasper to the inn, air mattress blown up and her tablet set up so she could watch the movie she downloaded last week. The home inspector had already tested the electric out, so she knew it worked. It would be better for her to get into the house while daylight still held. A little less obvious too, considering that people expected work done at the inn during the day. A pair of headlights pulling in would not go unnoticed, especially by her sharp-eyed neighbors or anyone else watching the house.

Even though most crimes shows relied on hanging out at crime sites or even attending funerals to catch the culprit, Donna had her doubts. Why a murderer would return. If a person got away with a crime, wouldn't it be best to keep silent and hidden? It made sense to her, but then she was logical. The murderer could return if he or she thought something left behind that could serve as an arrow pointing the police back to the culprit. She dismissed the idea as she threw Jasper's bed and dishes in the trunk.

"Surely the police swept the place clean of any clues."

Jasper barked his agreement or possible inquiry about the end destination of his belongings.

A small overnight case joined the dog bed along with a lamp, a small television and a hamper of food. White chocolate macadamia nut cookies could help her overlook anything that went bump in the night since she'd be too busy inhaling a dozen or more.

"The police could miss a clue if it didn't fit into their theory about the killer." The thought both scared and excited her. Another human possibly close by capable of cold-bloodedly killing someone was the scary part. If a clue existed, she could piece together the case and solve it. A sense of impending triumph put a bounce in her step as she chucked her uniform and a pair of slippers into the car.

It reminded her of the Sherlock Holmes game she used to play with her brother. The gameplay happened on a laminated surface with boredom as the worst result. Her top teeth rested on her bottom lip as she considered the possible outcome of the same game played with live characters.

Her dog, unaware of her mental cogitations, jumped into the passenger seat. "Just a minute, Jasper. I have one more thing."

Donna ran back into the house wondering where she'd hid the needed item. *Hid* was the appropriate word because she hadn't wanted to see it, despite Daniel's insistence on having it. The dining room chair served as an impromptu stepladder as she reached for the top of her china cabinet. The elaborate cherry scrollwork disguised the recessed area behind it. Sizable enough for something small and yet so obviously out in plain sight that a burglar would never look. A knowledgeable robber would know her china should be worth at least a thousand, but china must not be a fencible item.

Hardly the usual fence scenario with criminals with hats pulled low shading their faces dragging in heavy boxes of china to sell. The fence would hold the china up to the light, inspecting the thinness of the dish or turning it over for the marker stamp. Of course, he had to distinguish between bone, fine and porcelain china too. So few people could. Even the assistant at the upscale home furnishings store appeared baffled when she asked if any Spone china had passed through the store. She certainly had no desire to have any of the bone china that creator Spode created from human bone ashes from a crematorium, but she wouldn't mind seeing it. She had even heard of a family that made up a set of dishes from their deceased relative. Put an entirely new angle on having dinner with grandmother. The thought sent a shiver down her back. Not a good thing when standing on tiptoes on a chair.

Her fingers reached past the dusty scrollwork. She didn't need to see. The smooth cylinder and textured grip told her she'd found what she needed. Dust decorated the gun she swore she'd never use. Her brother managed to get her to a firing range deep in some subterranean area that could have doubled as a dungeon. A half dozen other grim-faced women took aim at the paper man-shaped torso with the bulls-eyes drawn over the chest area, not exactly on the heart. A clean shot would do enough damage to the internal organs to stop anyone in their tracks.

Daniel had drawn a few stares as he entered the room with her, not the usual kind, but rather the ones aimed at coiled rattlesnakes and mechanics who inflated car repairs. The targets at the end represented cheating husbands, abusive ex-boyfriends, stalkers and the bad luck to live in a crime-ridden neighborhood. Unwittingly by being born male, Daniel couldn't understand the feminine world where women often had to be on guard. Still, she had to give him credit; he did try to protect her and bought her a gun. An expensive extravagance could have substituted for a number of birthday presents.

Even though it wasn't her idea to go to a shooting range, she found herself following Daniel's instruction. Her hands sweated at the idea of holding a gun. Daniel kept returning the pistol, reminding her it was hers, not his. A slight tremor in her hands betrayed her anxiety. Not acceptable, she had to pull on her big girl panties and get the job done. The woman beside her had pelted her target with a steady barrage of center shots with her semi-automatic weapon. Obviously, she had no anxiety issues when it came to firepower.

Because they both donned headphones to protect their ears from multiple gunshots, she and Daniel communicated through gestures. He held up his index finger, which she knew meant first. He pointed to his chest, mimicked inhaling, but held his breath while shaping his hand into a makeshift pistol with his thumb and index finger. The third finger bent then straightened as it functioned as a trigger. Her brother's cheeks deflated as he mimed exhaling. Inhale before you shoot, exhale afterward.

She'd sucked in a huge gulp of air before pulling the trigger firmly and then exhaled after the bullet hurtled toward the paper man. The first two shots went wide, not even hitting the outlined torso. Not good, not good at all. Ms. Killer Instinct stopped shooting long enough to throw a pity smile her way. No interpretation was necessary.

Daniel stiffened beside her. Living with her a good part of his life exposed him to her natural competitiveness. Although, her younger brother didn't usually face it head-on. He may have witnessed a few competitions where snotty *I'm all that* girls thought they could run over her because she didn't come from a wealthy family or knew the right people. The social registry didn't matter on the soccer field or in the chemistry lab.

The image of Heather Donahue with her plastic smile and double Ds taunted her. Never got to drive in driver's ed because the instructor was too enraptured with her charms. Instead, Marcia and she stared out the back window waving at people behind them, especially if there were cute boys in the car following them. The instructor failed them both, probably afraid to put them on the road with no skills. It was her first experience with failure through no fault of her own. Her lips tightened as she imagined Heather at the end of the shooting alley.

Donna aimed higher as she sighted across the barrel since her eyes and gun hand were a good foot apart. A tidbit she remembered from a crime drama featuring a woman in the police academy. Instead of Heather, the image of her driving instructor with his receding hairline and half-open mouth as he ogled his student appeared. His expression morphed into shock as she plugged two bullets smack into his torso.

Her brother gave two thumbs up and a grin. *Wow. What changed?* He mouthed the words.

A shoulder shrug served as her answer as she turned back to the target. She took turns imagining people who had wronged her in some way. Of course, she knew she would never shoot anyone. It took on the form of therapy, releasing festering anger through the years. Maybe therapists would have more success if they used a carnival-style shooting gallery instead of the usual couch in their office. Who knew? It might actually lead to less violence.

Target practice had taken up three more off days before Daniel declared her proficient. That's when the gun went to its home on top of the china cabinet. Her hand wrapped around the weapon and brought it down within view. Her hand covered most of the piece with only the molded handgrip peeking out and the very edge of the barrel. It was hard to believe something so small could be so deadly.

She eased off the chair, pointing the gun away from her. Of course, she knew better than to store it loaded. The clip and the extra ammo resided in a separate hiding place. A news statistic stated 70 percent of homeowners had their own guns used on them.

Ammunition. Where would it be? Not anywhere, close to the china cabinet because that would make it too easy for a robber. A quick search of closet shelves and the interior of a large china teapot she seldom used yielded nothing. Jasper wandered into the house through the open garage door and whined his displeasure about the unsuccessful ammo search that hogged all her attention better spent on him.

"You're right, we need to get going." He made a mincing movement with his feet that indicated excitement before pivoting and heading for the garage. The gun went into her tote with a mental note to pick up ammunition. Not tonight, but sometime soon. Jasper would be her early warning system, scaring off any possible home invaders.

Truthfully, she didn't want to shoot anyone. Enough time spent in the emergency room demonstrated the damage a single bullet could do to vulnerable human flesh, which solidified her decision. It didn't matter if the shot was deliberate or the result of horsing around. Dead was still dead whether you meant it or not. Then there were the critical sites that could disable a person. Her head shook slowly side to side. No way could she live with that type of karmic guilt. Maybe it would be enough to yell, *I have a gun!*

With the car packed, she slipped into the driver's seat. Had she turned down the heat? Certain she had, she shifted into reverse and rolled out of the driveway, wondering if her neighbors were watching. Probably not, she wasn't one who merited a twitch of the curtains. Good old predictable Donna went to work every day and came home to her little yapper. No one knew an adventure awaited her. At best, it would be a sleepover with Jasper. Then again, something could happen. A tingling danced up and down her arms and across her shoulders. The same feeling she got when the roller coaster climbed the hill, knowing a swift descent and a dark tunnel awaited her.

Her foot hit the brake at the foot of the driveway. *Should she go back in and look for the ammo?* An audible sigh filled the car and this time it wasn't Jasper. While she had several excellent traits, her few idiosyncrasies such as continually losing items drove her crazy. She could look all night for the bullets and never find them. On another day, when baskets or patterned hosiery was her focus, she'd stumble across them. More room, that's what she needed for better organization.

What if someone did break in? This inconvenient fear monger who kept inserting unwelcome thoughts in her head needed to go. Logically, she should plan for the worst-case scenario. Nine one one on speed dial might work. As long as she was inserting speed dial numbers on her phone, she could put in Mark Taber's name. No reason to expect him to come running in the middle of the night, but he could be on duty. Yep, that's what she'd do.

The drive went fast as she lectured Jasper on expected behavior. The pooch spent most of the trip decorating the passenger window with his nose art creations. "Remember, Jasper, no accidents. I realize this is a new place, but we need to keep it nice. No one wants to stay at a B and B reeking of dog urine."

Food smells created by the various restaurants dotting the route resulted in Jasper's animated sniffing along with a slight drool, he paused and gave her a reproachful look.

"Yes, I know you're trained, but accidents can happen."

The dog's attention returned to the fast food restaurant bathed in vibrant neon lights. Donna noticed his actions but continued talking if only to reassure herself."

"Well, at least there isn't any carpet to worry about." Three levels of wooden floors except the ceramic-tiled bathrooms and the linoleum-lined kitchen and foyer. The wooden floor would benefit from refinishing, but she had to draw the line at closets and storage rooms. Oriental carpets would cover the polished floors. A period book she snagged at the library book sale mentioned that the very wealthy would pile carpet on top of carpet making a plush surface while demonstrating their wealth. Estate sales or even online garage sales could provide her with the needed rugs. After all, the rugs didn't have to match since they were in different rooms.

Her driving had reached almost a Zen-like state where she could make the correct turns without too much thought. Her contemplation moved onto the linoleum. "The foyer floor with its faded and pitted linoleum. Could be original."

Jasper whined a little and scratched at the window. Donna's foot tapped the accelerator until she reached four miles an hour over the speed limit. Surely, no one would pull her over for that. If an officer did, she'd explain her dog needed to use the facilities. A laugh escaped her lips as she imagined the reaction of a stoic cop trying to keep a straight face.

"We'll be there soon, boy." Normally, the worst thing you could do to a person who had to go to the bathroom was mention it. It might apply to dogs too. Another drawn-out whimper had her changing back to home renovation mode.

"Did you know when Linoleum was invented it was super expensive? It cost more than marble tile." No sound from her companion, but at least he wasn't whimpering, which could be a good sign. Think good thoughts. Jasper had never had an accident in the car before.

"It was such a big deal that they installed it on the grand staircase of the *Titanic*." The reflective street sign announcing her street glimmered as her headlights caught it. Her goal was to make it before nightfall, but the sun had already dropped, leaving a shadowy twilight in its wake.

"Some light is better than no light."

The car bumped up the driveway, dipping and swaying as the

tires took some minor potholes as she maneuvered around the larger ones. Another significant expense and not one she could sidestep either. Parking off the street, especially with her bizarre tape-measuring neighbor, ranked higher than curb appeal. A review that mentioned a visitor's car being towed wouldn't garner her any stars.

The car came to a halt at the kitchen entrance. No welcoming lights inside or outside the house, which puzzled her. Hadn't she deliberately turned on the exterior porch light as she left? Could be that Daniel had turned it off, unaware of her plan to return. Even if she weren't returning, the light would still serve as a security measure.

Oh well. She opened the car door, considering the location of her flashlight when Jasper used her lap as a launching pad, sinking his needle-sharp nails into her thighs before jumping. *Guess he really had to go.*

Bent at the waist, she felt under the seat for the flashlight. Finally, her fingers snagged the cylinder and drew it out at the same time Jasper started barking. *Great,* she'd hoped her overnight stay would be a secret. Nothing better to announce a clandestine visit than a barking canine. Her hand still clutching the flashlight, she lunged out of the driver's seat to find and hush her pet.

The tenor of Jasper's barks changed and moved away from the house, but she took the time to turn and lock the car with her fob before shoving the keys in her pocket. The rapid barking meant her dog was in pursuit of a rabbit or squirrel. She jogged by ragged shrubs and turned at the landscaping barn, which served as a euphemism for the half tumbled down shed that shielded a rusty mower. An item on her list to tear down, especially since her taxes went up for each building on her property. Whatever Jasper was chasing would take him onto the adjoining property.

A long shadow appeared to her right side, which she dodged. The faint light of the newly risen moon, along with the ambient lighting from the street lights, turned the early evening into a gray landscape filled with dark shapes. Some were identifiable as trees or houses, but not all. Her toe caught on something, sending her to the ground with a bone-rattling plop. The flashlight bounced out of her hand with the fall and flicked on as it hit the ground.

Geesh, the flashlight. Why hadn't she turned it on? Donna stared at the flashlight's yellow beam as she pushed herself up into a sitting position. Jasper's barking stopped abruptly. Whatever he was chasing had eluded him. Her housebound pooch often thought himself a great hunter but hadn't managed to catch anything the entire time she'd owned him. Not that she wanted a dead rabbit or a chewed-on bird presented to her as a gift, she didn't.

She sat for a few seconds catching her breath and waiting for Jasper to return. Her eyes went back to the yellow beam illuminating a footprint in the grassless stretch of the yard. The beam highlighted the grooves and lines of an athletic shoe in the soft earth. A good sized print, obviously an adult's, but whose? Someone who had no business around her house, that's for sure.

Agitated panting announced Jasper as he trotted back to her side Her pooch was never much on the actual chase. His mode included a loud, short pursuit. Perhaps, he was more guard dog than she originally suspected. Her hands scrambled for purchase on the uneven ground as she pushed to her knees. It would have been helpful if she had seen her unwelcome visitor. No doubt, it would have been a less-than-friendly meeting. Her fingers massaged the back of her neck as she considered the possibility of coming face to face with a possible felon. Her sense of unease increased as she reached for the flashlight.

The girl detective scenario deviated from the script she had written in her mind. Her left knee, which took the brunt of her fall, ached. Yeah, physical injury chasing her dog hadn't been part of the plan. The slam of a house door sounded in the distance. Probably just a nosy neighbor kid; she'd already experienced what lengths a teen would go to. It would make a good story at school, especially with some embellishments like a ghost.

The faint memory of a ghostly figure demanding she find his killer needled her into action. She reached for the flashlight and turned it back toward the way she came. Long, twisted roots stretched across the ground like the gnarled, knobby fingers of an old crone, which made it surprising she had only fallen once.

The footprint nagged at her. A slow wave of the light revealed only a single print due to the reappearance of tufts of grass and the multitude of roots. No path to follow that would lead her to the possible killer, but more likely to her self-styled teenage reporter. Might as well unpack the car and get settled in. A sharp stab of pain went through her knee, causing her to stumble at its suddenness. Tightening her muscles, she managed to stay upright. "I'll have to ice my knee."

Most likely there wasn't any ice in the fridge and she didn't feel like a road trip to get any. A bath and two painkillers should do the trick. Although the thought of sitting in a bathtub in a house where a man had died left a damp residue on her skin as if touched by ghostly hands as opposed to the evening dew.

The round sphere of light spotlighted her feet and about a yard around them. Plenty of obstacles to trip up an unwary homeowner. The footprint made her wonder about her visitor. Made her question if her uninvited guest had any trouble making his or her way through the obstacle course. It could have been luck, youth or a deep familiarity with the terrain that allowed her visitor to dodge known tree roots. A sparkle reflected the light back to her. *What was that?*

The toe of her right foot nudged whatever it was into the light. The bag sported plenty of sequins in various colors, a grade-school girl's dream of total sophistication. It glittered under the flashlight's beam. *Strange.* What child abandoned her pack? Perhaps it wasn't just teens who had used the previously vacant house as their own personal space. Her reaching hand almost had the bag until she realized it could be evidence.

Her hand fell to her side as she regarded the bag half-hidden by the dark bushes. Would any self-respecting felon use such an eye-catching bag? She doubted it. Still, she considered how she might retrieve it without putting her fingerprints all over it. A nearby stick served as answer. The diameter of the stick was bigger than her thumb but had the lightweight feel of something that had been long dead and all the life leaked out into the ground in the intervening time.

The jagged tip went under a strap of the bag. A shimmy of the stick moved the strap down farther to the meatier section. Okay, she had it. Inhaling, she lifted it. The rod bowed under the weight. Donna had to use her second hand to grip her first hand to support it. What could be in the bag?

She'd moved about a foot when the stick broke, sending the bag crashing to the ground with a clunk and a shatter of glass. Just enough to send Jasper into a barking frenzy. *Great.* She had probably just destroyed whatever was in the bag. Strangulation wasn't the result of being in contact with glass. The bag could be a red herring. A slight, sweet smell came from the bag, almost gagging in its intensity. Her hands served as an impromptu fan. "Ugh."

The smell dissipated quickly in the night air. Even so, there was something familiar about it that stroked an old memory. Two of her high school girlfriends and she had indulged in a pity party due to not having prom dates. Part of the celebration included drinking sickly sweet strawberry wine that she threw up later in the holly bushes of her own home. Her mother had blamed it on Joe, the raucous teen next door. What she needed was gloves and not some puny stick. As a nurse, she had tucked in her glove compartment a plastic bag with latex gloves and a mask in case she came into contact with blood or airborne pathogens. With the gloves on, she could pick up the bag.

The first thing she did after grabbing the bag was to open the back door. The empty house had a breath of expectancy about it, as if waiting for someone or something. *Crazy.* If anyone else had said such a thing, she'd point out that buildings didn't have feelings. The second thing she did was turn on the radio she had left behind to break the silence. The third thing was call Tabor.

"Hey, I know it's late, but I may have information."

"Go ahead."

She explained briefly about Jasper's chase, the footprint and the bag. "I think there may have been a recent trespasser."

"You are where right now?"

"At the inn, where else would I be?"

The long sigh carried over the phone. "Okay. I'll be there in ten."

Chapter Fourteen

THE SUDDEN DISCONNECT miffed Donna, but Mark hadn't launched into a lecture on the stupidity of camping out in the building. Daniel would have. Still, it was her house and she could do whatever she wanted, although the idea of an impromptu sleepover had paled a little when she fell.

In the intervening time, she moved the bag to the kitchen counter, noticing when she swung it out of Jasper's range that it was more the size of an adult backpack. Not the hiking kind, but the average "I don't have enough junk for a suitcase" type. The tingling sound it made when she moved it confirmed broken glass.

A few more trips gathered the rest of her supplies. By the time Taber arrived, she'd have her room set up. She pulled the unwieldy airbed up the stairs to the first bedroom. Difficult, but not impossible, but some type of lift would help a wheelchair-bound patron or an unusual amount of luggage. Her lips twisted as she considered some diva arriving with six pieces of matching luggage. It made no sense, but high-maintenance women seldom did.

The first bedroom earned the honor of being her home for the night. It could use some dusting, but the overhead light worked. The ugly cheap light fixture rested left of center of the ornate ceiling medallion. It spoiled the look of the entire room. Wall sconces would look better and bathe the room in a more flattering light. The right ambiance would ensure a good review and a possible return business. The fixture earned another squint-eyed glare.

"More expenses. Additional wiring." She nodded to the dog, who followed her up. "That doesn't come cheap either. No doubt the electrician will tell me he can't wire anything new into the old wiring because it's out of code."

The air bed box resisted her tugging but finally ripped, sending her flat on her back for her efforts. Donna unfolded the mattress before attempting inflation. The electric pump gave a wheeze and a gurgle before erupting into a loud whine that set Jasper into barking mode. The flat plastic mat grew into something that resembled a king-sized bed if it were made out of plastic and covered with a terry-cloth top. The pump shuttered to a stop.

"That's it."

She unplugged the pump as she watched her dog cautiously sniff the perimeter of the bed. The sheets fit a little looser than she expected. It could be the smooth plastic sides didn't provide any friction to adhere to the material.

A loud shout from downstairs startled her.

"Donna!"

Taber, of course. "Up here!" she shouted back as she made her way to the stairs. Her hand smoothed over the banister as she considered the possibility of a chair lift marring the elegant symmetry of the staircase.

The good detective sported jeans and a hoodie, an unexpected fashion choice. It worked, except for the scowl that accompanied it.

"Why did you leave your back door wide open?"

"I didn't." Her denial was barely out as she considered her various trips into the house. There'd been more than a half a dozen, but each time she'd intentionally closed the door. She had thought she locked it, but a few times the knob twisted easily under her hand proving it didn't always catch.

"It was open when I drove up."

Donna skirted the man as she darted toward the kitchen. The empty kitchen counter where she'd left the bag mocked her.

Gone. Possibly the only lead she had for her murderer was in that bag. Her open palm slapped the kitchen counter, causing pain to radiate through each finger. She made a fist, checking for the possibility of broken bones.

Taber had followed her into the room. "What are you doing?"

"Reacting to my stupidity in an obviously stupid way." If only she had taken a few seconds to check the door, she'd still have the backpack.

A furrowed brow and a softer expression replaced his scowl. "Are you okay? Can you get me up to speed as far as what is going on here?"

"Mmm," she stalled as she reviewed the events in her mind. "Daniel and I were working on the house today."

"Caught the smell of primer when I entered. Then what?" He circled his hand for her to continue.

Her first impulse was to tell him if he wanted her to get on with her story that he shouldn't interrupt. Her nostrils flared a little as she struggled to suppress the comment. Think polite and hospitable B and B owner. Being the congenial innkeeper might be the hardest part of owning an inn.

"I noticed how interested the neighbors were about someone moving in. They wanted specifics. I thought if the murderer is a local, he may return to the house to either erase evidence or plant some. The best deal would be to sneak in and stay overnight. That way I could catch the perpetrator."

Taber's mouth drew down at an angle. "Your brother was okay

with this?"

Her hands fisted before she rested them on her hips. She considered lying, but it would be her luck that Taber would feel the need to talk to Daniel all in the course of the case. "I'm an adult and a property owner. Besides, we aren't joined at the hip."

"Ha, it means he doesn't know. Wouldn't approve." His arms folded against his chest ready for a confrontation.

"What is this, the Victorian period? I don't need a male family member to rubber stamp all my decisions." Why had she ever found him attractive in a rumpled sort of way?

He flung out one arm, gesturing to the house. "I figured if you were so in love with the Victorian period that you might embrace some of their sensibilities. I didn't realize things would have to be spelled out for you." Color crept up his neck, giving him the ruddy glow of a hard drinker or rising blood pressure.

"What do you have to spell out? The house is no longer a crime scene. It's my place to do with as I want." This was the real reason she didn't marry, because men were so sure their way was the only way. She lifted her chin, daring him. Her brother would have recognized the look and backpedaled.

"True."

His acknowledgment made her forget what she wanted to say.

"I worry about you, more than I should. There is a killer out there."

Her cheeks rounded as she blew out a long breath. It was hard to be too mad at a man who worried about her. She wasn't sure when a non-related male had ever cared about her. "I thought that too, but now I think it is more teenage misadventure. The house has been empty for a long time. A great place for two young lovers to meet even if was on my back porch."

"Don't dismiss this too soon. I know you want everything tied up in a neat package, but it bears investigation."

Instead of acknowledging his remark, her gaze went over his shoulder to a rough spot on the wall that primer failed to disguise. The corners of her mouth pulled down. Yeah, of course, she wanted this all tied up. Thought the real work would be in renovation, possibly running the place, not avoiding a killer who also moon-lighted as a home squatter.

Conflicted with what to do about the bag stealer, she wondered how to make her impromptu camping trip sound reasonable. "I stopped by the store to get a few things for my stay. When I arrived here, Jasper jumped out of my car and started chasing someone or something. I followed with my flashlight until I stumbled. When I did, I saw a footprint. Didn't think too much of it since my property may have been teen rendezvous central as long as it was vacant. On my way back to the house, I spotted a sequinned bag, which I assumed belonged to a child. Still," she drew out the word, empha-sizing it, before continuing, "I used precautions as to not disturb evidence." No reason to mention dropping the bag and breaking the contents inside if the bag were missing.

Mark lifted two fingers to his lips in what Donna had already mentally dubbed his thinking pose. His eyes rolled upward as he organized information. "Good job," he finally commented. "I assume the bag owner retrieved it from the kitchen."

"Probably." Her shoulders slumped forward as her knee throbbed, reminding her of her fall. "Who else would want it?"

Mark threw her a sympathetic smile. "It probably belonged to a teenage couple planning to use the house for a romantic tryst. They had to come back for the bag in case you informed their parents."

Her nose crinkled as she imagined a anxious teen boy slipping into the kitchen to retrieve a bag that his girl friend insisted he'd get back. If the young lover had been a real jerk, the girl would have retrieved the bag. Something didn't work about the whole scenario. "Why would they think I would inform their parents when I had no clue who they even were?"

His hand went up and stroked his chin. "Good point. Teens seldom think in the grip of hormone overload. Could have left a license or some sort of identification in the bag. Being a good neighbor, you'd walk the bag home, deliver it to who ever answered the door, which would probably be a parent, then all hell would break loose."

"It could happen." She agreed, although she hadn't even thought that far ahead. The man had a point, a valid one.

"Too bad about the bag. Would have liked a peek in it." He held up a finger. "I want to make a cast of the footprint."

His statement poked at her, drawing her back into the present moment. "Don't you have a crime scene investigation unit?"

Taber's eyes lit up before he erupted into a hoarse chuckle. After a few seconds, his open palm covered his face as he managed to still the laughter. Silence hung between the two of them for a few heartbeats, allowing the sounds of the house to fill in the stillness. A dripping sound came from nearby along with the sounds of nails scraping against the wooden floor. *Creepy.* It could be the sound-track for a teenage slasher film. The drip could be a body bleeding out. Of course, as a nurse, she realized blood flowed as opposed to dripping. Tell that to her imagination and the goose bumps on her arm that united to put images to the sounds.

Jasper entered the room with a noticeable clicking as he sniffed the floor searching for a conveniently dropped morsel. That explained the clicking. *Good.* One less thing to worry about. Taber knelt and scratched her dog between the eyes, which resulted in a tail-wagging frenzy. The image of the detective wriggling his rump instead of the dog surprised a chuckle out of her.

"What's the joke? Is it because television fools you into thinking every town possesses a crackerjack CSI unit or that I'm the unit?"

Unwilling to share the mental image of the good detective waving his backside like a wet duck, she decided to agree. "Yeah, something like that."

"Ah." Taber continued petting the dog. "Don't worry too much about it since I actually attended classes on evidence detection and retrieval as a uniformed officer and a more recently as a detective. I know the difference between visible, plastic and latent prints."

Visible sounded self-explanatory enough. The other two not so much. "Tell me."

He grinned at her inquiry. Then his brow furrowed as he backed out of the kitchen, motioning for her to do the same. Jasper followed, his nails scratching the wood with every step. Tomorrow, she'd cut his nails or at least get them trimmed.

"I just realized our culprit could have left behind visible or latent prints if he entered the kitchen."

Donna's head whipped around as she stared into the shadowy kitchen for an identifiable footprint. None that she could see, especially with the forty-watt bulb that came with the house. Most people would consider it an energy-saving method. It could be, but it also hid some imperfections in the wall and ceiling. Maybe it had been installed by the real estate agent on purpose. Tomorrow, she'd replaced all the light bulbs with stronger ones.

Taber peered over her shoulder. "Don't see anything, but that doesn't stop the latent footprints from being there. Best thing we can do is not walk across the kitchen floor."

"Why?" Outside of hovering in midair, she saw no way she could cross the room.

"There are latent footprints on the floor, rather like fingerprints. I could dust some fingerprint powder over the surface. I'd prefer the fluorescent powder since using a black light makes it easier to see. At that point, we can photograph the print."

"At last, a break in our case." Her hands went together in a clap as she pretended to ignore the way Taber's bushy eyebrows shot up at the use of "our" when referring to the case. It really was their case, even if he didn't think so. "I've seen the powder used on television shows. Why didn't they use it when they first found the body?" Good chance the case would be solved already.

"Wouldn't have worked with everyone milling around. Dozens of footprints, most overlapping another one and would have taken hundreds of dollars of dust and countless manpower hours without anything to show for it."

Her brief exhilaration suffered an abrupt landing. A mental movie of various footprints running all over her kitchen resembled educational videos about the spread of germs. In this case, it was more about the smearing of evidence. "Wouldn't some of the same issues still be present in my kitchen?"

Taber's lips tugged down as if he watched the same mental movie with the colored footprints stepping over one another and often creating new colors as their footprints overlapped. "Could be a problem. I still think we have to try. Right now, we'll close the kitchen door and wait until we get enough powder to ghost the floor. I do have the equipment to make a plastic print impression in my car.

Both Donna and Jasper followed the detective to the front door, watching as he twisted the deadbolt free. Anyone inside could easily leave the house without too much trouble or drama. Her eyes remained on the closed door after it swung shut. A person could probably brazen it out with the house on the market while comings and goings of the house inspector, the agent, the mortgage assessor and herself. The murderer could have left by any door. All he or she had to do is act normal, not creeping around like someone who might fear discovery or intent on murder.

Jasper stared at the door, keeping a dedicated vigil for a man he'd recently met. Donna glanced at the door expectantly. *Was this how the murderer felt? Expectant? Knowing someone was on his way. Of course, the victim had no clue he'd been summoned to his death.*

A shadowy side parlor beckoned as a hiding place. She slid into it, trying to think like the killer. Was the victim told the door would be unlocked? The soon-to-be dead man may have wandered slowly through the house calling out the name of his host. *Possible.* Her lips twisted to one side, which didn't explain why the man ended up in the uppermost parlor.

Most people would have left, not hearing an immediate answer to their call. Something compelling made him stay or at least search the house thoroughly by moving upward. The sound of the door opening along with Jasper's greeting signaled Taber's return. Her initial motion to step out and join her dog in recognizing the man stopped.

"Donna, I got the kit. I'm gonna need your help to hold the flashlight." Taber's voice echoed slightly in the empty hallway.

Her lips pursed as she forced herself into silence. The red second hand on her illuminated watch swept past fifteen seconds, then twenty.

The wooden floors creaked slightly, allowing her to trace his movements. He headed first to the kitchen. A slight clicking indicated her dog followed. This meant the killer could easily follow the victim as he wandered the house. The murderer probably abandoned his shoes somewhere and moved silently on sock feet, avoiding the boards that creaked excessively. That meant whoever the killer was had been in her house more than once.

Who had access to her house? The real estate agent, of course, but didn't that apply to all of the ones who'd shown the house to prospective buyers? They punched some number code in the box and were able to obtain the key. Was there a homicidal agent in town? The thought had her re-examining her own. Maybe the woman wasn't just sly about unloading houses.

Then again, the number pads pushed on the keybox would have shown more wear than the other keys. Four numbers that could only be used in a little more than a dozen combinations. Anyone could have come up to the side entrance, which was conveniently shadowed by trees and tried various combinations until they hit the right one. The key might have been lifted and copied too.

Half dozen crime dramas used vacant houses on the market as places for illicit affairs, murders and body dumps. Her inn could have served for all three. Donna's hand pressed against her chest as she felt outrage on the house's behalf. Wasn't being used as a former bar, enough of an indignity.

Taber's silhouette filled the open doorway, blocking most of the light and making his expression unreadable, but his tone made visual inspection unnecessary.

"There you are! You took about two years off my life. Didn't you hear me calling?"

"I did."

Taber started to turn but swung back for a double take. "What?"

"It was an experiment. If I told you what I was doing, then it wouldn't work." Her shoulders went up in a shrug, realizing as explanations went that it was lame.

"Come again?" He stepped back, allowing her to move into the lighted foyer.

Her canine glanced up. Most people wouldn't consider it a judgemental glance, but she'd lived long enough with her dog to know that even he questioned her actions.

"Sorry if I scared you."

He shook his head in denial. "Not exactly, but I was somewhat concerned. In the end, I figured you'd have an explanation."

She cocked her head, rethinking her foray into crime re-enactments. "Well, I was wondering how the man got all the way upstairs. He was murdered there, not dragged up the stairs. Something had to compel him up there. He must have been meeting someone. I wondered how far the man would search if the killer had arrived first and hid."

"Hmm," Taber commented. His bent finger rubbed at the lines between his eyebrows. "Not a bad train of thought. Still, I wish you'd told me what you were going to do." He held up his free hand palm out while his left arm cradled a full white plastic bag with writing stamped on it. "Yeah, I know it wouldn't work as well if I knew."

She nodded in agreement. At last the man understood. "I think I may have discovered something."

"What?"

Why did she have to mention anything before she had it fully thought out? "Well, maybe two things. First, I believe the killer was in the house, hidden, waiting and able to trace movements just by the creaking of the floor." She held up two fingers when it looked like he'd reply.

A silent killer creeping about wouldn't be all that startling of a discovery. "My second point is the better one. The man's willingness to search for his host demonstrates how much he cared about him or her."

A loud snort had her narrowing her eyes at the man and retorting, "Okay. Give me your theory."

He bent and placed the bag down on the floor. Jasper circled it, darting in for a sniff and acting as if it might come alive suddenly. "I doubted if the two or possibly three involved were in some tawdry love triangle. It's been my experience that murder happens due to betrayal. Call it payback. More often, it's money. A falling out of thieves. I'm not entirely dismissing a crime of passion, but the man would notice whoever he expected to be there wasn't. His first response would be to leave."

His words didn't gel with the desperate man searching the rooms to find his beloved. "Why would he leave?"

Taber acted shocked at her ignorance. It irritated, but she decided not to mention it this time. Next time, she would.

"Save face, of course. If he was involved in some hot and heavy clandestine affair, there's a chance that either partner can pull out without warning. If he arrived and thought no one was here, then he'd leave. It would keep him from being the one that was dumped. Understand?"

"Now, I do. Even though, I consider myself a realist I still have issues with someone killing his or her lover. C'mon now, they were having an affair, which means they weren't married. It couldn't be a dispute about community property." She refused to elaborate, unwilling to expose her hidden soft, sentimental side.

Another dry, humorless chuckle filled the air. "Working in homicide, the first thing I discovered is the loved ones are the first people we look at when looking for a culprit. The husband decides a divorce is too messy. A wife discovers her husband's infidelity. The grand-children agree it is taking too long to get their inheritance. There's a fragile line between love and hate."

"That's awful." The familiar statement she'd heard more than once. Still her stomach rolled with the words. In the heat of the moment, a person could turn on someone he professed to love. Daniel declared he'd hunt down her missing bridegroom and pulverize him. At the time, she wanted him to. The image of her brother choking the man who cast her aside along with all their dreams for the future gave her some small satisfaction. On some level, she recognized it wasn't meant to be and hung onto the impulsive teenage Daniel's arm the way a tick attaches to a dog to prevent any retribution.

Yep." Taber agreed as he bent to pick up his casting mix. "You got a big flashlight? The bigger, the better. If not, I have one."

She held up one finger, indicating he should wait as she dashed back to her bedroom where she'd hauled most of her supplies, including an oversized camping flashlight. A person could do surgery with such an intense beam. The hefty battery weighed more than the actual flashlight did. Flashlight in hand, she made her trip back down the stairs.

They left by the front door with her goal of keeping Jasper in-side. Unfortunately, she hadn't shared the info with Taber, who held the door open for the canine, who squeezed out while throwing a backward glance over his shoulder at her.

"Be quiet this time," she warned the dog.

"I didn't say anything." Taber raised his eyebrows as he spoke.

Seriously, living only with her dog had caused her to revert to talking to the animal as if he really understood her. The way the canine angled his head and regarded her with a long stare almost convinced her that he did. All the same, people labeled pet talkers as nutso. This small idiosyncrasy made everything else she said suspect.

"I know. I was talking to Jasper. He may have chased off the trespasser with his barking. He tore through the shrubbery hot on the trail of something. Initially, I thought it was a rabbit, but maybe it was a person."

"Hmmm." Taber stared at Jasper as he disappeared around the hedges. "As for the bag, tell me about it."

A porch light came on next door. *Great,* her undercover mission had just gone public. The blinds opened as a curious neighbor peered through them. "We're being observed."

"Really?" The detective turned in the direction of the peeking neighbor and waved. "Don't blame them for looking. You would if someone was killed in the house next to you."

Good point. Her lips twisted up as she tried to consider her neighbors' plight. "Yeah, I hate to admit it, but you've got a point. I don't have to like it. Personally, I just want it to be over with. I want the culprit caught and I want this forgotten. There's a big difference between a house with some charming legend attached to it and a place where a murder happened."

She pointed in the direction she'd glimpsed the footprint. As least, it was where she thought it was. All the overgrown hedges tended to look alike. The light hit the area under the leafy branch. A few stones, a residual bit of wood mulch, but nothing else.

"Not here." *It had to be here.* The flashlight beam moved ahead as she hurried to the next bush. It had to be here. Maybe it was too dark to see anything. Although, she saw it earlier when she fell. "I need to start at my car and walk. There has to be an imprint where I fell."

Could it all be a figment of her imagination? It could be Taber doubted her, but all the same he followed with a bag of foot-casting material. The flashlight beam came across a set of footprints, actually several. "Look!"

"Hmmm." He knelt to examine the print. "Come here." His cupped hand motioned her closer.

Two steps had her legs practically brushing the squatting detective. With any luck, they could follow the prints to possibly the killer's home or hideaway. She leaned forward, resting her hands on her knees and trying to see what he was doing. "Are you going to cast a print?"

"Not yet, but I have an idea." He stared at her foot, then back at the print. "Put your right foot in the right print."

"Well," she spoke as she wondered about the wisdom of ruining the evidence. Taber didn't look the least bit worried. A closer examination showed that whoever's print it was had the same type of boot she did. In fact, about the same size foot. Her eyes narrowed as she stepped into the print. A perfect fit. Heat moved up her neck despite the frosty wind that rattled the tree limbs overhead.

"Okay. You got me. Still, I saw a print. It couldn't be mine because I hadn't walked there yet." Her shoulders went back as she steeled herself for ridicule.

A slight groan accompanied the man's rising. He rubbed his hands slightly on his pants, ridding his palms of dirt. His right hand massaged his neck as he spoke. "I believe you, but it's easy to be fooled by your own prints. Most rookies make the same mistake. Let's go find that print."

Donna didn't like being compared to some fresh-faced rookie straight out of the academy. Then again, she'd never gone to the academy so maybe it wasn't as big of an insult as she imagined.

The flashlight's beam illuminated their feet and about five feet in front of them. Any neighbors and the possible killer could pinpoint their location and deduce they were searching for something. Not good, not good at all, not the covert operation she had hoped to conduct. Then there was the missing backpack. "Do you even believe there was a bag? That I didn't just make it all up to somehow lure you to the house?"

His husky laugh touched something inside of her, making her vaguely uncomfortable, but not in a tainted food way, but more of driving down an unknown road feeling. Who knew what the next turn might bring.

"Nope. You're not the frivolous type to make up things. Besides, I did smell the lingering odor of chloroform in your kitchen. No reason for you to have it in your cupboards, is there?" His face turned toward her. Even with the tree branch shadows falling across his face she could still detect a slight smile.

Ah, a joke, a tease, she might have missed it. "No, you do know they don't use chloroform in hospitals anymore." Why hadn't she recognized the smell, instead of putting it down to overly sweet wine? When was the last time she'd smelled it? She couldn't remember.

"Didn't know that." His hand wrapped around a drooping branch for her to pass under. "When did they stop using it?"

Her shoulders went up in a shrug but realized he might not be able to see it. "I do know it was before I became a nurse. Of course, it didn't happen all at once. It caused complications such as harming the liver, coma, even paralysis. Basically malpractice city. Anesthesiologists already have some of the highest malpractice insurance. Add in chloroform and no one could afford the insurance to practice medicine."

"Good to know. So only people who use chloroform are criminal types then. Kidnappers, murderers or people up to no good or those who order it online for whatever purposes they might conceive." The light touched on some impressions. A large indent with two smaller ones at the front that had depth. "I found where you fell."

Her nose crinkled up at the word *fell*. It made her sound like one of the women in the commercials for health alert bracelets. The only reason she fell was her effort to capture her wayward dog. As if on cue, she could hear the snuffling sound of her dog nearby. Most of the time, Jasper never went far enough for her to worry about it or paper the neighborhood with missing pet posters. Right now, she needed to see the footprint more.

The light bounced around the area until it landed on an athletic shoe print. A relieved sigh escaped her lungs. Thank goodness, the print existed. Things were getting to the point where she doubted her own observations.

Taber eased to his knees and pulled some wooden slats from the bag and formed a square around the print. "I'll have to cut out the ground too. Once it's dry, the dirt can be brushed away. The impression can be inked and then applied to paper for a clearer print."

It made sense. She nodded as he spoke, but managed to keep the light on him and the print. The ridges resembled athletic shoes but narrowed toward the heel. Didn't make sense. Something familiar about them flitted at the edge of her memory. A sharp yip, then a continual growl indicated Jasper had cornered something. *Great.* The light swung as she turned toward her dog, causing a muttered curse from her companion.

"Oh." She turned the light back and considered briefly telling Taber that he could do it himself. After all she was the one with a ginormous flashlight. Still, he was the one who knew all the procedural maneuvers to catch the criminal. She stayed in place wondering what havoc her dog was creating now.

The casting bag wheezed and emitted a puff of plaster dust as Taber squeezed and twisted between his hands, which forced her to ask. "What are you doing?"

He gave her a long-suffering look—the same one doctors gave her whenever she questioned their orders. Uninformed was not the same things as being stupid, she reminded herself. Instead, she raised an eyebrow, not knowing if he could see it in the dark.

"The bag," he said, then hesitated to wait for her nod of acknowledgment before continuing, "has a water capsule inside that contains the right amount of water. All I have to do is squeeze it to break it. Then I squish and twist it to mix it. Finally, I tear off one end and squeeze it out."

"Like frosting," Donna added, only getting a long-suffering glance for her comment.

After tearing the bag open, he started on the outside of the print and not the print itself. Before she could ask, he explained. "If I started on the print the weight of the plaster could spread the print. I am creating a base that will support the plaster over the print, saving its integrity."

"Okay." She stored the information away. Sure, she could use it later. Part of her listened for the sound of Jasper, who was never a stealthy pup. *Nothing.* "I'm worried about Jasper."

Taber smoothed out the top of the plaster form with another slat of wood before he rocked back on his heels and stood. "Wouldn't worry about your dog too much. Chasing a rodent would do him good."

Not a very subtle slam on her dog's weight. Sure, exercise would benefit him. Not allowing him so many samples of her cooking would help too. The need to locate her pet overrode the need to defend him. "That's just it. I should hear him, especially if he's chasing something. He tends to bay when he's on the trail of something. That's the beagle in him."

They both stood, listening to the tree limbs crack and shudder above them in the breeze. Everything else was still. No car noise, no ambient noise of television laugh tracks seeping out from the well-insulated houses. Not even the footsteps of the dog walkers, but it was late. Too late and too cold for anyone to be out who didn't have to be.

Her heart clutched a little. He might be an overweight, ill-behaved dog to most everyone else, but he was family to her. Outside of her brother and mother, her only family. "Jasper." The wind carried the name, softening the slight tinge of panic she recognized.

Taber touched her back. "We'll look together." Their feet crunched frosted leaves and broke fallen twigs. In the stillness, they sounded like a herd of elephants.

Using the flashlight in a sweeping motion, they discovered Jasper's body on the other side of the house. Her hand pressed to her chest, as she felt a cry percolating in her throat. *No, it couldn't be.*

Taber's flat palm motioned her to wait while he knelt beside her dog. His head lowered as he bent at the waist. Donna's feet stayed put, but she leaned forward as much as she could without toppling to see what the man was up to. Was he trying artificial resuscitation on her dog? She'd have to take back all the mean thoughts she'd ever had about him.

Still squatting, he turned his head toward her. "Chloroform." He spat the word in disgust.

Chapter Fifteen

"JASPER." SHE SQUATTED beside her dog and picked up a limp paw. "He's still alive?" Even though the detective already checked, something about the canine's stillness bothered her. It wasn't uncommon for hospital personnel to mention a patient was critical as opposed to dead. The reasoning was such information shouldn't be delivered over the phone. The end result was the loved one drove like a maniac to be by their already deceased relative's side, hoping to gain a few last words of insight or forgiveness. A cruel practice in her opinion and she wasn't totally sure the police didn't employ the same methods.

Her open palm moved up the dog's warm body where a steady heartbeat continued. Slower than normal, but his heart did beat. *Thank God.*

Taber, still kneeling beside the dog, spoke, reminded her of his presence. "I think we need to get him to the 24-hour animal hospital."

Donna blinked a few times, trying to keep back the tears. *Be strong. Jasper's a dog. Most people think dogs are just objects.* "Okay." She gulped, trying to clean out the ball wedged in her throat.

One arm slid under him while the other cradled his head, but she couldn't pick him up from a squatting position. There had been no previous occasion to pick her dog up. Either he jumped into the car on his own or she gave him a boost.

"I'll take him." Taber's shoulder touched hers briefly as he inserted his arms under the dog and stood with no problem. "We should make sure the house is locked up before leaving."

The well-lit house drew her eyes, but she glanced back at the silhouette of Mark and Jasper moving away in the dark. "Not sure why I should bother to lock up. It doesn't seem to keep some people out."

"It will keep out the majority." Mark's voice was loud in the cold air. "Besides insurance will balk at paying if they discover the doors were unlocked."

True enough and it served as a motivation for her to sprint to the front and side doors and lock them. By the time she reached the car, the comatose Jasper was stretched out on a jacket in the backseat. Did he place the dog on the jacket out of kindness or to cut down on dog hairs? Mark's worried expression made her decide it had to be a kindness.

Donna slid into the back seat and slammed the car door. The car nosed into the street as Mark spoke. "The hospital is on Walnut and 9th. It's a little expensive, but I doubt that matters to you."

"It doesn't." She shook her head in the dark, surprised he'd even mention the price. "How do you know about it?"

He coughed followed by the sound of cellophane rustling, then it stopped. It was easy to deduce the man reached for a cigarette but stopped on her account. "Well," he started but swore as a motorist shot through a red light in front of him. "I'm not solving murders every day."

"Don't tell me you moonlight for the animal hospital?" The conversation distracted her a little as she kept a hand on Jasper, willing him to live.

"Nope. You'd be surprised how many people straggle in with an ailing pet in the middle of the night. Occasionally, we get a 911 call from a child whose pet has been hit. Normally, there is a fine for making a false 911 call. To the child, it is an emergency. If I'm nearby, I've taken a few pets to the hospital. I've also found out the majority of the parents wouldn't pay for the visit or couldn't pay. They told their child nothing could be done. However, the child believed someone could help."

The words were delivered dispassionately, not giving her a hint of his feelings on the matter. A softie, someone who cared about animals and children, hid underneath his gruff, hard-bitten exterior. No wonder he told her about the price. "Afraid you'd be stuck with the bill again?"

"Not really," he said, answering her unspoken question about who paid all those other pet bills.

The man had several layers. Who knew what existed under his cynical, chain-smoking exterior? If only he'd quit smoking, he could extend his life span. Everything he owned, including the car, would have to be fumigated. The mental work of creating a non-smoking Taber with more color in his cheeks occupied her thoughts for a few seconds. "Why do you smoke?"

Oh no, another abrupt question she was trying to refrain from asking.

"Why do you ask personal questions?" he fired back in a slightly amused tone.

Excellent rebuttal, she'd have to give a point on that. "It's who I am."

"Same here."

Stupid answer, the point she gave him before she'd take back. "It's not who you are. You weren't born smoking. If you were, your mother would be the one screaming, not you."

His dry chuckle turned into a rasping cough. She wanted to point out to him that was exactly what smoking did to him, limit his ability to do ordinary things such as laugh. This time, she kept her mouth shut. No one else was volunteering to take her dog to the all-night animal hospital.

"You're not one who will take a simple answer." He drove in silence for a few minutes before he started speaking. The quiet served more as a bond than a barrier between them. "Hmm, I began smoking when I was thirteen."

"That's young. More chance of addiction in the teen years."

"Don't I know it."

"Why?"

Silence from the front seat made her wonder if he'd heard her. "My father was a policeman. He was killed in the line of duty responding to a domestic call. My mother dissolved into a million pieces and couldn't help me figure it out. I started hanging out with a rough crowd. I decided the bad guys lived longer while the good guys were mowed down like ducks in a shooting gallery."

"You're a cop, I mean a detective. What changed?" It was hard to imagine him as some teenage thug, especially with his soft heart.

"Someone broke into our house. We weren't exactly rich, but they took the few things that had meaning to my mother, including my father's gun and wedding ring. The police came and took the crime very seriously. They tracked down the teenage thug who happened to be one of my so-called friends. I decided then I didn't need friends who would steal from me. The smoking stuck, unfortunately. I couldn't rid myself of it as quickly as I did my friends."

"Did you ever see any of those friends again?" Donna couldn't think of any felonious friends she might have, but she did run across plenty of backstabbing girlfriends. They remained the same when she saw them years later.

"Yep."

Not exactly informative, the neon animal hospital sign announced her time to find out more about her reticent companion was coming to a close. "What did you say when you met again?"

"You have the right to remain silent."

"Oh, not exactly hugs and hand slaps all around."

"Nope. More like frisks and handcuffs. The funny thing was not all that much time had passed. Maybe seven years, but none of them remembered me. That's how much I mattered. You'd think my name would have stayed in their minds, but it didn't."

The car bumped up to the emergency entrance where doors slid open and a woman dressed in scrubs wandered out. "Hey Taber, what do you have for me tonight?"

"A dog intentionally chloroformed in an on-going crime investigation."

"An officer?" She bobbed her head and peered into the back seat.

Taber answered with a slight nod as he climbed out of the car.

Donna was unsure what she meant until she remembered police dogs were officers too. An overweight puggle hardly qualified as a police dog, but it took all kinds. If it guaranteed faster service, then Jasper was an honorary officer for the night.

The door swung open as the woman and another attendant scooted a small gurney near the car. Its raised sides prevented the occupant from rolling off. There was a restraint to buckle the animal down. She watched as the two people worked as a team as they removed her canine from the car and placed him on a gurney. Not so different from the crew at her hospital's emergency room.

The car door slammed as Taber resumed his seat. "I'll park the car, then we'll go in and see what the prognosis is."

She sat in silence wondering if she should have said something, but his words formed a statement, not a question. The car stopped and he was at her door, handing her out before she had time to even think. He held out his arm to her and she gladly took it, grateful for the support. All her life, she'd been the capable, responsible person. People knew she'd be there and would get the job done. This sudden weakness that made walking a conscious endeavor was new to her. Couldn't say she liked it. No, didn't like it at all.

Fluorescent bulbs cast a harsh glow on the molded plastic chairs in the waiting room. A red-eyed woman waited, clutching a dog coat to her chest. A weary elderly male had a small animal carrier at his feet. They both looked up at their entrance, then looked away, either avoiding her anxiety or afraid of exposing their own.

The large clock on the wall ticked loudly, counting off the slow passage of time. Donna picked up a two-year-old magazine and tried to read about the problem of coydogs, but the article didn't hold her interest.

The swinging doors opened with the entrance of the veterinarian. "Jorgenson, Sunny," She called out the name and the woman sprang up. The vet approached her and wrapped one arm around her shoulders and guided her through the swinging doors. Never a good sign.

Donna's hands were lax in her lap. Taber's warm hand enveloped hers. "He's going to be all right. The extra weight will help him ride out the chloroform."

She wanted to respond her dog wasn't fat, but he was. "Thank goodness he isn't a tiny frou-frou dog."

They sat holding hands, saying nothing. The doors swung open again. This time an attendant came out, not the vet. She walked up to the two of them and smiled. "Officer Jasper is doing fine. We'd like to keep him overnight for observation, but we do not expect any complications."

The breath she'd been holding whooshed out like an arctic wind racing over the tundra. "Can I see him?"

★

AFTER ASSURING HERSELF that Jasper was all right, Taber drove her back to the inn. Before she could get out, he grabbed her hand. "I don't want you staying here."

"I have to. How else are we going to catch the killer?" The dash lights were bright enough to illuminate his displeasure at the use of the word *we*.

"We aren't. It's my job. Your job is to remain alive to take care of Jasper."

She shook her head in disbelief at the man's stubbornness. "I'm not a dog. I'm aware there is danger. I even have a gun." The fact she had no bullets wouldn't make a convincing argument. Already, she had her doubts. "Someone needs to look after the casting too."

"It's done. I'll cut it out, then I'll follow you home to make sure you get there."

The look she shot him should have slapped his alpha attitude, but it appeared to have no effect. Instead, he walked around the car and opened her door.

"Get your flashlight and I'll let you observe real police action."

Her eyes rolled on their own, not sure if he was patronizing or trying to be humorous and sucked at it. "Okay, but I'm still staying here." The audible snort he made, she chose to ignore. Right now, they'd get the print, then she'd handle the man who had the brass to think he'd tell her what to do. No man ordered Donna Tollhouse around. If she chose to do something, that was different.

The area around the house felt darker, creepier, without Jasper snuffling about. As a guard dog, her pet was a dismal failure. Still, she felt safer with him around.

The two of them carefully retraced their steps, but darkness made everything harder to distinguish. Every tree, every overgrown shrub, every protruding tree root resembled the last one. The two of them made a slow circle of the house until they reached the front. "Where did it go?"

A two-by-one-foot rectangle of plaster should have been very noticeable. The whiteness on the dark ground should have caught her eye. Taber slowly turned in a circle, then pointed to her car. "Let's head to your car and we'll start there. We'll find where you fell and the footprint cast."

This technique worked well on crime dramas, but she didn't see it working well for their situation. Maybe daylight would reveal what night hid. Might as well humor the man if she planned on staying here tonight. Her original idea didn't appeal. Even with Jasper present, the idea of an overnight stay felt questionable, but she had a crime to solve.

They reached her car. She stood waiting for a signal from Taber, who held the flashlight. Her cupped hand held up to her ear indicated she had heard Jasper barking before she sprinted off. As she jogged, she tried to remember where she fell when a tree root caught her toe, almost sending her to the ground. "Ow!" *Great.* Strengthening her voice, she called out. "Found it."

Taber reached her in a few steps. "Good reenactment."

Her nose crinkled, but she held back a retort. The light moved to the side where she initially saw the print, expecting there to be a plaster mold, hard enough to cut out of the ground. Instead, the light bounced over some specks of plaster, a broken wooden slat and a scraped-out hole in the ground.

It was gone. "Someone stole the footprint!"

Taber swore as he knelt to examine the area. "Made a clean job of it too. Scraped away any visible print."

Mentally she recreated the image in her head of an athletic tread design that narrowed to a small heel. "It was a high heel sneaker with a wedge heel. It was a large size too. That means the killer is a woman with a large foot and bad taste."

"You got all that from the print?" A grudging admiration came through the question.

"Yes. What did you get?"

Emotions shifted across his face as he looked over his shoulder at the surrounding houses. "I thought the print was a weird shape. The fact the criminal came back, grabbed the bag out of your house, probably watched us cast the impression and then stole it, proves she lives close by. Chloroforming your dog was just enough to get us to leave."

"That means she probably wasn't trying to kill my dog."

"True." Taber stood, but continued looking at the hole where the print had been. "Looks like the work of an amateur with so many mistakes." He held up his hand when Donna sighed.

"Impulse killers don't think things through. They tend to react more. The fact you surprised someone with a bag containing chloroform isn't good." Taber's eyes narrowed while his mouth formed an uncompromising line. Probably the face he used when handcuffing trash-talking felons.

A neighbor-turned-killer just happened to be hanging out at her house with a backpack loaded with chloroform. It could be a simple retrieval mission. The cops missed the bag when combing the yard for clues. Of course, none of them went face first to the ground for a better look. "Do you think she wants to use the chloroform on me?"

His face somehow grew sterner, if that were even possible. He turned, peering at the nearby houses. His hand rubbed over his face in what she termed the mulling-over action. "Actually no. How would she know you'd be coming back tonight?"

The man had a point. "Okay. I can accept that. You believe there was a bag." He nodded, so she continued talking, crossing her arms due to the cold wind and an uneasy feeling that accompanied the breeze. "She had to retrieve the bag, but the police never found it. It must have been hidden somewhere in the house. Loose floorboard, secret nook."

A branch snapped behind her. Just wind, it tended to snap the dead limbs. Another expense she hadn't planned on, an arborist. No doubt, they didn't come cheap.

"That makes sense. For some reason, the murderer has some prior knowledge of the house. We'll have to look into that angle. Tell me about the bag." He touched her elbow and pointed toward the house.

Her agreement took the form of walking toward the house as she spoke.

"Ah, the bag. I didn't see it for that long. The front was covered in sequins. The rest was pink. My first attempt to pick it up ended with me dropping it and breaking something inside."

"What?"

She hadn't taken the time to open it, figuring she'd already be guilty of tampering with evidence. "Now I know it was the chloroform, not wine and wine glasses as I initially thought."

The back porch light showed that Taber's brow smoothed, but a few lines remained sketched out by sun and time. "I guess we know why there wasn't a struggle. She surprised him and knocked him out with a saturated cloth."

Enough crime dramas featured victims incapacitated by a whiff of the sickly sweet liquid. "Yeah. That's probably what happened. We know the killer was a woman with a big foot, which means she's either tall or decent sized. She also wears high-heeled sneakers and carries a glittery backpack worthy of a twelve-year-old."

Taber had his foot on the porch step as he turned to look at her. "Don't forget she has easy access to the house and apparently the ability to observe all the comings and goings, which means she has to live…"

The whine of a bullet whipped by her face, grazing so close it left the acrid smell of powder behind. Before she could even react, Taber fell backward on the step with a grunt. The sound of footsteps running through the underbrush created an urge to follow and bring down the troublesome killer, but with what? A moan propelled her into action as she reached the wounded detective's side. Her scarf served as a compress on the shoulder wound while she took his pulse. Racing, no surprise there. His skin was grayer than she liked, but that was to be expected too.

"Take cover," He grunted the words with effort. His breathing grew rougher.

"I'm calling for help." She ignored his headshake. Did the man expect her to leave him bleeding on the ground as she ran for cover? Her hand trembled as she reached for her cell phone. Luckily, she could thumb dial the three numbers while holding the compress in place.

The operator came on the line. "State the nature of your emergency."

"Officer down. The shooter is still in the area. Ambulance and support needed." She gave the house number automatically. The operator asked her to stay on the line.

"Do you know the name of the officer?"

"Detective Mark Taber." She glanced at Mark to see how he was doing and the man rolled his eyes. He hissed under his breath, something about never hearing the end of this. Sirens wailed nearby, signaling that help was on its way. It should be enough to scare the murderous, high-heeled sneaker wearer for a little bit.

The police arrived before the medics, peppering her with questions. Most she couldn't answer. A few gave her suspicious glances when she mentioned the high-heeled sneaker wearer and chloroform. One older cop with a graying crew cut sniffed his disbelief at her answers. He acted as if he thought she'd been the one to take a pot shot at Mark.

Seriously. She needed this now. All she did was try to find the murderer and now she'd be jailed for shooting an officer. "If I decided to shoot Taber, it would be a clean shot. I don't do sloppy jobs."

"Donna. Stop." Taber had pushed himself up in a half-reclining position and placed his hand over the compress she was still holding in place. "She was about eight inches from me. If she had a gun, I wouldn't be talking to you now. I'm not even sure the shooter was aiming for me. Could have been aiming at Donna."

The accusatory officer folded his arms and agreed. "Yes. That makes sense."

What makes sense? she wanted to ask. Did it make sense she didn't shoot Mark or the fact someone wanted to kill her? Probably the later.

Medics arrived and took over Taber's care, hustling him into the back of an ambulance. No, they were not persuaded to let her ride along even if she was a nurse. A female officer, noting her agitation, stepped closer and spoke in a low whisper. "Memorial Hospital."

That's all she needed. She headed for her car, but Officer Gruff and Disbelieving stopped her by stepping in front of her. "Where are you going?"

Would he keep her from sitting vigil on Mark, afraid she might hurt him? "Home. I told you what I know. You can get ahold of me if you want to ask me anything else. I'd just be in your way if I stayed." Her lips pulled up into an inane simper that she momentarily hated herself for, but it did the job.

He stepped to the side and waved her on. *Good gravy*, playing the silly female card did work. As she unlocked her car, she wrestled with both her indignation that the officer accepted her as a brainless nitwit and her worry over Mark. Buckled in, doors locked, she slowly reversed down the driveway, passing the flashing lights. As she pulled into the main street, she passed the few curious neighbors out on their porches in their hastily donned coats and robes. It felt like they were glaring at her, but that had to be her imagination. She wasn't the one who brought all this ruckus and notoriety to the neighborhood. That honor belonged to another resident.

Chapter Sixteen

A CAR HORN blared as she stole the right of way. "Get over it, you hesitated!" She knew the driver couldn't hear her, which was probably just as well. Her metamorphosis into the type of rude driver she couldn't stand wasn't something she wanted to acknowledge.

Her examination revealed Mark's wound had clotted even though the bullet rested deep in his shoulder. No exit wound. The fact that Mark was coherent said something, not sure what. Could be he had a high pain tolerance, or it wasn't the first time he'd been shot. The possibility had her squirming in her bucket seat as she eased into the hospital parking lot. First Jasper, now Mark. The killer had a lot to answer for in her book. The Tollhouses were not a family to just let things be. Okay, correction, she wasn't someone to just let things be.

When one of Daniel's previous gal pals sued him for child support, Donna was the one who forced the paternity test, not her brother or even his ineffectual lawyer. Turned out the twins had two different fathers with neither being her brother. It was worthy of a tabloid talk show. That brush with fatherhood slowed her brother down and made him a bit more discriminating about his female companionship. Although, he would have supported the kids no questions asked, taken them to the park and attended their school functions. Overall, he would have been a decent father, which was probably the reasoning behind the legal maneuver. All the same, family took care of their own.

Why was she rushing to the hospital? Mark wasn't family. He'd be in emergency room triage by now. Might even stay there for an hour or two depending on how heavy the workload was tonight. Only close family would be allowed in. Did he even have family around here? All she knew was he wasn't married. No way she could bluff her way in as his wife. The man would be coherent enough to insist he didn't have a wife. He did have a sister, though.

After parking the car, she half-jogged to the lobby and through the swinging doors to the emergency room since the receptionist wasn't at her desk. A nurse immediately stopped her and gave her a stare down.

"Where do you think you're going?" The woman fisted her hands balled and placed them on her hips.

Donna, familiar with the move since she had used it numerous times herself, experienced no intimidation. "I'm going to my brother, Detective Mark Taber. He was shot in the line of duty." She didn't have to force the slight breathiness that accompanied her statement.

"Oh, the cop." The nurse relaxed her arms and her face followed suit.

Donna corrected her, "Detective," and earned a glare for it. The man worked hard for the title. He should at least get to use it. Plenty of physicians got miffed when not addressed as doctor.

The nurse turned and she followed, mentally vowing to keep her mouth shut. She'd been working on that all week without success.

Curtains separated the various examining areas. It was the sign of an older, poorer hospital. Why hadn't they taken him to her own hospital, which had better facilities? Her lips twisted as she regarded the curtains. Could be the police insurance was only honored at this hospital, or it was the closest. Probably the later.

The nurse announced in a strong voice that carried just the slightest edge of skepticism, "Your sister is here."

The hospital bed folded near the top, allowing Mark to sit in an upright position. His shirt was off and a thick white bandage wrapped around his shoulder. A magazine rested across his lap and a pair of reading glasses perched on his nose. His mouth dropped open at the announcement. Donna waved behind the nurse's back, hoping to get his attention.

"Eileen is here," he said the words slowly. "I could always count on my older sister being there for me."

Her eyes narrowed because she was fairly sure he'd put an extra emphasis on the word *older*. His acceptance of her identity switch was all she needed as she swung around the nurse and pulled up a chair. Plenty of people claiming to be a relative had faked her out before. The only way you truly knew was if a patient refused to see them. That could happen with actual relations too.

"Sister," Mark said, the corners of his mouth twitching a little as he held back a smile, "so good of you to come."

Seated in the chair, she reached for his free hand, the one without an IV catheter in it. Her fingers curled around it automatically, squeezing it, assuring herself he was still alive. A slight beep indicated his heart and blood pressure were monitored. *As it should be.* A casual glance at the leads attached to his body confirmed that protocol was being followed.

"Should I assume now since I'm helpless on my back, you're checking out my masculine charms?"

Her eyes shot up from the leads to his laughing eyes. "Brother, I'm shocked you'd say such a thing." A perusal glance did note he had a hairy chest, not a waxer like so many modern men. She preferred men being themselves as opposed to emulating some fashion model, not that there were all that many men in her life. *Focus, Donna, bullet wound.*

She angled her head toward his arm. "Bullet still there?"

"Of course." His hand pulled from her grasp to touch the bandage, wincing when he did. "Hurts too. Already took some X-rays. A lot of times they leave the bullet in, especially in combat situations."

The desire to examine the wound clawed at her, but Mark's sister would never do such a thing. "Bullet's evidence."

Mark nodded. He started to push up his slipping eyeglasses but whipped them off instead. "I said as much to the ER doctor. The surgeon that will remove it is home sleeping as you should be."

"Maybe so." The illuminated hour hand on her watch pointed to eleven. She'd expected it to be much later with everything that had happened tonight. On a typical night she'd be changed into her nightgown, in bed and reading her latest murder mystery. No nightgown, but definitely a murder mystery that she and Mark were both living. Reality tended to be more messy and dangerous than reading about it.

The nurse peeked back in and mentioned as she held the curtain open for two orderlies that a room was ready. She glanced at Donna, who remained seated by Taber. "Visiting hours are way past over. You can return tomorrow at 8 a.m."

The bum's rush, she recognized it. She stood, reluctant to leave the obviously tired man. Besides, she had no clue what he had on under the covers. The man deserved some privacy. "Okay," she spoke, trying for compliance. "What time is surgery?"

"Seven." The nurse volunteered the information without thought. Why wouldn't she? A sister would want to know.

She reached across the bed and touched Mark's cheek. "I'll be back."

His facial muscles showed some slackness, evidence that a pain-killer or muscle relaxer had been administered, probably both. "I know," he mumbled the words before his eyelids closed.

Walking away was difficult, but she had no reason to stay. It wouldn't do her any good to stand guard by his bed. Maybe someone should. A call to the police department wouldn't be out of line. She had the phone in her hand even before she hit the parking lot. Her first call was to work.

"Emergency. I won't be in tomorrow."

The answering service did not pry into the nature of her emergency, which was good. She wasn't explaining. Her job was to call the head nurse for a replacement, but the head nurse was her. The phone dinged in her hand. "Of course." A brief glance revealed the answering service number.

A few minutes later she convinced her fellow nurse, Shannon, to take her shift since it was her off day and she needed the extra money for her son's tuition. Call it taking advantage of a single mother, but she knew her go-to people when it came to extra shifts. The digital dashboard clock read 11:22, too late to call Daniel, but she punched the two for speed dial anyhow. He'd be upset if he heard about the shooting from someone else.

Maria answered the phone with a suspicious, "Hello?"

Oh, it sounded like some former companions hadn't got the memo Daniel was married or didn't care. "It's me, Donna."

A sigh greeted her, then a friendlier greeting came across the airwaves. "Sorry, I should have known. Got a drunken bootie call last week. The woman couldn't even tell she wasn't talking to Daniel. It, ah…"

"Made you slap the snot out of my brother." She didn't always understand why Maria was still uncertain of her brother's loyalty. After all, he married her, but she didn't really have time to shore up her sister-in-law's self-confidence. "Is Daniel awake?"

Not that it mattered, she'd have Maria wake him up.

"Yes, he's sitting beside me watching some vintage football game." The tone of her voice expressed her bafflement at her husband's behavior.

Her brother's voice sounded in her ear. "What's up?"

"A lot." She went through the short version from someone hanging out at the house, scanty details of the middle and ending with Taber getting shot and going into surgery in the morning.

There was a lot of angry breathing on the other end of the phone, but Donna kept going, not allowing her brother a word in edgewise. If she stopped, she might cry. That was for other people, the weak, the overly sensitive and those who just needed the sympathetic attention.

"Where are you?"

"Home." Pretty much true, she thought as she drove into the driveway. The garage door came up, allowing her to pull in. Good thing she wasn't working tomorrow. Life certainly threw her a curve ball today. Make that two curve balls and then ran her over with a steam roller.

"How are you?"

"Exhausted. I'm going straight to bed, but figured I'd call you because if you heard about the shooting you'd be mad I didn't tell you."

Daniel cleared his throat. "You're right," he acknowledged gruffly. "What are your plans?"

"Mark's surgery is at seven in the morning. I'll be at the hospital maybe earlier. I could not convince the police to put a security detail on one of their own. They insisted the hospital has security." She couldn't believe the force could be so negligent. She'd worked in a hospital long enough to know how well security worked.

Stalkers, non-custodial parents with no-contact orders, even exes determined to see how bad off their former spouse was made it to a post-op floor with little trouble. She considered herself the last line of defense. Did her job well. Sent the people packing, but she couldn't be at the hospital twenty-four/seven, but she could be by Mark's side tomorrow.

No canine frenzy of happiness greeted her when she opened the door. The foyer light she usually left on, wasn't. Could be she forgot in her hectic leave-taking. The bulb could have burned out, too. Even though the package advertised it was a three-year bulb, they never meant used continuously. Her keys clattered to the floor as she missed the bowl. Should pick them up, but it seemed too much work. Besides, tomorrow she'd remember where they were.

A pang of loneliness hit as sure as any hypodermic needle driven hard into her skin. A long sigh escaped her as she examined the mess from her sudden departure in the dim light thrown by the exterior security light. She'd deal with it tomorrow.

The knee she fell on had stiffened up, making her walk more like a peg-leg pirate. If she didn't ice it before bed, she probably wouldn't be able to bend it the next day. Sleep, sweet dreamless sleep, beckoned more than holding a bag of frozen peas on her knee. The house felt wrong. Difficult to put her finger on it, but something wasn't quite right. Excluding the mess she left and the absence of her dog, a cold breeze circled around her, touching her face before blowing a paper off the table. The sliding glass door was partially opened.

Exhaustion tugged at her, dulling her senses. Did she close the door when she left? Of course, she did. Otherwise, she'd have an incredibly high heating bill. Did she lock it would be a better question. Probably not. *Great.* All she needed was a burglary to top things off.

Her favorite cast-iron skillet sat on the counter. Obviously not a cooking ware savvy thief or he would have taken the skillet. Cast iron didn't come cheap. A tiny sound pierced her lethargy. Something moving, maybe caused by the wind. She took a silent side step to the counter and wrapped her hand around the heavy skillet handle. The sweet smell of chloroform alerted her to the location of her visitor. Gripping the handle tightly, she spun, swinging the pan at chest level.

Thump! A curse in the shadowy room, a stumble, but not a fall and the distinctive sound of a trigger pulled back. Donna dropped to the floor before the bullet shot through the air where she used to be.

A groan came from the area near the fridge where the shadows were the deepest. Whoever it was had just felt the aftereffects of battering by quality cast iron. Donna's body, flattened against the floor, made a smaller target, but eventually the shooter would investigate. No reason to lie there waiting for imminent death. Donna tried to get a visual of where she was and where the shooter lay.

The rounded edge of the stove pressed into her calf, which meant she was only five feet from the back door. All she had to do was work her way back out of the house, jump in the car and leave.

Oh yeah, the keys. Maybe she'd come across them as she backed out. Holding her breath, she wiggled back an inch. Her coat caught on the stove drawer, making the effort harder and not exactly silent.

"Stop right there. No getting away, you know." The raspy female voice sounded somewhat familiar. Not in the someone she knew way, but someone she had talked to at one time.

Stopping didn't seem like a great option, but the shooter knew where she was. Sweat beaded on her face as she considered her options. The ignominy of being killed in a home invasion was not how she wanted to go. Her right hand moved behind her, checking out the area when it encountered the hard handle of the skillet. It must have bounced when she dropped it.

It served her once. It could serve her again. Taking a tiny breath, she visualized throwing the pan at the culprit who resided near her fridge. Good chance she'd hit the person or create the distraction she needed to get outside.

"You're hard to kill for such an old-school chick. Surprised me." There was the sound of movement and a slap of an open hand against the fridge.

The woman was attempting to stand, which would put Donna at a distinct disadvantage. Flat on the floor, she'd be little more than a cockroach. The woman continued to talk, demonstrating she didn't know her exact hiding place. The light switch rested by the back door. If she had turned it on when she came in instead of wondering why the foyer light was out, she could have been dead already. The light would have illuminated her as an easy target, not that she wasn't one right now. She had to get up and run. All she had was a skillet, which she could throw, but would more likely fly through the air and miss the woman. What else could serve as another weapon?

If she were by the china cabinet, she had an arsenal of expensive porcelain frisbees to throw. Near the door, close to the stove, what was there?

"Being an old chick, figured you'd stick to old-school ways."

Wasn't it bad enough she was trying to kill Donna? Did she have to preface everything with the adjective *old*?

Donna moved into a squatting position without a sound or an ominous creak of the knee. Who's old now, she wanted to taunt but knew better. Definitely time to keep her thoughts to herself. Too bad no one told her own personal nemesis the same thing. The woman's voice grew louder, indicating she was moving closer.

"I know your name. Your brother introduced himself and told me your name too."

Thanks, Daniel. It never paid giving out too much information. *Act now!* Her inner SWAT team persona screamed. In a flash, she remembered the knife block on her counter filled with precision blades that could cut through aluminum and a frozen roast.

"If you would have left things alone, then I wouldn't have to kill you. I figured the police would let the case go cold since no one cared about the dead man. No outraged rich family fueling the investigation. Just you. All I had to do was…"

Donna jumped up, threw the pan that earned a curse, but no oomph of pain. A bullet went wide, just barely missing her arm by inches. The other woman still couldn't see her or was a poor shot. Donna lunged for the counter where she knew the block was, picking up a handful of knives and throwing them at the backlit form conveniently standing in front of the window.

"What the hell?" A knife clattered to the floor, indicating a miss.

Inhaling, she held her breath as she took aim with the boning knife. It had the length and feel of the knives she used to throw as a kid. Before settling on nursing as a career choice, she had considered circus performer.

The torso would be the widest target, but she didn't want to kill her. Lower near the thigh would disable her, giving Donna the needed time to hotfoot it out of there. The knife rushed through the air as the ambient light caught the shine of the gun barrel. Both weapons gleamed together for a second until the knife pierced the woman's gun hand. The weapon tumbled to the floor with a hollow thud. Sirens sounded in the background.

Tires squealing outside along with the abrupt cessation of the siren announced the cavalry had arrived, but she wasn't safe yet. The knife stick made her culprit even more bloodthirsty. The black blob on the floor had to be the gun. Donna threw herself on it. The solid circular metal form pressed into her stomach. Too late, she'd realized she'd thrown herself onto one of Jasper's dishes. He tended to push them around once they were empty, hoping to remind her of their unfilled state.

Great. Where was the gun? A voice yelled outside the sliding glass door. "Police. Freeze." The first one had a flashlight, but it didn't stop him from stumbling over her prone body. At least he caught himself before he fell. The second one had enough sense to flick on the lights.

Donna blinked at the sudden brightness, then looked at the woman with two grim-faced cops holding her arms. The light bounced off her black sequined shirt and shiny spandex pants. Donna's eyes trailed down to the high-heeled sneakers. Ah yes, how a stripper dresses to commit crimes. She must have missed that fashion advice.

The woman twisted in the officers' hold. She managed to toss her long blond hair back before smiling at the officer. "It's all a mistake. That woman," she said, angling her head in Donna's direction so there would be no question who she was referring to, "she's crazy. Stabbed me with a knife and threw a skillet at me."

Words rushed to Donna's lips but never left, as she stood transfixed by the woman's elongated neck with just a tiny bulge of an

Adam's apple. That was usually the hardest thing to change in sexual reassignment surgery. They could shave it down some, which helped with the more pronounced ones.

One officer held her potential neighbor as the other cop cuffed her. An idea was starting to form, but she chose not to share her deductions She asked a question instead.

"How come you know your way around my inn so well?"

A smirk screwed up the killer's face before she gave a short laugh. "Burns you, doesn't it?" A medic stepped over to examine her hand, which resulted in her kicking out at him.

"Not too serious," the medic announced, backing out of kicking distance.

Another police officer, wearing latex gloves, edged the gun out from under the table and into an evidence bag. No way she'd have located that gun in a timely fashion. As it was, she'd sport a dog bowl shaped bruise for a few weeks. Good thing the police showed up since it appeared that her limited knife skills wouldn't have saved her.

One officer, a little older than the rest, seemed to be barking out orders. Must be in charge, or people let him think he was. She sidled up to him and waited for a break in shouting. He glanced over at her, giving her the opening she needed.

"Who called the police?" She suspected the retired music teacher across the street who kept a sharp eye on the neighborhood activities.

"Taber asked us to drive by. You thought he'd be vulnerable in the hospital, but he considered you a much more likely target. When in route, a 911 came from your neighbor."

The words struck her like the anvil that Wiley Coyote was always trying to drop on Roadrunner's head. "Why didn't he tell me?"

Her indignant exclamation right into his face was the definition of confrontational. She took a step back, cleared her throat and said in a much, softer, milder voice, "He didn't tell me. It might have been hard since he was falling sleep."

The man nodded his head. "It's the drugs the hospital shot him full of. Be thankful, he shook off the effects long enough to call for help."

The man saved her life.

"What about me?" A whine entered the stripper's voice. One of the officers read her the Miranda warning as they escorted her out of the house.

Donna watched her go, still batting her eyes heavy with false eyelashes at the younger cop. Honestly, they couldn't see it. Put an enormous amount of blond hair and a rack in a man's face and he missed the obvious. Well, maybe not the obvious. She'd seen drag queens in her college days that made better women than this one.

The police cars peeled off, causing the neighbors to wander back inside their houses. The captain nodded at her. "You going to be okay here?"

"Yeah, sure, you got the killer." Her words reassured her somewhat. No reason she couldn't go to sleep in her own bed. The man was almost out the door when she finished her thought. "Unless there's an accomplice."

As tired, battered and bruised as she was, the thought sent a thrill of fear up her spine. *Great.* The captain gave her questioning look as she scooped up her keys. "Wait until I lock up, I'm going to my brother's house."

He not only waited for her but followed behind her in his squad car too, for which she was incredibly grateful. The policeman couldn't see her lips or hear her chanting, which was just as well.

"I'm strong. I refuse to fall apart. I can do this."

She felt like the little pig with the straw house and needed her brother with the brick house to let her in. Her closed fist hammered on the door while the police car idled in the distance. "Let me in, let me in," she murmured as she knocked. Maria answered the door in a robe, her eyes barely open, indicating she had been asleep.

"What's up?"

Not bothering to answer, Donna pushed inside, slammed the door, shot the deadbolt, then twisted the handle lock.

Daniel padded in barefoot in a pair of pajamas she knew he hastily donned. Not that she wanted to know her brother's sleeping habits, but a previous girlfriend felt everyone needed to know they were always nude. "What's going on?"

She ignored her brother's question and sprinted for the over-stuffed club chair. The one her father always used to sit in. The leather squeaked as she plopped down, then the shaking started. Her hands gripped her arms, trying to control the tremors.

Maria's voice sounded distant. "Daniel, she's going into shock."

Her brother knelt by the chair and embraced her. "It's okay, Donnie. Everything will work out." He turned his head slightly and called out to his wife. "Get me a blanket and the brandy."

Two drinks later, her shaking had subsided enough to explain her sudden appearance. "They caught the killer."

"That's good." Her brother gave her a measuring look. "Why would that upset you?"

"Caught her in my house, trying to kill me." She shook her head, barely able to imagine minutes before she was fighting for her life.

"Oh my God!" Maria yelped and scooted over to the chair to pet Donna's shoulder as if she were a cat. People did odd things in the name of comfort. There were worse things.

"Taber saved my life. He called the police from his hospital bed." She shook her head, trying to imagine Mark swimming up from a drug-induced haze to call the cops. His sharp mind put together the killer's most probable actions quicker than she did. Her mouth quirked as she recalled she almost walked into certain death tonight.

Her trembling stopped, but a weariness overtook her as she leaned back in the chair and closed her eyes. Daniel hovered over her as Maria spoke. "The poor dear, she's been through so much. I wonder if this B and B idea should just be shelved."

"No!" She answered without opening her eyes. Her brother snorted before adding, "Sounds like she's back to normal. C'mon, sis, you'll want to go to bed, especially if you're going to be at the hospital for Taber's surgery."

Her eyes snapped open. "You're right." She stood and allowed Maria to herd her to the guest room even though she was familiar with its location.

"I even got feather pillows for you."

"I appreciate it." She smothered a yawn behind her hand as she opened the bedroom door. "See ya in the morning."

Chapter Seventeen

THE BITTER COFFEE gave off a slight burnt aroma that caused Donna to place it back on the table. "You'd think they could come up with a fresh pot as opposed to this stuff that must have sat on the back burner for two days distilling until it was an undrinkable sludge."

Daniel gulped the rest of his coffee before setting the empty cup down. "It's okay. Besides your nerves could do without any more caffeine."

Her brother might be right but it didn't mean she had to agree. Instead, she stood and paced around the small waiting room. A slight hint of cigarette smoke lingered despite all the NO SMOKING signs posted everywhere. Normally, she'd be going into a rant about the dangers of smoking, but for a moment she wondered if a cigarette could help ease her anxiety.

Daniel looked up from the magazine he was flipping through. "As a nurse, you realize it's a simple operation."

She pivoted and pinned her brother with a disbelieving expression. "Are you serious?"

"What?" He shrugged his shoulders. "What did I say?"

She took a few more steps, then turned and threw her hands up in the air. "People die everyday in simple operations. Last week, a woman expired during liposuction. Liposuction for Pete's sake."

Daniel threw the magazine down and stepped over to her and

wrapped an arm around her shoulder. "I know it's hard, but…"

A nurse appeared in the open doorway. "Are you Mark Taber's sister?" She glanced at Donna.

"Yes I am and this is his brother."

The nurse eyed Daniel longer than needed in Donna's opinion, but she didn't question her assertion. "Good news. Taber came out of the operation with flying colors. He's in recovery now. We're waiting for him to wake up, then we'll take him to his room. Then you can see him."

Thirty minutes later, Daniel and Donna slipped into Taber's room. The man, surrounded by pillows, smiled at the two of them.

"My family keeps getting larger and larger. I always wanted a brother."

Donna maneuvered around her brother to check Taber's monitor and chart.

"Does it meet your specifications? Am I progressing as I should?"

The man was chatty, but people reacted differently to anesthesia. Most just zoned out, but apparently not Taber. Even though he looked slightly awkward in his thin hospital gown, he still managed to look heroic.

"You know you saved my life last night."

"That's what I heard. I thought we were getting kinda good working together and I didn't want to go to the trouble of breaking in a new partner." He grinned and winked at Daniel, which made her wonder if he were joking.

"Go ahead and joke." She leaned over and kissed his unshaven cheek. "You're still my hero."

"Aww." He reddened under her praise.

Daniel slipped up beside the hospital bed. "I need to thank you too. I'm very grateful for you saving my sister."

"No problem, just part of my job. I'm glad the culprit is behind bars. Can you tell me anything else?"

"I figured you'd know more than I do."

He shook his head. "Tried. Called before the operation. Wouldn't tell me anything. Maybe I can get some info now."

A cough sounded, causing them to turn in the direction of the door where the officer, who escorted her to Daniel's, stood. "I came by to see how you're doing and find you talking shop."

Taber smiled and motioned him in. "The man I wanted to see. Tell us about the case."

"Hmmm." The man pulled up a chair. "I think I need to sit for this."

Taber rubbed his hand over his face. "That bad."

"Bad. Weird. Unexpected. We brought in Bambi Dillow. She was kicking and screaming, complaining about how hard you were to kill." He nodded in Donna's direction.

"I heard that part before she left. How did she get in and out of the inn?" It would be good to know how to protect herself.

"A while back her mother was the cleaning lady and had keys to the place. Felonious tendencies show up early. Little Bobby decided to copy all the keys to let himself in and out of the houses his mother cleaned."

Daniel's brows lowered. "Bobby? I think I missed something."

Taber shook his head. "Fooled you, did she? I didn't have much contact with her, but I still thought her walk looked too practiced."

Donna didn't care about her walk, natural or not. "What was her excuse for depositing a dead man in my place?

"The vic was her cohort in crime. They'd conducted several robberies together, usually in affluent neighborhoods. When things got hot, they both decided on plastic surgery. Our friend in jail thought it would be cool to be female. Not sure if that was something he-she always wanted or what, but for enough money you can find someone do the surgery. Especially proud of the results, Bambi picked up work at The Lion's Den where she met the doctor."

"So why turn on the dead guy?"

"The best we can figure out is the marriage between the doc and her was the real thing. Love, the whole bit. Apparently Russ, the dead guy, had gone through his money and thought Bambi's change in the address was an attempt to work a new scam in a different neighborhood. According to her, he was trying to blackmail her into ripping off her new neighbors. Somehow, she made it sound like offing her former partner was a community service."

"I don't understand the doctor. Couldn't he tell that she'd had a lot of surgeries?"

The captain shrugged his shoulders, "Could know, but didn't care. Gotta go." He waved as he turned to go.

Daniel looked at his watch. "I'm going to have to get on the site to make sure the guys keep working. You want me to swing by the inn later?"

"Of course, I should have Jasper by then."

"Are you going ahead with the inn?" Mark asked.

"I have to. The property value was low before, but murder tends to drop property values even more. Gotta fix it up. Once it is open, you get one free weekend. Figure it's the least I can do."

"Sounds great to me, but try to not stumble over any dead bodies in the future."

Donna winked, before adding, "Herman Fremont thinks there's something hidden in the house that may have resulted in a couple cold case murders. It might bear looking into. If nothing else, it would give The Painted Lady panache.

She pivoted, putting her back to the injured man before she smiled, knowing the effect her words would have.

A slight edge could be heard in Mark's voice. "Wait, don't do anything until I can help."

Ah, she loved a mystery, especially when assisted by a particularly heroic detective.

The End

Donna's Secret Weapon
Macadamia Coconut Chocolate Chip Cookies

Gather these ingredients first.

2 cups of butter-flavored shortening (do not substitute butter)

1 ½ cups of packed brown sugar

1 ½ cups of granulated white sugar

4 medium eggs

4 tsp vanilla extract

4 ½ cups of all-purpose flour (sifted)

2 tsp baking soda

1 tsp salt

2 cups of semisweet chocolate chips (Spurge on this ingredient because cheap chocolate doesn't cut it.)

1 cup flaked coconut

1 cup chopped macadamia nuts or macadamia nut pieces

Directions

1. Preheat oven to 350 degrees F (175 degrees C).
2. In a large bowl, cream together the butter flavored shortening, brown sugar and white sugar until smooth. Beat in the eggs, one at a time, then stir in the vanilla. Sift flour adding in baking soda and salt. Then stir in flour mixture into creamed mixture one cup at a time until well mixed. Fold in the chocolate chips, coconut and macadamia nuts. Roll dough into 1-inch balls and place them 2 inches apart onto ungreased cookie sheets. (It is better to use parchment paper if possible.)
3. Bake for 8 to 10 minutes in the preheated oven. Allow cookies to cool on baking sheet for 5 minutes before removing to a wire rack to cool completely. Leaving them out will make them crunchier as opposed to immediately wrapping them up for storage

Drop Dead Handsome

Coming March 2016

TWO MONTHS AGO, Daniel's idea of a reunion special sounded like a good idea. The local winery put reunion stickers on their bottles of table red after she provided the stickers and bought three cases. Each room got a gift basket of wine, chocolate, bath salts and a candle for a romantic getaway. The baskets rested on a foyer table. Originally, she thought leaving them in the room would work, but she wanted to make sure the guests each received their baskets personally.

The guests started arriving at three, sometimes, in groups, or even singles. Even though some of the names sounded vaguely familiar, no one recognized Donna or at least acted as if they did. Her sister-in-law, Maria, had taken the brunt of the reservations since people tended to reserve online and she served as the webmaster.

Only two rooms left, she checked to see the guest names. One was a single rented to Terri Gentry. No, it couldn't be her high school nemesis. An urge to scream landed on her as fast as a dropping spider the same time the front door opened. Her mouth rounded in disbelief. Fate had a wicked streak a foot wide. The sunlight spotlighted the man as if he were a singer ready to solo. The broad shoulders, height and cocky saunter told her who it was. His face remained in shadow as he walked in the foyer.

Wyn Lansing, the same male she spent her junior year making a fool out of herself for. Her father joked that Wyn must have made up his name to sound successful. At the time, she thought her father cruel, but now she wondered if it could be true. The popular senior even took pity on her while she stood on the sidelines and asked her to dance at the winter formal. For a brief interval, she considered herself Cinderella. Instead of the clock striking midnight, his date returned from the bathroom. Not much happened after that, besides a handful of greetings at school followed by a threat from his girlfriend, Terri, to disembowel her. If that wasn't bad enough, the twit started a rumor she had an STD.

If Donna had bothered to check the guest list before now, she would have sent Terri and Wyn an apology note claiming to have accidentally overbooked. No real worries since no one had actually realized she'd been in their graduating class. As a service person, she must be invisible until they needed something. Even then, no one remembered her name, calling her everything from *miss* to *inn keep*.

"Donna Tollhouse, as I live and breathe, it is you." Wyn walked forward with his arms held wide as if expecting to sweep her up like fast moving combine cutting through a cornfield.

The one person she didn't want to remember her. Her traitorous lips tilted up as the handsome man came closer. His wavy chestnut hair hadn't changed much, probably dyed it. The crinkles around his eyes possibly made him even better looking. It gave him character. She and her girlfriends had blessed him with the nickname *Drop Dead Handsome*. They were certain that his classic profile and charm would be enough to cause a woman to drop in a dead faint. Of course, she didn't know anybody that had, but he certainly set feminine hearts aflutter.

When he was almost upon her, a woman with a sullen expression and struggling with a suitcase entered after him. "Wyn, you left me to carry the luggage."

Donna took a slight step to the right, avoiding the over friendly greeting. Did the appearance of who was obviously his wife cause her sudden action? *Of course not.* Fact was she was never that good of a friend with Wyn, despite her fantasies.

"Welcome." She smiled at the two of them. "So glad to have you here."

Wyn grinned back at her and held out a hand, which she shook, glad the moment of awkwardness passed.

"Couldn't believe it when I saw a note that you were running The Painted Lady Inn. I knew right then we had to stay here."

Her smile felt tight and plastic as she held it under the baleful woman's gaze, "Ah, yes, so glad you did." She reached for the reunion basket and swung it so forcefully that the bath salts flew out hitting the nearby wall, bursting the bag and scattering across her refinished floors.

Great. Carefully, she placed the shaken basket on the floor and reached for the next one. Terri wouldn't get bath salts. *No great loss there.* "Here, let me try it again," she joked as she tucked the room key in the basket and handed it over.

Wyn took the basket from her making sure his hand brushed hers and gave her a broad wink. Oh, no, this she didn't need. Right in front of his wife too.

"Breakfast is served between nine and ten." With any luck, her face didn't show any of her emotional turmoil. There had been rumors about Wyn running through women the way most people did tissues. Apparently, it was true, which explained his wife's attitude.

"Why couldn't we have stayed at a hotel?" The wife's shrill voice carried as Donna went to retrieve a broom and dustpan. Too bad, they hadn't.

His low-voiced response thankfully didn't carry. At least, the man could use discretion sometimes. Donna knew for a fact how loud a voice could penetrate. Daniel and Maria had carried on a practice conversation in the open areas as Donna moved from bedroom to bedroom checking the acoustics. It wasn't soundproof, but she was betting on the guests sleeping as opposed to having footraces in the hall.

By the time, she had the salts swept up and the broom stowed, Terri had arrived. The woman swept in with the same arrogance that Cleopatra must have shown entering Rome. A disdainful head tilt announced she'd been in grander accommodations. No mistaking the woman, she looked the same, only tighter as if her skin had shrunk making her face all angles without any soft curves.

"Hello, Gentry, Terri, I have a reservation."

An urge to remark the fact she was in the inn made a reservation self-evident. She repressed the comment. "Yes, you do. Welcome to The Painted Lady Inn. Here's your gift basket." She pushed the remaining basket in Terri's direction.

The woman pawed through the contents as her lips pulled down in a frown. "The bath salts that were mentioned in the special are missing."

Before Donna could answer, Terri continued.

"No way, I can carry my luggage and the basket upstairs. I guess it is too much to expect a backwater establishment like this would have an elevator?" Her sneer announced she already knew the answer.

"Here at *The Painted Lady Inn*, we strive for authenticity." It seemed a better answer than *No, we don't have an elevator.*

Terri raised both eyebrows as she stared down at Donna, who had picked up both the woman's suitcase and basket. Normally, the woman wouldn't have anything on her height wise, but with her hunched over like Quasimodo, the hunchback of Notre Dame, she was at a disadvantage.

What did she have in the suitcase? Bricks? She stood, straightening her back and retaining as much dignity as possible. "You're in 2B."

"Hmm. Should I assume there's no running water?"

Count to ten. She inhaled deeply. While she didn't think it was possible, the woman grew even more malicious with age. "Excuse me?" Maybe she hadn't heard right.

"If you're trying to return to Victorian times, then they wouldn't have running water."

Ah-ha, she had her there. Terri had never been a stellar student. Her graduation depended more on her father being on the school board than actually doing work. The woman needed assurance that the owner of a stately Victorian home such as the inn would have had indoor plumbing, but she needed the woman's six hundred dollars more. Technically, she'd already spent the money on linens. "We do have running water. Cold and hot."

Perhaps Terri didn't hear the sarcasm in her voice. Donna only heard it because she knew it was there.

"Has Wyn Lansing arrived yet? He's the one who told me about the inn." She inhaled deeply as if she were readying herself for some deep, dark confession. "I'm only staying here because of Wyn."

Ick. Didn't need to know that. Sure, the wife wouldn't be big on her husband playing musical bedrooms. "Just arrived about ten minutes ago."

"Perfect!" The woman clapped her wine tipped talons together.

"I can't wait to talk about old times."

Talking must be code for something else. The wife looked like she could knock Femme Fatale off her skyscraper heels. She didn't have to be a mind reader to know what the next question would be. "He's in 3G."

The woman minced up the stairs humming a dated song under her breath. *Yeah, easy to mince when you weren't carrying anything. Two more steps, she could do it.* "Here we are," she pushed out the words trying not to sound winded even if she was.

Donna pulled the key out of her pocket and opened the door. "Here's your sitting room with daybed, table, chair and television."

"Television. How authentic." Terri tittered as if she just made the greatest joke ever.

Too bad the room wasn't on the third floor where she could point out where she found the dead man who haunts the inn. Although, he didn't really haunt the place. Since she had found his killer, he should be good for at least one haunting. She knew exactly whom she'd choose to haunt, too.

Donna moved down the slender hall and gestured to the bathroom. "Your bathroom comes equipped with a claw foot tub." The slipper tub had taken three men to wrestle it upstairs.

"Quaint."

The woman managed to degrade an expensive tub with one word. She'd love to toss her out of the inn, but she was well aware the woman would go online and write a scathing review. Worse yet, she'd be the type to file some civil suit for emotional abuse. It was past *time she returned to the foyer.* She gestured to brass bed piled high with pillows. "Your bedroom."

"Oh good, a four poster!" Terri grasped one brass finial and shook it, rattling the bed.

Don't say anything. Don't say anything. She kept up her mental chant as she exited the room and made her way down the stairs. This weekend might end up with another murder in her house. Unfortunately, she'd know the killer personally.

By the time she'd reached the bottom floor, Maria stepped through the kitchen door. "Sorry, I'm late. I stopped by the store to pick up extra snack items since you have a full inn."

Not trusting herself to speak, she pointed to the kitchen where they both headed. Inside the bright room, Donna pointed upstairs and pantomimed choking someone.

"That bad, huh?" Maria unpacked individual bags of pretzels, chips, crackers and trail mix.

The sight of the packets reminded her of her original vow to only served homemade goodies. There would be a plate of individually wrapped brownies and cookies at each snack station. Her image of carefully arranged goodies on a china plate died a swift death when one guest took the plate of cookies meant for the entire floor. She found the evidence when she cleaned the room. Painstakingly wrapping the treats made it clear that they were not for one room only.

"Yes." Donna shook her head as she helped, sorting out the nibbles for the three different snack stations. "Fate must hate me. To allow the two people I probably least wanted to see from my graduating class to show up here."

"Sorry." Maria finished one basket and pushed it to the side. "You could have given me a list if you wanted to avoid murder and mayhem."

Her eyes rolled upward on her own. "Nothing that melodramatic. I'm afraid there might be some bedroom hijinks. The fact I gave up my room to accommodate more guests means I won't be here to put a stop to it."

Her sister-in-law snorted and then rolled her eyes as she finished a second snack basket.

"I could do something about it!" She hadn't a clue what, but the last things she wanted was *The Painted Lady* to gain a reputation as a place to hook up.

"Mmm," Maria threw her a sideways glance as her lips tilted up slightly, almost a smile, but not quite, more of a smirk. "Maybe you could call up that handsome detective you've been seeing."

"We're friends, that's all. Maybe I could," she hesitated trying to think of a reason to get Detective Mark Taber to her inn in the middle of the night without an actual crime.

"Seriously, Donna, I was joking. The last thing you need is another murder at the inn."

Author Notes

- If you enjoyed this book, please lend it to a friend.
- Write a review.
- Do you have an idea for a story or a character name? Love to hear it. I can be reached through my website at www.morgankwyatt.com
- Want to get free books, read excerpts before everyone else, receive special members only swag and giveaways? You need to be on the mailing list. Go over to my website and sign up. (I don't sell my mailing list and guard it as well as I do my chocolate.)
- Do you like humor with your suspense? Check out Suspicious Circumstances: Love or Deception.
- Love to meet you, check out my personal appearances on the website too.
- Can you do one more thing? Go out and have an amazing day.

M K Scott

Made in the USA
Lexington, KY
26 July 2017